MW01124501

Chaser

A BAD HABITS NOVEL

BESTSELLING AUTHOR
STACI HART

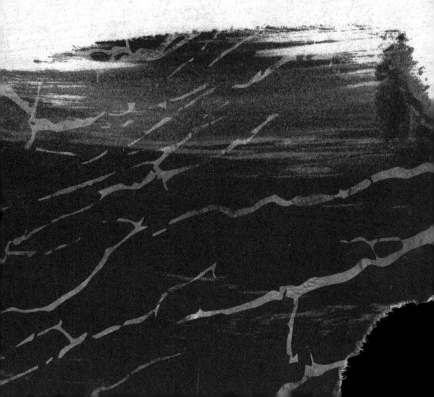

Cover design by **Quirky Bird**

Photography by **Perrywinkle Photography**

Editing by **Love N Books and Rebecca Slemons**

Book design by **Inkstain Interior Book Designing**

BOOKS BY
STACI HART

HEARTS AND ARROWS

Rereleasing in 2017

CONTEMPORARY ROMANCE

Hardcore

With a Twist

Chaser

Last Call

Wasted Words

Tonic

A Thousand Letters—February 2017

SHORT STORIES

Once

Desperate Measures

*To **Brooke**.*
You're welcome.

Charming Bastard

MAGGIE

Cooper grabbed me by the hips and dragged me to the end of the bed where he knelt. I gasped — somehow, I was completely naked, but he was fully clothed, smiling up the line of my body, that crooked smile of his that made my insides turn into mush. My thighs rested against his shoulders, and his eyes were smoldering hot, locked onto mine as he closed his lips over me and sucked. Hard.

"*Whoamygod.*"

That's what I tried to say, at least, but I think it sounded more like *Humuguh*. Not that Cooper needed clarification. His eyes closed, dark lashes against his cheeks, fingers digging into my hips as he licked and sucked, sending tremors up my thighs when he moaned softly against me.

My eyes slammed shut, and my chin pointed at the ceiling as my fingers twisted in his dark hair. Within seconds, I was rocking against him with my heart doing its best to escape my ribs and the rest of my body begging him to keep going.

He broke away. I cracked my lids, which weighed about seven

pounds each, and glanced down at him. His face was turned toward the closed bedroom door, with alarm written in every angle.

And then I heard the front door close.

Lily.

Cooper looked back at me, blue eyes wide, and we stared at each other for one stunned second before bursting into action. I rolled out of bed with wobbly knees, and he stood, scanning the room for a place to hide.

Here's the problem: No one knew Cooper and I were hooking up.

Here's the bigger problem: My brother, West, might actually kill Cooper if he found out.

It wasn't because Cooper was one of West's best friends. I mean, I guess that was part of it — calling West overprotective was like calling a great white shark 'cuddly.' The real issue was this.

Cooper was a player.

I don't mean he dated around. I don't even mean that he slept around. What I mean is that his level of hookup was beyond my ability to comprehend. Cooper was heir to a billion-dollar fortune, though that money required nothing to maintain. No job, no responsibility, which meant he partied nonstop. He'd dated — read: *banged* — every model and socialite in the New York major metropolitan area. I knew because I'd seen the details splattered all over gossip magazines in nearly every grocery store I'd ever been in.

No one would approve of the affair, particularly not my brother. God only knew what West had seen when they were roommates at Columbia — enough that West had sworn me off of Cooper for eternity. If he found out, he might ship me back to Jackson. And I'd have a hard time keeping it from West if his girlfriend found out. His girlfriend who had just dropped her keys in the dish by the door.

"*Hide,*" I hissed, as I pulled on my flowery bathrobe, and Cooper blinked at me as I spun toward the door.

I bolted out of the bedroom and closed the door behind me, smiling at Lily with what I was positive were crazy eyes.

"Hey, Lily." My voice was a little too high, and I smoothed my crazy blond curls.

"Hey, Maggie." She didn't seem to notice I was acting squirrelly, just strode into the kitchen to fill up her water. Her legs were a mile long and lean, dancer's legs, and she had the nicest butt ever. Rewards for being a professional ballerina with the New York City Ballet.

"You're home early today. I thought you had a show?" My face seriously felt like a plastic mask as my heart jackhammered and my brain scrambled through places Cooper might have hidden. There was no space under my bed — that area was strictly reserved for my shoes, of which I had many — and the closet was about big enough for a mop.

I hoped to God Lily would leave to go meet my brother without needing anything from our room. And then I died inside because there was no way in hell that was an actual possibility.

She twisted her long, blond hair and threw it over her shoulder. "No show tonight. Maybe you were thinking about tomorrow?"

I let out an awkward laugh. "Oh, maybe I was."

Lily finally glanced up as she screwed the lid on her water bottle, and her eyes narrowed the second she really saw me. She looked me over. "Why are you in your bathrobe?"

"Oh … well, I just got out of the shower." My cheeks were on fire.

"How come your hair isn't wet?" Her brows shot up, and her mouth fell open in a gaping smile when she figured it out. "Oh, my God, is Mr. M in there?"

"No," I blustered, but she looked at me like she knew exactly what I'd been doing seconds before she walked in the door.

"You liar." She laughed and bounded past me to throw open our bedroom door. Her face fell as she scanned the room, and I stepped into the doorway behind her.

Cooper was nowhere to be seen.

I let out the breath I'd been holding. "See? Not lying. I was just masturbating."

A laugh bubbled out of Lily. "I love you. Sorry to interrupt. Let me just grab some stuff and I'll leave you to it."

I smiled, but it was half-assed as I scanned the room for any sign of him. There was nothing, just my rumpled, fluffy bedding and my clothes in a pile at the foot of the bed. I was all of a sudden very glad he'd kept his clothes on.

And then I saw the closet door. It was only open a crack, but we rarely went in there — it just wasn't big enough to use for anything useful. I knew for a fact that it was closed before I'd left the room.

My heart went nuts again as I took a seat on my bed as far as I could get from the closet in the hopes it would divert Lily. "How was work?"

She set her bag on her neatly made bed and turned for her dresser. "Long and difficult and amazing, as usual." She dug through her drawer. "What'd you do today?"

Cooper. I threaded my fingers in my lap and squeezed to help me focus. "I made some headway on jobs, have a few leads. I decided my vacation is over. I've been in New York for three weeks and haven't done anything but sightsee and sleep."

"And Mr. M. You've been doing a lot of him." She snickered.

I blushed, thinking about him hiding in the closet. "Yes, and him."

"I'm happy for you, though. After everything that happened with Jimmy, I'm sure this is a welcome change of pace. No commitment, and all that." She tossed some clothes into her open bag.

The last thing I needed was commitment after breaking up with my fiancé. On our wedding day. After I caught him porking my maid of honor. "Definitely," I said with a smile and swiftly changed the subject. "What are you guys up to tonight?"

"Dinner, then Habits. You should meet up with us."

"Maybe I will."

She held up some lingerie and waggled her eyebrows at me before stuffing it in her bag.

I wrinkled my nose and laughed. "He's still my brother, you know."

"Which is why I won't tell you what I'm going to do to him when I put these on."

"Thanks for sparing me the visual," I added flatly.

She laughed as she zipped up her bag and slung it on. "Well, I'm off. Hope you're next. You know where the batteries are."

I blushed again. "I'm good, thanks."

Lily waved as she passed by. "Bye, Mags. I'll text you when we get to Habits."

"All right. Have fun." I called after her, not moving until I heard the door close. I let out a thousand-pound breath and hopped off the bed.

When I pulled open the closet door, I busted out laughing. Cooper was almost sideways in the closet, his long body bent like the saddest version of Tetris I'd ever seen around a stack of shoeboxes, a pair of snow boots, a small suitcase, and a few dresses that hung mostly in his face.

Somehow, he didn't look affected, just smiled crookedly at me, his dark hair mussed and hanging a little in his face. "You found me."

"You look ridiculous," I said with a laugh. "Come here."

He hauled himself out of the closet and stepped into me in almost a single motion, slipping his hand around my waist. "I wasn't through with you."

My body was pressed against his once more, and I smiled up at him. "That was too close."

"I know. But I can't say I didn't enjoy listening to you and Lily talk about me like I wasn't hiding in your closet."

My hands slipped up his chest and around his neck. "I bet."

"So," he pulled me a little closer, "you call me Mr. M?"

"Well, it was Mystery Man, but that ended up shortened to Mr. M, which I think is funnier anyway, given that's your actual initial."

"Maybe I should come up with one for you so I can talk to your brother about us."

"Ew." I laughed and batted at his chest.

"Mystery Woman. Miss W. Works both ways." He backed me up, smiling when I hit the bed. I hung onto his neck as he lowered me onto the mattress. "So what else have you told Lily about me?" His fingers found the tie of my bathrobe and tugged.

My heart fluttered as I watched his hand slip under the fabric and up to my breast. "Oh, just that you're a rocket in the sack."

He smirked and opened my robe slowly, deliberately, exposing my naked torso. "Is that so?"

Our legs tangled together, and I smiled at him innocently, even though I was already aching for him. "Mmhmm. I like to make everyone jealous with tales of your prowess. Well, except Lily. I've gotta be careful or she'll start talking about her sex life, which involves my brother."

He laughed and trailed his fingers down my stomach.

"We can't do this here again," I said, needing to make the point before I lost my ability to form coherent thoughts.

His hand skimmed lower, sending a riot of goosebumps across my skin. "Agreed. But in my defense, I only came over to give you back the panties you left over at my place. Although I can't say I wasn't enjoying the thought of you walking around Manhattan with no panties on."

I giggled, breathless. "I'm sure that's the only reason why you came over."

Cooper chuckled, eyes on my lips. "You think you've got me figured out, don't you?"

The butterflies in my chest took off, and I waved them away. "Isn't it that simple, though? No strings. And anyway, we've only got two more weeks before time's up."

His eyes were still fixed on my mouth, and I tried to read his reaction, but he gave away nothing. "You and your rules."

The rules were everything — they were the only way I could guarantee I wouldn't get hurt again. I smiled to cover the reminder. "Two weeks. So show me what you've got while you can."

His blue eyes met mine. "Oh, I plan to."

Something about his words, about the way he was looking at me held me still. He was like a snake charmer — when he looked at me like that, like he could *see* me, I swear I'd do whatever he asked. I was sort of helpless in that way. And as his eyes burned a shade darker, he pressed his lips to mine and showed me plenty indeed.

Strings

COOPER

An hour and change later, I trotted down the stairs of Maggie's building with my hands in my pockets and my heart skipping. I hadn't wanted to leave, but I'd kissed her goodbye anyway, appreciating the feeling of her body against mine. I shot her The Smile — the one that made her cheeks flush, the one that got me what I wanted and served as a mask, when I needed one — and then I snuck out of the apartment in the hopes I wouldn't run into any more of our friends, since the majority of them lived in that building.

I smiled to myself as I stepped out into the crisp Manhattan night, thinking about her, picturing her stretched out on her bed with her eyes closed, curly hair a mess, imagining the feeling of her fingers in my hair and her hot skin against mine. Making her feel good had become my new favorite hobby.

No one could say I wasn't successful when I put my mind to something.

The affair had been going on happily for two weeks, though only under a myriad of ground rules, all set by Maggie. No commitment, no expectations. No dates or gifts. Four weeks, and we'd go our separate ways. The biggest rule — we had to keep it a secret. Because of West, she'd said, and she was right. If he ever found out, he might never speak to me again. That is, if he let me live. And he was the best friend I'd ever had.

I'd agreed to her terms without thinking twice.

I'd been doing the 'no strings' thing my entire life, but I should have known it wouldn't be easy with Maggie.

"Cooper?"

It was nearly dark, and I looked up to find Lily and West arm in arm-in-front of me — West, tall and dark, hair tied in a knot, smiling at me from behind his beard, and Lily, tall and fair, eyeing me suspiciously.

I smiled back to cover my surprise. "What's up, guys?"

"Hey," West said. "We're just heading to Habits."

Lily's eyes narrowed. "What are you doing over here?"

I shrugged and lied. "I was on my way to see if you guys were home—"

"Then why are you going the wrong way?"

"You didn't let me finish. You *weren't* at West's, so I left. Was just about to text."

West started walking and clapped me on the shoulder when he approached. "Well, now you don't have to."

Lily was still maddogging me. "Who doesn't text first?"

"Me." I smirked at her and winked as we walked toward the bar. "What are you guys doing tonight?"

West pulled Lily a little closer. "Probably just Habits for a bit, then home."

I made a face. "But it's Saturday night."

He chuckled. "Yeah, well, not everyone parties every weekend like rock stars."

"What do you mean? That's exactly what everyone our age does on the weekend, rock stars or not."

Lily leaned into West. "I've got to work tomorrow at ten-thirty. West can go out though."

I shook my head. "She gave you permission, man."

He laughed. "No, thanks. She's been at the theater almost every night, and tonight I've got her to myself. You're on your own, pal."

I smiled, wondering if I could get Maggie to come over just as my phone buzzed in my pocket. It was a text from Jules, my assistant. She'd been organizing my life for me since I was seven.

Hey, just a reminder about the photo shoot with W *Magazine. They said they'd meet you at the marina at 4:30 tomorrow to set up on* Midnight Caller.

I sighed. I hadn't told anyone about my nomination for *W's* twenty-five most eligible bachelors, mostly because West would never let me hear the end of it once he found out. I wasn't even sure why I'd agreed. I think I'd been so surprised that I didn't even consider turning it down. Although if I'd have known they wanted to shoot on my sailboat, I might have refused.

I texted her back. *Thanks for keeping me honest.*

Somebody has to. I emailed you a list of their requirements. Sure you don't want me to come with you?

Nah, I can handle it.

All right. The journalist is Elena. The stylist will have all the clothes, so just show up in whatever.

Naked, then. Got it.

I'm sure the photographer will be pleased. Really, though. Try to keep your pants on.

No promises.

Ha, ha. Let me know if you need anything.

Will do.

I hesitated with my phone in my hand. West and Lily were chatting, which meant they weren't paying attention to me. I stared at my screen for a moment before pulling up Maggie's name.

I found myself smirking as I typed a message. *Just ran into West and Lily.*

My phone buzzed within a second. *WHAT?*

Don't worry, secret's still safe. We're going to Habits. Come meet us.

My phone was painfully silent for a few seconds. *Didn't you see enough of me tonight?*

No such thing.

She was quiet again before it buzzed. *I don't know. I really need to paint my nails. Maybe wash my hair. I've been meaning to rearrange my sock drawer too. It's a mess in there.*

Come on. I'll buy you a bourbon.

Pretty sure that's a direct violation of the rules. No dates, and no buying me stuff.

Don't make me beg, Mags. I realized I was holding my breath.

But it's so cute when you beg.

I smiled. *It's so cute when you give me what I want.*

You're impossible lol. Let me get dressed and I'll be there in a few.

If you're still in your bathrobe, I think you should come just as you are.

I'm sure my brother will think that's adorable. Now quit distracting me so I can get down there.

Hurry.

I slipped my phone in my pocket just as we walked through the heavy wooden door and into Habits. The bar was right around the corner from West and Lily's building. Between the proximity to their place and the fact that Lily and Maggie's roommate, Rose, was a bartender, we ended up there. A lot.

It was an old building with planked wooden floors and a dark bar balanced by clean white tile walls and big windows that faced the street. The food was good, and the drinks were strong. But the company was the best part.

We'd been hanging at Habits for years, ever since West moved in with Patrick after we left our dorm at Columbia. Once Lily moved in with Rose, the Habits crew was really born. Rose had been working at Habits as long as any of us knew her, and everyone gravitated there, including me. It was the first time in my life that I had a group of friends who were ... normal, for lack of a better word. No trust funds, no ski trips to Switzerland or benders in the Riviera. And their normalcy made *me* feel normal. For a while, at least.

Rose stood behind the bar, her long, shaggy hair hanging down her back, which was to Patrick. She was very busy lining up shot glasses and ignoring him. In true fashion, he was watching her with dark eyes, like she was the most interesting thing he'd ever seen or ever would see. I could feel the heat from across the room as he wrapped his tattooed fingers around his glass and brought it to his lips.

I took a seat at the far end of the bar next to Patrick as Lily leaned over to kiss Rose on the cheek.

"Hey, Rosie. You guys are dead tonight. It's too quiet in here."

"Tell me about it. I'm watching the clock in ten minute intervals." Rose jerked her chin at West and me, smiling with her hands on her hips. "What's up, guys? Whatcha drinking? The usual, Coop?"

"Please."

She reached for a rocks glass. "Whiskey or beer, West? We finally got Bulleit in."

He smiled and took a seat on the other side of Patrick. "I can't say no to rye whiskey. I'll take it neat."

"You've got it." She got to work making drinks. "Thank God you guys are here because I needed some company. Bob's not big on conversation."

We all turned to glance at Bob, who seemed to be napping on his usual high-top bar table in the corner.

West shook his head, chuckling. "That's the cardinal rule of public drinking. The minute you put your head down, the end."

Rose waved a hand. "He's harmless. Plus he's nice to everybody, and he's a damn good tipper. As far as I'm concerned, he can pass out in Habits any time he wants."

The door to the bar opened, and I looked over to find Maggie walking in, curly hair bouncing and cheeks flushed. She walked a tight line toward us in dark skinny jeans and a light denim shirt, camel ankle boots clicking on the hardwood. She could have belonged equally in a magazine ad or on a farm. I imagined her lying in a heap of hay, smiling up at me, and my pulse quickened.

"Hey, y'all," she said as she walked up, her Mississippi accent heavy. The second our eyes met, the flush in her cheeks deepened.

The Smile was one hundred percent unplanned.

Everyone said hello as she took a seat next to me. She was only a few feet away from me, but it felt like a million miles.

"Maker's and ginger?" Rose asked with a smile.

I admired Maggie's profile as she smiled right back. "That'd be great, Rose. Thanks."

She turned on her stool to face everyone and hooked a boot in the leg of my chair. I couldn't even look at her or my cover would be blown — my face would give me away.

"It's quiet in here tonight for a Saturday."

"Don't remind me," Rose groaned.

"Oh, I'm sure you'll get busy later, right?"

"Probably," she said as she handed Maggie her drink. "But I'm already in lax-mode."

"What's that?" Maggie asked and took a drink.

"Where you get lazy because you're slow and start thinking about going home. So then when you actually *do* get busy, everything crashes because you were checked out. It's all about the zone." She tapped her temple.

Maggie laughed. "I'd be the worst waitress ever. I can't multi-task to save my life."

West smiled over at her "That's true. I once watched her try to unload the dishwasher while she cooked dinner."

"Burned dinner," she added.

West chuckled and picked up his drink. "Lily said you've got a couple of leads on a job? We wouldn't want Rose to feel obligated to give you one after learning your fatal flaw."

"Funny, Weston." Maggie smiled and rested an elbow on the bar. "I found a couple of things today that I'm real excited about. Only a few at schools — the rest are charity outreach programs. I'm just so ready to get back to working with kids again. I only had a solid year of teaching before … well, before everything blew up. But I miss my Kindergartners." She sighed. "I'll see what happens this summer. Maybe I'll end up back in a classroom after all, but I'm excited at the prospect of charity work."

I wanted to ask her about her job search and felt guilty for not asking when I'd seen her earlier. Not that Maggie was overly interested in talking. I smiled to myself, considering ways I could go about changing that.

"Good," West said. "Seemed like you were gettin' bored."

"Maybe a little. I don't know if I'll ever see everything I want to see in New York, but I put a big ol' dent in it. And I never thought I'd get through the pile of books on my tablet, but I did. It's a terrifying, hollow feeling to have an empty to-be-read pile, I'll tell you that much. I feel like my bookshelves are empty."

West raised an eyebrow. "Get real books and you won't have that problem."

Lily laughed and made a face at him. "No, you'll have an entirely *new* problem — where the hell to put all your books."

"Yeah, West still hasn't figured out the answer to that." Patrick raised his glass to me. "Didn't expect to see you at Habits tonight, Coop."

I spun in the stool and leaned back against the bar, hanging my arm next to Maggie's, feeling the small distance between us like it was tangible. "I was in the neighborhood. Figured I'd stop in and see what you guys were doing."

Patrick smirked. "It's Saturday — don't you have some club opening or penthouse party to go to?"

"Right?" Lily added, her blue eyes bright. "Fun, fancy, rich people stuff."

I shrugged. "I haven't decided yet. Keeping my options open."

"Oh, the high life." Lily took a sip of her water. "Astrid's around too. We came to meet her."

I saw Maggie stiffen in my periphery before she took a long pull of her drink.

See, Astrid was my 'girlfriend,' which is in air quotes because the entire thing was a cover. Lily's older sister and I had a long-standing arrangement. We'd dated at one point, but it never went anywhere because a) I'm a terminal bachelor and b) she met Sam. He'd been burned by the media and was a part of the social elite, but after what he went through, he wanted out. And Astrid was definitely in — an 'it girl' model who'd been living The Life since she broke out at eighteen.

So Astrid and I kept 'dating' to throw their scent off of Sam. We met a few nights a week at hot spot clubs and restaurants and appeared together whenever we had an event to attend — all in an attempt to keep the rumor mill spinning. I had full permission to see anyone I wanted on the side, so I did, which kept people buzzing with speculation that I was stepping out on her.

It was one of our favorite jokes.

Astrid was my unlikely confidant, one of the only people who I could trust with anything and everything. She knew about Maggie and was the only one of our friends who really got what it was like to live The Life. We were both in the same place, and she understood the pressure that came with everyone knowing who you were. It was a relief to have someone who I could be completely honest with in a world centered around wearing masks.

Maggie knew Astrid and I were a show, which was more than the rest of our friends knew. They at least thought Astrid and I hooked up, and we let them. In fact, I encouraged it. It was too easy, and Astrid needed my help. She hadn't even told Lily — she was just too scared to lose Sam. She'd been hiding him for a long while, and she'd keep doing it or risk losing him. But I didn't think Maggie fully believed me when it came to the ruse with Astrid. In fact, I didn't think Maggie believed much of what I said.

It was my own fault. I'd built the image over years, through the course of my adult life. It was what *everyone* thought, and that was how I liked it. But who knew what West had told her. Probably recounted the worst stories in his arsenal, and he had a cache that could take down my love life indefinitely.

I was still lost in thought when the door opened once again and Astrid walked through, tall and skinny like all the models I knew, dressed mostly in black with her blond hair twisted into a sloppy knot. She smiled and took a seat at the far end of the bar next to Lily.

"Hey, guys. Hey, Coop."

I winked at her and raised my glass.

Maggie tipped her drink back until it was empty and set the glass on the bar top. Her cheeks were pink, though she smiled warmly at Rose, avoiding eye contact with me. "Can I get another?"

"Sure," Rose answered, not seeming to notice Maggie's discomfort.

I made myself look away, but I couldn't stop my smile. She always got weird around Astrid, which shouldn't have made me feel like a boss. But it did. I took a sip of my scotch.

Lily turned to Astrid. "What are you doing over here?"

"I was just nearby and wanted to say hi."

Lily rolled her eyes. "God, do you guys just wander around New York all day doing nothing?"

I snickered. "Sometimes."

She shook her head at me before hooking her arm in West's. "I can't wait until this summer when we have a little time. I usually hate the end of the season. After working so much, a break is weird, like slamming on the brakes when you're going a hundred miles an hour, so I usually end up at the theater every day anyway. But this year, I'm looking forward to it."

West looked down at her and smiled. If they'd been cartoons, little pink hearts would have been floating between them. "We might go to Mississippi at some point to see Mom and Dad."

"I really want to go to the beach, too." She perked up. "Ooooh, could we go sailing, Coop? Maybe go up to the Hamptons?"

"Sure," I answered. "Just say when."

Lily looked to Maggie. "You've got to go sailing, Maggie. It's my absolute favorite thing about summer, lying on the boat all day in the sun, the salty air, the sea — it's amazing. And Cooper has a beach house in the Hamptons like a good rich boy." She sighed. "I could stay there forever." She eyed me, suddenly very serious and with a hint of authority. "Promise, Cooper?"

I thought of Maggie on the porch of the Hampton house at sunrise with nothing but my tailored shirt on, and I smiled. "Promise."

"When does the ballet season end?" Maggie asked Lily.

"At the end of May this year, sometimes at the beginning of June. We always perform A Midsummer Night's Dream as the last show of the season. You guys should come."

"I'd love to," Maggie said. "Maybe West can be my date."

"Or we could all go." I took a sip of my scotch and glanced at her over the rim of my glass. A small smile played at the corner of her lips.

"We should definitely all go," Rose chimed in. "We don't go to the ballet together enough."

Patrick smiled at her. "No, we don't."

"Well," Lily said, "I've got tickets with everyone's name on them."

"Oh, Cooper," Astrid said, "speaking of tickets — a courier dropped off my invitation to the Met Gala earlier today. Tell Jules I said thanks."

"I'll let her know you got them."

Lily perked up. "I'd almost be willing to date Cooper if it meant getting to go to the Met Gala."

I snorted.

"What's the theme this year?" Lily asked.

Astrid leaned forward, looking like a girl. "It's called *Spellbound: From Fairytale to Fashion*, and I have this idea for my dress, but I don't know if I'm going to be able to talk someone into designing it for me."

Maggie was drinking again. I watched her, hoping she'd look at me, but I had no such luck.

"Oh, man I want to go *so bad*. Some day." Lily sighed. "I can't wait to hear about the exhibits."

Astrid grinned and touched her arm. "Come dress shopping with me next week. I've got appointments with Givenchy and John Galliano. You know you want to see the inside of their boutiques."

Lily's eyes stretched wide. "Uh, yes, please."

Maggie set down her empty glass with a clink and dug her phone out of her bag. She glanced at it for a brief second and turned to the rest of us with a smile I didn't buy. "My mom just texted me and needs me to call, so I'm gonna run." She laid some cash on the bar and stood.

Lily frowned. "You just got here."

West was frowning too. "Is Mom okay?"

Maggie waved a hand. "Oh, I'm sure she's fine, just a dry cleaning emergency or something silly. I'll see you guys later."

Her eyes connected with mine only once before darting away, cheeks flushing as she turned and walked out.

My brow dropped, and I slammed the rest of my scotch. "I think I'll head out too."

"Good," Astrid said with her eyes on me. "I'll come with you."

Lily huffed. "God, everyone wanted to hang out, and now you're all leaving."

Rose looked desperate as she pointed at Lily and West. "You two can't leave too. What the hell will I do all night?"

"Don't get into any trouble." I chuckled as I stood.

"Have a good night, you guys," Astrid added.

"You too, I guess," Lily pouted.

"Bye, sister." Astrid kissed her on the cheek, waving at Patrick and West before heading for the door.

I held it open for her, and we stepped onto the sidewalk as I texted my driver.

Astrid watched me. Eyed me, really. "What's up?"

I shrugged and slipped my phone into my pocket. "Not much. What's up with you?"

She rolled her eyes and smiled. "Nice try, asshole."

"Nothing's up."

"I didn't know you'd be at Habits," she prompted as we passed under a street light.

"It wasn't planned. I was at Maggie's and ran into West and Lily on the way out."

"Close call."

"Not as close as when Lily came home and I had to hide in the closet."

A surprised laugh shot out of her, and she gaped at me. "Dangerous, Coop."

"Trust me, I know." We stepped up to the curb where Bobby had just pulled up in my black Mercedes. I opened the door for Astrid.

"Sometimes going over to her place is the only way I can see her, and I wanted to see her."

She slipped into the car. "It's not that simple. If Lily had caught you—"

"I know, Astrid." I climbed in after her and closed the door with a thump. "Hey, Bobby. Could you take us home, please?"

He nodded at me in the rearview. "Sure thing, Cooper."

Astrid dug around in her purse for her phone. "I mean, it's not like I've never seen you act recklessly before, but this is next-level. Even for you. What's it been now, two weeks?"

I leaned against the door. "Ever since we all went to Noir."

"I don't know how you ever convinced her. I was certain she was one hundred percent anti-Cooper."

I smirked at her. "No one's one hundred percent anti-Cooper."

"Well, she was at least a steadfast eighty percent."

I chuckled. "I don't know how it happened. There was just this moment when Tricky was hauling West out of the club, and I just … I don't know. It sounds crazy."

She raised an eyebrow and folded her hands on top of her bag. "Try me."

I thought back to that moment at the club, her small face turned up to mine, eyes wide and open. "When she looked at me, I just knew she was all I wanted that night. But it was more than just that …" I said, half to myself. "It happened that way the first time, too, at her reception. It was like deja vu."

"I still can't believe that you hooked up with her on her failed wedding night."

My brow dropped. "She was hurting, put on a brave face and found a way to get through what had to be one of the worst nights of her life. She needed an escape. I was her getaway car."

She sighed. "I know. I mean, I get it — I probably would have banged you too if I'd just caught my fiancé nailing my maid of honor.

20

Rebound sex is satisfying in its own right."

I shook my head.

"Sometimes you just need sexual healing. Does she know you're seeing other people too?"

"I'm not."

She gave me a look. "What do you mean, you're not?"

"It's part of the rules."

Astrid pressed her lips together to stifle a smile. "How long have you been … monogamous?" She busted out laughing and waved her hand at me. "Oh, my God. I can't even say that without laughing, Coop. What the fuck?"

I rolled my eyes. "It's temporary."

She let out a satisfied breath and shook her head. "I cannot believe you agreed to these rules."

"She might have suggested I wouldn't be able to do it."

"I'm with her."

"Clearly you've never seen me when I've put my mind to something."

She watched me with a know-it-all smile on her pretty face. "So what I'm hearing is that it's just a game to you."

"I like playing the game with her. It's not a big deal. I'm having fun. She's having fun. Why mess with a good thing?"

"Because your best friend will murder you." Her smile fell a hair. "Are you sure you can handle this?"

"Of course I can. I've got it under control."

She raised an eyebrow. "Do you?"

"I do."

She made a face like she knew better.

"West isn't going to figure it out."

"What if you end up liking her? What if she wants more? What if *you* want more? What then?"

I laughed again to cover for the fact that I didn't have an answer.

STACI HART

"What's this *more* you speak of?"

Astrid rolled her eyes and looked out the window, smirking. "God, Cooper. Don't you take anything seriously?"

"Not if I can help it."

The Life

MAGGIE

Within minutes of walking through the door, I was dressed in as much elastic and jersey as possible. My insane hair was tied in a little ponytail on top of my head, and I scowled at myself in the bathroom mirror as I slathered on an avocado mask.

If I was going to spend Saturday night alone, I was going to do it right.

I'd gotten all dressed up and paraded down to Habits to see Cooper, just like he'd asked, and then Astrid showed up all, *Ooh, look at me, I'm so pretty and tall and know a million designers.* Not that it mattered. Because it didn't. Cooper wasn't mine, and he wasn't even dating Astrid.

Technically.

He said.

I wrinkled my green nose at my reflection as I washed my hands. I looked like the Wicked Witch of the West. Green was appropriate because I wasn't fooling anybody. I was jealous as hell.

I took a swig of my bourbon — because you know the first thing

I did was make a drink — and headed into the living room with a makeup bag full of nail polish.

Doin' it right, y'all. Doin' it right.

I flopped down on the couch and turned on the TV, scrolling through the movies saved on the DVR until I landed on my favorite movie. *Mean Girls* always made me feel better. I sighed and dug through the bag, lining up the tiny glass containers in a row.

I was so annoyed, I was even annoying myself. I didn't know what I expected going down there. I mean, he'd just left here, and I was sure he had some fancy plans. He probably didn't even want to hang out with me. In fact, he was probably on his way to some club where he could hang out with socialites and actresses who were charming and beautiful and — *dammit*, I was jealous all over again. As if I'd ever stopped.

I picked up a hot pink nail polish and sighed. *Passion fucking Pink it is.*

The movie was already going, and I felt a little better when Regina George made her appearance. I was like Cady, and Cooper was like Aaron Samuels. And Astrid was Regina, obviously. Except she wasn't anything like Regina. In fact, Astrid really was a decent human.

I sighed again and shook the polish, my brain as noisy as the clinking of the little metal ball inside.

They weren't seeing each other, and I knew it. I really *did* trust Cooper. Mostly. It was easier when I was with him, but when we were apart? Well, then I just drove straight off into Crazytown, thinking about the *image* of him. The one plastered all over *US Weekly* and *Just Jared*. The one featured in my brother's favorite tales of debauchery.

Again, not that it mattered. Because we weren't a real thing. It was just for fun, a fling, a diversion, that was all. I was *not* ready to date. I needed it to be easy and simple. That was the theory, at least. I just wasn't sure what easy or simple was.

I'd been with Jimmy for seven years, since I was sixteen, so I'd never really had the opportunity to date, to play the field. I had no idea what I was doing once I'd left Jackson. Really, I'd had no idea what I was doing, ever. Catching your fiancé having sex with your 'best friend' on your wedding day was proof of that.

So now was the time for me to cut loose. New life in New York, full of oat sowing and being young and stupid. That was the plan. Cooper was a little close to home, but that was why I had the rules. And everything would be just fine. Pretty soon, I'd have Passion Pink toes and skin smooth as a baby's sweet little ass, which was nearly the same thing as being unstoppable.

COOPER

nodded to the doorman as I stepped into The Compass. It was built in the 20s, a beautiful deco building perched on 5th Avenue. The gleaming foyer was welcoming, warmly lit with gold and cream walls. I walked across the gold compass inlaid in the elevator well and hit the call button.

I'd grown up in this building and had walked the edge of the compass rose a hundred times as a kid as I waited for the elevator with my mom. The gold doors opened in front of me, closing once I waved my key fob over the sensor pad.

My phone buzzed in my pocket with a text.

Simone: Hey, stud. Where can I find you tonight?

I smiled to myself and slipped my phone back in my pocket.

What? If I responded, she'd never give up. In fact, I had dozens of unanswered texts stacked up in my messages.

I told Maggie I'd be monogamous, and I meant it.

When the doors opened again, it was to my private foyer. I walked across the black-and-gold starburst to the black door, unlocking it to step into my quiet apartment.

'Apartment' was maybe an understatement, but calling it my penthouse just smacked of douchery.

It had been my parents' 'starter home' — a three-thousand-square-foot penthouse overlooking Central Park. I'd inherited it and had it gutted when I redecorated, but I kept the flooring. Losing it would have been tragic, even though it was a little old fashioned. They were the original parquet floors from 1928, with intricate patterns through the entire apartment. My interior designer brought in dark leathers and deep colors to match, though all the design was clean, bringing it up to date without having to do anything destructive. The woman had talent.

She was a great designer, too.

I headed into my room and kicked off my shoes, reaching behind me to pull off my shirt as I made my way into my closet. The long space was lined with suits and coats, pants and tailored shirts, a few tuxedos. I had more shoes than I was comfortable admitting, and I walked past them all to the built-in drawers, digging around for a T-shirt and jersey pants. And when I was sufficiently comfortable, I headed back into my room, flopped onto my king-sized bed with a sigh, and grabbed the remote to my seventy-inch TV.

Cooper Moore — liver of The Life.

The Habits crew thought I was out living it up with the rich and famous. The rich and famous crew thought I was out just living it up. The truth was that I watched a metric fuckton of Netflix.

Don't get me wrong. I partied enough. I slept a lot. I went sailing. I read books. Okay, I read comics, but I read a *lot* of comics. I mean, what else is there to do? I can only survive so many brunches. I'd done the whole party all night, out until dawn, sleep all day life. Drinking, drugs, girls. Summers boozing my way through Europe with my childhood friend Ash and the rest of the elites we grew up with. I can't say it isn't fun — it's definitely fun. But it's empty. Like trying to exist strictly solely on a diet of candy and Mountain Dew.

Don't look at me like that. Try eating nothing but candy for one entire day and tell me how you feel.

For a long time, it was enough. In fact, I honestly hadn't thought all that much about my satisfaction with The Life until recently. Until Maggie, if I were being honest.

I didn't know how it happened, exactly. Maggie was just West's little sister, and for much of our friendship, she was just a kid in my eyes. The first time I'd met her was on the day we moved into our dorm, and she was just a sixteen-year-old, big-eyed, brace-faced kid, compared to my very adult eighteen. We weren't even living in the same universe. I saw her a couple times every year after that, but West was always around. We were never alone, never really hung out. Not even when I went to Jackson with West for Christmas, or when she came to New York to visit.

Plus, she always had a boyfriend. Not that it would have stopped me, if I'd really decided to go after her. But I had more respect for her than that. More respect for West.

But the night of her would-be wedding, everything changed. I saw her for the first time.

I don't know what made me turn around at the reception that night, but I did.

She was standing just behind the entrance to the party tent, staring at the parquet with shining blue eyes and her brow bent in pain. No one had seen her outside of her family since we all got word that the ceremony was off. No one had seen her in that dress — the dress she was meant to get married in.

The light was soft and low, illuminating her pinned-up curls like a halo, casting shadows across her arms and hands clasped in front of her as her fingers gently squeezed and twisted. The dress fitted her perfectly, the curve of her hips and legs swathed in lace, fitting her body close until it dropped behind her in a short train. My eyes followed the line up to the high collar, the loose cap sleeves, and to her trembling chin.

She took a breath. That breath stole mine.

I'd never seen anything so beautiful and broken. Not in all my life.

Her bridesmaids materialized behind her, smiling, and one touched her arm. Maggie's face changed, brightened to mask the hurt that had been so clear only a second before. She looked brave. And she was.

She said she still wanted to have the party. Said the booze had been paid for, and that we should drink it. God knew we all needed it, Maggie especially.

Everyone drank too much that night except me. I carried around the same glass of scotch for two hours, watching West get tanked as I tried to defuse his desire to find Jimmy and beat him unconscious. They danced to a new setlist that Rose compiled, jam-packed with girl power and pep. But at one point, a slow song came on, and Maggie stood in the middle of the dance floor to catch her breath, smile slipping as everyone paired off. I set down my drink, and in seconds, she was in my arms.

She'd smiled up at me gratefully, her eyes wet with tears. I made jokes, as I do, but with every step, she fell into me a little more until she was flush against my chest. West and Lily were dancing nearby, laughing. Patrick sat alone at the table looking world-worn, and Rose was at the bar. But Maggie was in my arms, and all I wanted in the world was to take away her pain.

It was late by then — most of the guests had already gone, the party having died down after a long night of drinking. And so we danced, shifting in a small circle with her arms hung around my neck and head tucked under my chin. My fingers grazed the tiny buttons on the back of her dress, and I squeezed, pulling her closer to me.

She leaned back when the song changed, and for a long moment, we didn't move. Just stood still in each other's arms.

"Come with me, Maggie," I whispered.

She nodded, never breaking eye contact.

I glanced around — everyone was occupied. So I took her hand, and we slipped out of the tent and away.

We hurried out of the garden and into the hotel, my heart thumping in my ribcage, holding her hand while we waited for the elevator with eyes on us, on her, probably thinking she was my bride, and part of me didn't mind. And then I stepped into the elevator and into her, until we were breathing each other, until my lips were on hers like they were meant to be there.

The doors opened, and I broke away, my arm around her waist as I swept her out of the elevator and down the hall to her honeymoon suite. She dug out the keycard with shaking hands and unlocked the door, and we slipped into the cool, quiet room. The door closed behind us, taking the light with it.

I reached for her arm, turned her around and cupped her face. And then I looked into her eyes and made her a promise.

"I'll make you forget he ever existed."

I kissed her with everything in my heart, hoping that if I did, she would be all right.

There are some things in life that can't be forgotten, no matter what you do, no matter how you try. I dreamed of my fingers unbuttoning the back of her wedding dress. My hands slipping down to her garters. Unhooking her corset. Her lips. Her eyes. The feeling of waking up with her against my chest, my fingers tangled in her curly hair.

But when she woke, she was flustered, embarrassed. Ashamed. She didn't have to tell me she thought I was a mistake.

I told myself that we were only caught up in the emotion from the night. I wanted to kiss her pain away, and for one night, I did.

So I turned the charm up to eleven. I made her laugh, made her feel like it was all right, that I felt just like she did. Gave her a final kiss and told her I'd see her around. And then I went back to New York and tried to forget about her.

I'd recently determined that it was impossible.

When I came home, I couldn't shake her. I dove back into my social life, but it just felt off. Different. I even called a couple of my sure things — the wild, late night girls who gave and gave and gave. But I was just … disenchanted, I guess would be a good word.

Then Maggie came back. I have to admit, when I saw her for the first time again, nothing went as planned. West had sent me to pick her up from the airport, and when I saw her, there was a moment, a long, stretched out moment where we slowed to a stop in the busy terminal, eyes locked on each other across a dozen feet. But then time started again. She brushed me off. So I needled her to cover for the fact that I was hurt.

After the failed reunion, we circled each other like magnets, the tension a force between us, keeping us apart.

Until the club.

Everything in my life had come easy to me — girls, friends, money, even my degree from Columbia. In fact, if I had to work for it, it didn't happen. There were only two exceptions to that: sailing and Maggie.

Her resistance amused me, mostly because it was so plain to see that she wanted me. Maybe I wanted her to admit that she was into me more than she'd say, more than she would be a no-strings hookup. Because I'd done those before. In fact, it was all I did. And *that* didn't feel like *this*.

I didn't want to break her. I didn't want her to submit. I just wanted her to admit it. Preferably to me.

Aside from all of that to intrigue me, there was the matter of her innocence.

She'd only been with one other man, the same one she'd been dating since high school. Which meant he'd had no time to learn anywhere near the number of tricks I'd acquired, aside from all the fucking around he did. I'd discovered that he didn't know anything about a woman's body. It was pretty standard missionary with the occasional request for what she found to be obligatory oral. But only for him. The asshole didn't even go down on her.

The thought made me irrationally angry.

I'd spent the last two weeks digging through my bag of tricks, showing her what it was like to have her body worshiped. There was something unbelievably fulfilling about making her happy, making her feel good. In fact, it was addicting.

She was addicting.

She'd left Habits in such a hurry, and she hadn't texted. I glanced at my phone, wondering how mad she was for only a split second before picking it up and shooting off a text.

Hey. You left too soon tonight.

My phone buzzed after a second. *Sorry. It's hard to be around you sometimes when everyone's there, you know?*

I do. Intense. Did Astrid have something to do with it?

Nah.

I smiled as I typed out a response. *She wouldn't mind if you came with me to the Gala instead. Imagine it. Me in a tux. You in something sparkly with a long zipper for me to unzip.*

That breaks the cardinal rule. No dates. I'm not equipped for public consumption via paparazzi.

Oh, trust me. You are.

Nice try, Coop. Although I wouldn't mind seeing you in that tux.

I settled back in my pillows, still smiling. *We could go as friends.*

The rules are in place for a reason, Mr. Moore. Thanks for checking up on me.

You know she's just a friend.

I know. And anyway, it's fine as long as you promise you're not banging anyone else.

I promise. I wouldn't lie to you, Mags.

You'd better not. Pretty sure I could get West to commit a felony by telling him we're hooking up.

I chuckled. *I like feisty Maggie.*

I bet you do. Sleep well, Coop.

I'd sleep better if you were here, I typed back, not wanting to let her go.

Ugh lol. Rule breaker.

Rule enforcer.

So I'm the cop and you're the robber? I feel like this makes a lot of sense. Tell me you have handcuffs.

Omg, Coop. And what do you rob? Unsuspecting ladies of their hearts?

I smirked. *And panties. Among other things.*

LOL.

Night, Maggie.

Night, Cooper.

I set down my phone with a sigh, relieved that she was all right and a little high from talking to her. I might have also imagined her lying in bed, smiling at her phone like I had just been.

I scrolled through Netflix, trying to decide how best to spend my Saturday night. I was all caught up on *Arrow* and *The Flash*. I'd watched *Firefly* at least six times and *Doctor Who* three. Maybe I'd watch *Supernatural* again, or *Star Trek: The Next Generation*.

What, did you expect? Porn? Cooper Moore — International Man of Mystery.

I blame my father for the sci-fi addiction. He was always working, even when he was at home, but one night a week, we'd pile onto the couch and watch sci-fi together. Star Trek was our favorite, but when I quoted Spock at school in the second grade — an elite private school packed with bluebloods — my best friend Ash made a huge joke out of it.

And that was when I decided to keep it to myself. West only knew a little, just about my comics collection, though I'd occasionally make a reference that would get me eyed. But the fact that it was my own little secret made it that much more comforting. Like a security blanket of nerd.

The secrets that I had made me feel safe. If I kept enough of myself hidden, I couldn't get hurt. In a world where everyone wants something from you, it was easier — smarter — if you play it close to the vest.

So that's exactly what I did.

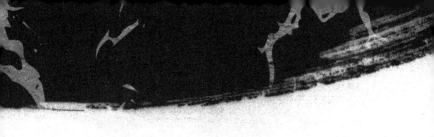

Grown-Ass Woman

MAGGIE

stretched and rolled over in bed the next morning, sighing at the serenity of the morning. Everything was still and quiet, though I could hear Lily in the kitchen. Our room was bright, the light diffused by the curtains, everything soft pinks, creams, and grays. Lily's bed was across from mine, her wall graced with a display of ballet shoes from important performances. She'd scribbled the date and show on the toe of each pair and hung them on her wall, the most recent being her *Swan Lake* debut.

The shoes framed a large painting of a ballerina in the shadows, only parts of her body visible — profile, shoulder, tutu. I admired it often — the darkness and lightness of it, that it felt heavy and feather-light all at once. Patrick had painted it for her years before, after he went to his first ballet. He'd painted something for everyone. In fact, most of the art in our apartment was Patrick's work.

My mind drifted to the day ahead, wondering what I'd do to occupy my time. I'd be alone again — Lily would be at the theater, West would be at Columbia grading papers as part of his TA duties. Rose would sleep most of the day. So I'd fill out applications and look

for something to occupy my time, besides Cooper.

It had started off casually, but in the last week, we'd ramped up to seeing each other every day, without fail. The closer we came to the end, the more … I don't know, *frantic* I felt about him. Like the binge brownie session before a diet. I told myself it was just because he did stuff to my vagina that I'd only read about in Cosmo. It was forbidden and exciting — there was something thrilling about being near him with everyone around, knowing they had no clue we were seeing each other in the buff, on the daily.

Plus, Cooper was thrilling on his own. He was a walking dream — tall and dark, rich and charming, cheerful and reckless.

He was dangerous.

That made him infinitely more appealing. All the more reason for the rules.

My phone buzzed on my nightstand, and I picked it up to find a text from Cooper. I smiled thinking about him lying in his gigantic bed, thinking about me.

Sleep well?

I texted him back. *Decent. You?*

I had this dream about you last night.

I snickered. *Oh, yeah? What about?*

Come over and I'll show you.

My cheeks heated up. *I'd love to, but I've got some stuff to take care of today.*

Ah, yes. The job hunt. What's on deck?

I've got a few things working. Gotta fill out some applications and send some emails.

I want to see you.

My heart skipped. He was just so … direct sometimes. I think it affected my pulse rate. *You just saw me yesterday.*

Well, I want to see you again. Come over tonight.

Maybe. What time?

I'm tied up until 8 or 9. Don't say maybe. Say yes.

I wanted to go so bad. My brain screamed at me to cut that shit out. *I'll text you later.*

So, yes?

Bye, Cooper.

See you tonight, Mags.

I rolled my eyes, betrayed by my smile as I closed the app, only noticing then that I had an alert for another text. From Jimmy.

Seeing my ex-fiancé's name alone still threw me into a spin. Never mind when I read the actual message.

Been thinking about you.

My heart pounded so hard it hurt, my breath coming a little too fast. I closed the app. If you'd scrolled back through his texts, you would find a long, one-sided grovel-fest. I hadn't responded once. I felt like I deserved a medal or something. Ice cream, at the very least.

Jimmy had been thinking about me. I almost laughed at the thought. And then I wished I had the balls to text him back: *I won't be thinking about you at all while I'm banging Cooper Moore tonight.*

I flipped off the covers and climbed out of bed, no longer feeling happy and comfortable there, looking for some distance as I made my way through the apartment.

New York apartments were nothing like what I was accustomed to. In Jackson, your apartment would be at most forty years old, built in that 70s or 80s style with the bar behind the sink and mirrored closet doors. In Manhattan? The buildings were much older, mid-century or before. Which meant they were tiny. Our kitchen opened up to the living room, which had just enough room for the essentials — couch, coffee table, TV, and a table and chairs. But Lily and Rose found a way to set it up so it didn't feel cramped, with a style that was somehow girly while still maintaining an edge.

Must have been a New York thing. I'd never achieve that level of chic on my own.

Lily smiled over her shoulder at me as she stood in front of the stove, pushing eggs around the skillet. She was so pretty, big, wide set blue eyes and long, blond hair hanging against her back in waves.

"Morning," she said. "Hungry?"

I smiled back. "Sure. Is there coffee?"

"Mmhmm," she hummed as she looked back at the eggs. "Made a full pot."

I grabbed a mug and poured the steaming coffee in. "How'd it go last night? Stay at Habits late?"

"Oh, not super late. Astrid and Cooper left just after you did. When West and I left, Tricky was still there making Rose squirmy."

I pushed away the thought of Astrid leaving with Cooper. And then I pushed away the thought of tackling Astrid and slapping her. "Poor Tricky. I wonder if he tried to talk to her." I poured a scoop of sugar into my coffee and gave it a stir.

"Doubtful. I wish he would, even though I have no idea how Rose would handle it if he did."

I took a seat at the table. "Doesn't she want him? Deep down, at least?"

"I think so. But see, once Rose makes a decision, that's pretty much it. Especially where her heart's concerned. He's got a lot of work to do if he really wants her to hear him, and I don't think he has any idea where to start. Giving her the smolder face isn't going to be enough."

I chuckled. "My God, all those tattoos all over? I'm not usually into that, but damn. Plus, those fuck-me eyes he gives her — I don't know how she can stand it."

"Me neither. She's got ironclad willpower." She dumped the eggs onto a plate. "Scrambled okay?"

"Perfect."

She handed me the plate with a napkin and fork. "How are things with Mr. M?"

"Thanks, Lily." I laid the napkin in my lap and picked up my fork. "Mr. M is as sexy as ever. He wants to see me tonight, so I may not be around."

She smirked at me as she cracked eggs for another round. "That makes it almost every day for the last week."

"Not that you're keeping track or anything."

"Clearly I'm not at all interested or curious about this guy in any way. And I'm not at all dying to know who he is, or what he looks like, or where you met him, or all of the millions of things you haven't told me. I'm very indifferent about the whole thing."

I laughed. "Clearly."

"So, none of those pesky *feelings* have developed, have they?"

I took a sip of coffee. "We're just having fun, that's all. There's nothing more to it. He's a lot like Jimmy, which makes it impossible to take him seriously."

"But, I mean, how alike are they *really?*"

I thought about how to phrase it in a way that wouldn't tip her off, taking a bite of eggs to stall. "Well, they're both manwhores, even though Mr. M is up front about it. And they're both charmers. They have a knack for making me feel special and pretty, even though I don't believe they want anything real from me. Just … magnetic, you know? They have charisma. You just want to believe them so badly. Which is scary, because apparently I'm gullible."

Lily pushed the sizzling eggs around again. "I dunno. You trusted Jimmy. That doesn't make you gullible."

"Says you. Anyway, I see Mr. M coming from a mile away. I won't be fooled again. I've got his number, and I know his game. I'm armed with foresight and a set of surefire rules to keep things casual. As long as I can just enjoy that little sliver of him I know I can handle, everything will be okay."

"Oh, I'm sure you can handle his sliver just fine."

"Not half as well as he can handle mine."

She giggled. "So, how does it work? Like, do you guys talk and hang out, or do you just go cowgirl up and then split when it's over?"

"We talk, but dates aren't allowed, per the rules. We hang out at his place sometimes too, but nothing much, really. I just get freaked out if I stay there too long or we talk about serious stuff."

She plated her eggs and sat next to me, arranging her napkin. "So you really don't have *any* feelings for him?"

"I mean, I like him. I enjoy talking to him. And I'll admit, he is such a good kisser that I sometimes forget all about the rules."

Her full mouth didn't stop her from snickering.

I pushed my eggs around my plate before scooping up a bite. "But I'm just another notch on his bedpost. He's just using me, and I'm using him too. It works."

"As long as you can keep that mentality, you'll be just fine."

"I'm being a modern woman. Like Carrie Bradshaw with a less impressive shoe collection. Using my vagina the way it was intended to be used — by a super hot vagina wizard."

She broke out laughing just as a knock rapped. The door opened, and West walked in.

My brother was apparently a dreamboat, per every hetero girlfriend I'd ever had. He was well over six feet of long and lean, with blue eyes like mine. We didn't look all that much alike, weirdly — he had the stature of our dad and the coloring of our mom, while I looked the opposite — just like my mom but blond like my dad. He'd been living in New York for six years, and in that time, he'd grown a beard, a man bun, and an affinity for flannels and oxfords.

"Hey," West said with a smile. "What are you two giggling about?" He walked across the room and bent to lay a kiss on Lily's lips.

"You don't want to know," she answered and stretched to kiss him once more.

"Hey, Mags." West took a seat next to me at the table. "I'm glad you're up. Brought you something." He pulled what looked like a pink flashlight out of his pocket and handed it to me.

I set my fork down and took it, curious. "Why are you giving me a flashlight?"

He chuckled. "It's a Taser."

I huffed. "I have mace. I don't need a Taser. I'm not together enough to walk around with something this dangerous. With my luck, I'll accidentally tase an old lady asking for directions or something."

"You've been running around the city without one for long enough. Don't fight me on it — just put it in your purse and thank me for looking out for you."

I rolled my eyes.

"Just do it and I'll shut up."

I gave him a look. "Thanks, West."

"You're welcome." He smiled, looking smug. "What are you doing today?"

"Hitting the pavement. Or internet, as it were. I figure that should take up a good chunk of the day."

He sat back in his seat and hung an arm on the back of Lily's chair. They looked so good together, like they belonged on the cover of a magazine. "Where all are you applying?"

"Some elementary schools and a handful of charity reading outreach programs. There's one in particular that works with kids who live in homeless shelters. I wouldn't get paid, but it would be so rewarding. I just can't imagine the life those kids live, not after growing up with a stable family in the suburbs."

"God," Lily said, eyes wide. "You don't always think about how many homeless *kids* there must be in the city."

"I know. I read on one website that there are more than twenty-five thousand homeless kids in the New York Metro area. It's crazy. A lot of them live in community houses with their families as they try to get back on their feet. I think I'd really enjoy it, bringing books into their lives." I sighed and scooped a bite of eggs onto my fork. "I can afford to volunteer for the summer, maybe see if there's something I can do with them on a long-term scale. And in the meantime, I'll keep looking for a teaching job for next school year."

"Sounds like a solid plan," she said.

West eyed me. "Sounds dangerous."

I rolled my eyes. "God, you're the worst, Weston. I'm a grown-ass woman armed with pepper spray and a hot pink Taser. I'll be fine. I'll be at the shelters during the day with a million other people. Anyway, I don't even have the job yet, so just leave me be."

He made a face and folded his arms across his chest. "You don't even know how to use the Taser yet."

I picked it up and inspected it. "How hard could it be? Push this zap button." I pressed it, and it crackled so loud, I jumped. My eyes widened, watching the electricity snap between the prongs. I let the button go. "Yeah, I'm betting that alone will run off the rapists."

Lily snickered. "He makes me carry one too, you know. He bought it for me years ago."

I gave my head a shake in commiseration. "He is so overbearing."

West's eyes narrowed. "*He* just doesn't like to think about his girls walking around New York without him."

Lily patted his forearm and leaned over to kiss his cheek. "I think it's sweet."

"Thank you."

"And a little pushy—"

He frowned.

"—but sweet."

He sighed. "Are you about ready to go?"

She shoveled her last bite into her mouth and hopped up. "Sure am. Let me grab my bag."

West stood and pushed in his chair. "Good luck today, Mags. Let me know how it goes."

"I will. Cross your fingers for me."

Lily beamed as she walked back in with her bag, and I watched them clasp hands and look into each other's eyes, smiling like there was no one else in the world but the two of them. I was somehow elated for them and filled with jealousy all at the same time.

Lily smiled over at me. "Have a great day. I'll see you tonight, okay?"

I sighed and smiled back, feeling tired out of nowhere. I picked up my coffee. "Sounds good."

They waved over their shoulders as they left the apartment, which was suddenly very, very quiet. And I was very, very alone.

I pushed back the chair as I pushed down my thoughts, grabbing Rose's portable speaker to turn on music. And then I put on a smile and cleared off the table, humming as I washed the pans and dishes.

Being alone wasn't all that bad. There was something nice about solitude, doing something mundane and responsible and grown up. Today I'd start building real roots in New York. Find an undeniable reason to stay forever. Because even though I was here, I still felt like I was in limbo. Finding a job was the first step to digging into my new life.

I dried off my hands and set up my laptop, feeling determined. Opened my email sitting straight as an arrow at the kitchen table. Pulled open my bookmarks feeling like a boss and fired away. Before I knew it, I had applied to three public schools and four charity outreaches, which was the sum of everything on my to-do list for the day. I checked the clock.

It was ten.

I sighed, annoyed that I didn't have a single productive thing left to do. Eleven hours to kill before I saw Cooper. I chewed on my lip. Maybe I could explore the city some more or go to the library and check out a new book. I could read in the park — it looked like a gorgeous day. Or I could text Cooper.

Why wait all day if he was free now?

I only considered the question for a split second before picking up my phone and firing off a message. *Welp, that didn't take nearly as long as I thought it would. You busy?*

My phone dinged within seconds. *For you? Never. Want to come over?*

I smiled. *Be there in thirty-ish.*

Let me send Bobby.

I rolled my eyes. *You're just as bad as West. I can find my own way, thanks, boss.*

All right, you strong, independent woman. I'll be waiting.

My heart fluttered again as I hopped up and nearly skipped into my room to get dressed. I pulled open my drawers and dug through them. Had to be casual for sure. Not too fussy. Maybe I'd even still go for a walk and read in the park after seeing Cooper. Naked.

I stripped off my clothes and slipped into my favorite casual-but-still-sexy-because-it's-see-through black bra and panties, tugged on skinnies and a loose, striped tank. I reached under my bed for my white Converse, past all my gorgeous shoes that I never got to wear, because New York is dirty as hell, and shoved my feet in. And then I blew into the bathroom, stuffing a cardigan and scarf into my bag.

It wasn't that I was overly eager for no reason, it was just that I was already thinking about his lips. I could see them smiling. I could feel them against mine. I could see them closing over my —

Oh, for God's sake. Give it a rest.

I made a face at my reflection and picked up my mascara, then brushed on a little blush. My hair was a mess, which was nothing new, but I sprayed it with some expensive stuff my hairdresser sold me and scrunched it up, shaking out my roots. No one would ever accuse me of not having volume, that was for sure.

I headed out of the apartment, pulling on my cardigan and wrapping my scarf around my neck as I headed across the hall to West's. I knocked and waited. We all had keys to each other's apartments, though I still felt weird using mine to get into my brother's place. Patrick would have answered within a second — his hearing was ridiculous — so when he didn't, I unlocked the door and headed inside.

Their apartment had the comfortable, easy feel of a couple of guys who didn't give a crap about interior design, but their hobbies lent their own charm to the place. Patrick's art hung all over the walls, and the shelves were piled with West's books. He had so many, shelf after shelf, from the classics on up, hardbacks and paperbacks stacked in front of each other, slipped into the free spaces. Shakespeare was his favorite, the topic of his proposal for the doctoral program at Columbia.

I made my way to one and quickly scanned the shelves, settling on *Stardust* by Neil Gaiman, another one of West's favorite authors, and then I bounded out of the building.

I popped in my earbuds, smiling in the crisp spring afternoon, feeling like a legit New Yorker as I set out to walk the mile to Cooper's place by way of Central Park. I knew exactly where I was going without needing to check a map. My MetroCard was in my bag, which somehow felt like an official token of my authenticity, whether I needed it or not.

You know what it was? I felt like I had my shit together. Like this new, improved, cosmopolitan Maggie had shed her old skin and left it in Jackson where it belonged. New Maggie was just that — shiny and new and indifferent to everything that had happened before. I wanted to reinvent myself. No, reinvent was the wrong word. I wanted to *redefine* myself. And I had.

My whole life, I'd lived in the same town, known the same

people. Do you know what it's like to run into everyone you went to high school with every time you went to the grocery store? Or the post office? Well, it sucks. No one forgot that time in first grade when you sat on a brownie and had chocolate on your butt all day. They don't forget about the time Shawn Cross spit gum in your hair on the field trip to the zoo and Miss Jaret had to cut it out with a pair of safety scissors. And they *definitely* don't forget that one time you caught your fiancé nailing your maid of honor on your wedding day. In a *church*, no less.

But in New York? No one knew and no one cared. And that was a gloriously freeing thing.

The day was spectacular — that kind of day that you live for all year, where it's the perfect mix of blue sky and clouds, the air just crisp enough to be comfortable, carrying the promise of change. I made my way across the park with my eyes on the blooming cherry blossom and magnolia trees. I walked the path past the joggers and couples and around the Central Park Lawn, which was blanketed with people reading books, just sitting in the middle of the park, soaking it all in.

Once I hit the Met, I headed down 5th Avenue and to The Compass.

It was beautiful, the old, Deco feel of the 20s in every column, every angle, and I looked up, craning my neck as I tried to guess which windows were his from the outside. I smiled to myself, winding up my earbuds as I approached the awning to his building.

The doorman smiled at me. "Miss Williams?"

I blinked, startled that he knew my name. "Yes?"

"Mr. Moore added you to his permanent guest list. He told me to send you up."

I blushed. "Thank you so much."

"It's my pleasure. Allow me." He opened the door, and I stepped into the lobby, feeling a little fancy and a lot strange.

I'd been there almost a dozen times, but Cooper was usually with me, and we always came through the back entrance. But as I stepped into the elaborate foyer, I felt like a hayseed in my sneakers and jeans. To fit in there, I would have needed to be a little more Dior and Louboutin and a little less H&M and Converse.

I followed the doorman into the elevator well, admiring the golden compass on the floor between the two elevator doors. It always caught my eye, the elaborate starburst that made the compass rose, colored in alternating matte and shiny gold. It was like the cherry on the design sundae in such a brilliant building.

The elevator door opened, and I stepped inside. The doorman ducked in and waved his key fob over the sensor pad before hitting the P1 button.

He tipped his hat as he backed out. "Have a lovely time, Miss Williams."

"Thank you again," I called as the doors closed, and I leaned against the elevator wall, all of a sudden nervous, or intimidated maybe. Like I didn't belong. When the doors opened a moment later to his black and gold foyer, I felt even less sure of myself. But I walked across the space and knocked on his door anyway. And the second he opened it and I saw his smiling face, it was like nothing before that moment had ever happened.

Boss

COOPER

Her face lit up when she saw me, and I smiled down at her, the little thing in my big, imposing entry. I dragged her into my apartment before either of us spoke — all she could do was giggle as I pulled her into my chest.

Her blond hair was so curly, all I wanted was to bury my hands in it as she looked up at me, smiling.

"I only wanted to send Bobby so I could get you here quicker, you know."

Her cheeks were flushed, and my eyes followed the trail of freckles across the bridge of her nose. "It's a gorgeous day, and I'm glad I walked. But thanks, bossypants."

I moved her hair from her face, slipping a big curl through my fingers. "There's only one thing I'm the boss of, and right now, it's in your pants."

A laugh shot out of her. "Oh, my God, Cooper."

I chuckled and bent to pick her up, my hands on her ass, and she wrapped her legs around my waist, bringing her almost eye-level with me. One corner of my mouth pulled up in a smile. "Tell me it's

not true."

She laughed, her arms hanging loose around my neck. "Nobody's the boss of what's in my pants but me."

I leaned into her. "Let's see about that."

Her eyes closed, our lips only millimeters apart for a heartbeat before I closed the gap. Her lips were soft and sweet, mine strong and insistent, and I swept my tongue against her bottom lip, urging her to open her mouth. She did what I wanted.

The kiss was everything it always was with Maggie — a mix of recklessness and decision, playfulness and sincerity. Her kiss always told me more than she would admit with her words.

She tightened her arms around my neck, and I deepened the kiss, squeezing her tighter. I spun us, and she squealed, smiling against my lips as I walked blindly to my bedroom. I laid her down on my bed and arched over her, pressing my hips into hers.

My lips found her neck, and she sighed, slipping her fingers into my hair. I trailed a hand down her ribs to the hem of her tank and under. Up her hot skin, to her breast. The thin lace was a tease — I cupped her, thumbing her nipple that peaked under my touch. She sighed again, and I smiled.

"I can't get enough of you," I whispered against her skin, closing my lips to kiss her delicate collarbone.

"I know," she whispered back as I lifted her shirt.

My eyes were on my hand as it traced the curve of her breast, my fingers as they hooked the fabric and pulled, exposing her to me. Her hips rolled gently against mine, and I brought my lips almost to her nipple. I let out a breath, teasing her, and she arched her back, begging me with her body. So I waited a second longer, my lips still inches from her, knowing full well what I was doing to her.

I squeezed and closed my mouth over her nipple, sucking gently. Her fingers twisted in my hair.

I spent a long moment right where I was, with her soft breast in my hand and tight nipple in my mouth. My fingers skated down her stomach, to the button of her jeans that I popped open with one hand, to her zipper that I dropped. I kissed down her body until I reached the V of her open pants, laid a long, hot kiss just above the waist of her black panties before backing away. My eyes connected with hers, and when I smiled and she blushed, I felt like a god.

I reached for her heels and pulled off her sneakers, grabbed the band of her jeans and tugged until they were off and out of my way, then her panties. And all the while, she watched me, blushing like that with her bottom lip between her teeth.

I ran my hands up her thighs and pushed her legs apart, skimmed the tip of my nose up her thigh and spread her open. I licked up the line, pausing when I reached the top to suck, rocking my face against her as she whispered something unintelligible, her fingers roaming to her bare breast. Her legs tightened when I slipped a finger inside, then another, hooking them to press the sensitive spot inside, squeezing in time with my tongue.

Her back arched, thighs trembling, and I moved faster, steady, giving more pressure, matching the rhythm of my mouth and hand as her hips rolled against me. She came closer, closer as I spurred her on, on and on until she dragged in a breath, squeezing around my fingers once, tight, then in pulses. Her breath slipped out in a sigh, and she dragged in another, shallow, ragged as she came.

I slowed as her body relaxed, rolled my tongue gently against her, hands still splayed across her ass and hips. She ran a hand through my hair, and I broke away to kiss her thigh again.

Maggie mumbled something, and I looked up at her. She looked sated, fresh, her face soft and lips smiling, fingers absently stroking her breast.

I climbed up her body. "Hmm?"

She opened her arms, and I filled them, settling in against her. "I said, you win."

"Won what?" I laid a kiss on her neck.

"You're the boss of what's in my pants."

I smirked. "I know."

She ran a hand down my chest. "Why do you have so many clothes on?"

"I had a point to prove."

Maggie smiled and pressed, urging me back. I rolled over, taking her with me. "You're never naked enough," she said softly and sat, straddling me.

She crossed her arms and grabbed the hem of her shirt, pulling it over her head, leaving her curls bouncing. Her bra was next — I watched as she reached behind her and unhooked it, slid it down her arms and tossed it away. My eyes roamed her naked body, the soft curves of her breasts and stomach, her hips, her thighs. I slid my hands up her thighs as her fingers found the buttons of my shirt and unfastened them one by one, and she slipped her hands underneath, up my abs, my chest, my shoulders, so my torso was exposed.

Her eyes were on her hands as they trailed across my skin, fingers grazing my nipples as she dragged her fingers down to my pants and unfastened them. She grabbed the band of my pants, sending a shock through me when her nails grazed my skin, and my eyes locked on her bottom lip, caught in her teeth. My heart thumped as she moved between my legs and pulled my pants and underwear down my thighs, down my calves and off.

She settled between my legs, eyes down, lips parted, her arms around my waist, breath hot against the length of me. Every nerve in my body focused on her — she was close enough that I could feel her mouth, millimeters away. Her nose brushed the sensitive skin next to my shaft, and I closed my eyes, sucking in a breath when she licked the very top of my thigh, her cheek brushing against me.

I slipped a hand into her wild hair.

She ran the tip of her tongue up the length of me and kissed my crown, softly, sweetly. And when she closed her hot mouth around me and dropped down, I sucked in a breath, watching as I disappeared in her mouth. Her hand worked my base when she pulled out, her tongue rolling before she dropped down, again and again until I couldn't take it anymore.

I wanted the rest of her. I wanted all of her.

I whispered her name — it was all I could manage — and when she let me go, I rushed to meet her halfway, taking those swollen lips for my own.

My fingers shifted in her hair, and I broke away. "Lie down," I said, my voice rough.

I guided her to lay on her stomach, lifting her hips, angling her to me. Her cheek pressed against the bed, and her eyes closed as I stripped off my shirt. I touched the wet length of her, circling the bundle of nerves, and her lips parted again with a sigh.

God, I loved that sound.

I guided my crown to stroke up the line and back down, gripping her hip with my free hand when I hit the dip, flexing my hips and pulling her onto me until I filled her, felt her all around me.

I couldn't breathe.

Her thighs trembled as I pulled out slow and flexed again, harder. I hit the end, and she jolted forward with a moan.

My hands found the bend in her hips, and I pushed her away, pulling her back down onto me with a soft pat.

"*Yes,*" she whispered and slipped a hand between her legs.

Every motion, every thrust, every moan from her lips and quake of her thighs sent my pulse racing faster. And when she came again, I couldn't hold on. I slammed into her, my heart stopping for a long moment, and when it started again, it was all I could hear, my fingers squeezing her hips like I'd fly away if I let her go.

I drove into her a final time before leaning forward, pressing my chest against her back as she stretched out onto her stomach.

Her lids cracked open when I kissed her bare shoulder. "That's my favorite."

I brushed her hair from her face and smiled. "I know."

"I used to hate it from behind. It always felt so cheap … but not with you."

The thought of anyone making Maggie feel cheap made me want to find the asshole and explain a few things to him. With my fist. "I'm happy to make you feel expensive any day."

She chuckled and shifted, and I rolled over, propping my head on my hand.

"What's the rest of your day look like?" I asked.

She mirrored me. "I was going to go read in the park."

"Great. I'll come with you." I smirked, knowing she'd resist and knowing I could talk her into it anyway.

One eyebrow rose, and she shook her head. "That sounds like a date."

"How so? I won't buy you anything or even touch you. Just a couple of young New Yorkers, reading in the park on a perfect afternoon."

Her cheeks flushed, even though she was trying to look resolute. "Don't you have a thing to go to?"

"Not for hours."

"I'm sure you need to prep for that instead."

I shrugged. "Nothing to prep for. It's just some photo shoot I regret agreeing to."

She raised an eyebrow. "Oh?"

"It's not a big deal."

"Yeah, I do photo shoots all the time. Totally normal. Why do you regret it?"

"Because they want to shoot on my boat, and I don't think they'll respect my boat."

Her brow quirked. "Is it for a sailing piece?"

I hesitated. "No."

"What's it for?"

I eyed her. "I'll only tell you if you swear not to tell anyone, especially not West."

Her interest was piqued, eyes a little wider, the corners of her mouth turned up. "Well, I'm keeping everything else from him, so why not add to the list?"

I hesitated again. I hadn't spoken of it to anyone but Jules, and I was suddenly embarrassed. I thought about talking my way out of telling her, but part of me didn't mind that she knew. I took a breath. "I was chosen for *W*'s twenty-five most eligible bachelors."

Her mouth popped open. "Are you serious, Coop?"

My cheeks flushed, and I couldn't do a thing to stop it. "Yup."

She glanced away, shaking her head and said, half to herself, "I just banged one of the twenty-five most sought-after men."

"According to *W*."

She pushed me in the shoulder, smiling. I grabbed her hand and pulled her a little closer. She smirked at me. "I can't believe that. No wonder you don't want West to know. He's going to have a field day."

"Yes, he is. Which is another part of the reason I'm regretting agreeing to it. But I'm supposed to meet the photographers this afternoon. I've still got a few hours." I slipped a leg between hers and squeezed until her body was flush against mine.

She bobbled her head, eyes on the ceiling, and I knew I had her. "I dunno. I have some very important solo reading to do in the park."

"Come on, Mags. It's not a date. In fact, it breaks none of the rules. But if you really don't want me to go, we could always stay here." I squeezed her tighter.

"I just had two orgasms, which no one besides you has ever done to me, by the way. I don't think I could go another round if I wanted to."

"Is that a challenge?" I brushed my lips against hers.

She laughed. "You really are impossible."

"I know." I kissed her again. "Let's go."

"All right," she said with a sigh. "But it's not a date."

"Whatever you say, Mags."

She rolled away from me, dropping her legs to the floor to stand. "Whoa." She wobbled and reached back for the bed to steady herself. "I think my legs are rubber."

I headed into my bathroom, feeling nine feet tall. "Then my work here is done."

MAGGIE

paused with my shoe in my hand when Cooper walked out of his closet looking like a freaking model — black jeans and oxfords, a grey Henley half-tucked into his pants, body long and lean, a jaw that could cut stuff. He ran a hand through his hair and smiled at me.

Bastard didn't even have to try. It's like he just existed on some separate plane of sexy than the rest of the world.

"You ready?"

I blinked, smiling back as I pulled on my shoe. "Ready."

I followed him through his apartment as he collected his things, first his dark messenger bag, then a blanket that I thought might be cashmere. He folded it into a neat square and slipped into his bag, and I watched him, wondering absently how much it cost. It was so strange when I thought about it, which oddly wasn't all *that* often. Just moments that reminded me how different our lives were. But

Cooper was just … Cooper. I mean, he was superhuman in bed and had the bone structure of a Michelangelo, but he was just a man.

I picked up the scrambled Rubik's Cube that sat next to a marble chess set on the long table behind his couch. "I haven't seen one of these in years. The only way I can do them is by peeling the stickers off."

"It's not hard, once you figure it out."

I laughed. "No way can you solve this. I've never seen anyone do it."

He smirked. "Bet you a kiss."

I smirked right back and offered it to him. "Deal."

"Go ahead and mix it up."

I mixed it up even more than it already was and handed it over.

He took it, turning it over in his hands a few times before getting to work, spinning the cube around. My eyes widened with every turn as the colors came together, click by click by click until it was finished. He handed it over for inspection. It was perfect.

"You've got to be kidding m—" His lips were against mine, his tongue slipping into my mouth as he kissed me deep.

He broke away, and I was breathless. "Told you," he said as he let me go.

I blinked, trying to collect myself, a smile stretching across my lips as I watched him walk around the couch. My eyes found the chess set again, and I picked up a pawn to inspect it.

"This is beautiful, Cooper."

"Thanks," he said. "It was my grandfather's. I never could beat him. He was the smartest man I've ever known, and the only person who could beat me at chess." He chuckled and grabbed a hardback book off the coffee table in his living room with Batman on the cover.

I set the pawn back down and picked up my bag. "So, you're a DC man, huh?"

He smiled at me appreciatively and glanced at the cover before putting it into his bag. "I like them both, to be honest. But I find I enjoy DC more than Marvel, aside from X-Men. That's my jam."

I snickered. "Your jam." We headed to the door and into the foyer. "Batman seems a little obvious, though. I mean, super-rich dude uses money to fight crime?" I gave him a look and waved a hand over my opulent surroundings.

"Don't hate." We stepped into the elevator, and the doors closed.

"Oh, I definitely don't hate. Just saying, there are a lot of similarities between you and the The Bat."

He pressed L and leaned back against the rail as he slipped his hands into his pockets. "Bruce Wayne leads this double life — one where he has to pretend to fit in for the sake of appearance and another where he's doing what he feels he's meant to do. The sad thing about him is that neither one of those versions are real. They're two identities, both meant to mask who he really is, and he's lost somewhere between them. He's almost as bad as the villains — everything he does is driven by a blind part of himself that can't move on. He just chooses to do good, or what he perceives as good."

I shook my head, impressed. "Pretty deep, for a Batman rundown."

He smiled at me, and my heart sped up. "I've read a comic or two."

"Who knew? Cooper Moore, closet nerd."

He laughed as the doors opened. "You have no idea."

I stepped out first, smiling down at the ground.

"Something funny?"

"You just surprise me sometimes."

He pushed open the door to the building, and as I passed, he whispered, "I've got surprises for days."

I nearly swooned.

We stepped onto the sidewalk, and I felt a little higher, a little lighter as we walked to the corner, the park stretching out across the street, green and inviting.

"So, where did you apply?" he asked.

"Elementary schools and a few charities, but the job I really want is with Project Homestead. I'd be working with the enrichment programs director to plan and teach reading workshops, sort of like library programs for kids, except run entirely out of the shelter."

"Oh." There was a strange quality to the word, like that one syllable held layers of meaning.

"What?" I asked earnestly, glancing over at him.

"Their headquarters are near my house." He put on that smile of his that scrambled my brains.

"And?"

"And I was just thinking how convenient it would be if you were working there."

I laughed and shook my head as we came to a stop at the corner and he hit the crosswalk button. "Of course you were. Always thinking with your Mini Cooper, aren't you?"

He gave me a look that might have blown up my panties. "Oh, I don't think *mini* would be the adjective most people would use."

I wet my lips, scrambling for composure under the heat of his gaze. "No, you're probably right about that. But Giant Hammerhead Cooper doesn't quite have a ring to it, does it?"

He laughed, the sound deep and easy. "Guess not."

The city on this side of town was quiet, for New York, at least. The park seemed so peaceful, and we were far enough up 5th to have plenty of distance from the bustle of touristy Midtown. It was no wonder that the area was the residency of choice for, well, anyone who was able to live there.

I could feel him next to me as we crossed the street, even though we weren't touching. It was the first time we'd been in public together. Like *together* together. Not that it was a date or anything. Just a walk in the park with my fuck buddy. Totally normal. No big deal.

Discomfort snuck into my brain at the reminder that I shouldn't be hanging out with him like this. If it weren't for the gorgeous day and the fact that there was no way Cooper would give up, I might have tried to bail. Maybe. I didn't know how he was able to talk me into stuff. I mean, outside of him being the most charming bastard I'd ever met in my life. It was like I couldn't say no. The thought annoyed me.

Two weeks.

I stood up a little straighter as we turned into the park. Being with Cooper felt good, and I didn't want to fight it. I'd fought enough lately. Right now, I just wanted to coast. A smile played on my lips.

We wandered away from the packed lawn and down a path, cutting off into the grass a ways. We were deep enough that you could barely see the city. It was another great thing about this part of Manhattan. The buildings around the park weren't towering skyscrapers, but lower, older residences, which made the magic of the park all that much more spectacular. You'd barely even know you were smack in the middle of the biggest city in America.

Cooper stopped and looked around. "What do you think? This work?"

"Works for me." I took off my bag and sat down in the grass.

"Hang on, I brought a blanket." He pulled it out of his bag and unfurled it.

"That's too fancy to sit on."

"That's not a thing." He laid it down and stretched out on his back, watching me expectantly. When I didn't move, he patted the space next to him with what I could only call a come-hither smile.

I shook my head and laughed. "It's so wrong, Cooper." I got up anyway and lay down next to him on my stomach.

He pulled his phone out of his pocket and tossed it between us before reaching for his bag. It buzzed almost within a second, and I glanced over.

I didn't mean to pry. I really didn't. But I didn't expect to see boobs on his lock screen either.

Natasha: Missing you. Wish you were here.

Adrenaline shot through me. "Uh, I think you got a message." I sat up and reached for my bag.

He picked up his phone and laughed. "Mags, wait—"

"Nah, I'm good." I made to get up, but he grabbed my arm.

"Hey, hang on. Come here and look at this."

"I just saw plenty." I tried to get up again, but he pulled me down and moved so I had to look at his stupid, gorgeous face.

"Look through my texts."

I frowned. "I hardly think that'll—"

"Maggie, just do it." He put his phone in my hand.

I made a face at him.

"Like this," he joked, his voice overly patient as he unlocked his screen and opened his messages.

Text after text was stacked up in his phone — it looked like a laundry list of sex kitten booty calls. I scrolled back.

Jeanette: Where've you been, handsome?
Taylor: Saw Ash tonight, wished you'd been there.
Marie: When can I see you again? It's been too long.
Chelsea: Lonely tonight. Are you free?
Sarah: Come to Noir tonight. We're in VIP.

They just kept going. Part of me wanted to barf at the sheer number of women who had texted him with the apparent intent to bone. But a much bigger part of me was shocked that he hadn't responded to a single one. I looked over to find him still smirking.

"I told you I wouldn't see anyone else, and I haven't. I keep my promises, Maggie. Delete their numbers if you want."

My face scrunched up. "What?"

"Delete them. The numbers."

"What will you do when we're through?"

He shrugged and looked at his phone, angling his face just enough that I couldn't quite see his reaction. "Oh, I'll manage."

I handed it to him. "You don't have to delete them for me. I believe you."

Cooper took it and flipped over onto his stomach again. "All right, I'll do it."

I laughed and reached for it. "Don't, you'll regret it."

He stretched to keep it out of my reach. "Maybe. Maybe not." He was in a list in his contacts, selecting name after name.

"Oh, my God. Cooper, don't."

"You can't tell me what to do." He made a dramatic surprised face at me, moving his finger super slowly to the delete button before touching it.

The contacts disappeared.

I gaped at him. "I cannot believe you just did that."

But he just smiled. "Believe me now?"

"I already told you I believed you, asshole!"

He laughed. "I just deleted a hundred numbers from my phone to make a point. How am I an asshole?"

"Ugh. I don't know. You drive me crazy."

God damn that smile. "Then we're even." He reached into his bag for his book.

I just sat there for a second as he opened his book like nothing had happened.

I watched him reading, admiring the line of his nose, the curves of his lips and chin. His dark brow and long, black lashes. And then, I sighed and stretched out next to him.

I didn't get it. He didn't owe me anything. We'd agreed to the rules, it was true. And the rules were important to me. I really *did* believe him before he'd emptied out his contacts.

I guess I might have believed him a little more after that, though.

I reached into my bag and pulled out *Stardust,* laying it out in front of me.

He glanced over. "What are you reading?"

I raised an eyebrow at him. "Don't be that guy. Didn't you know that talking to someone while they're reading a book ups the likelihood of you getting stabbed by like four hundred percent?"

"I think I read that once," he said with a laugh and turned the page. It was a large spread, a detailed illustration of a dark street, all shadows with streaks of light from the lamps, Batman in the shadows with just enough light on him to catch the details of his silhouette.

"Pretty sure there's a statistic about reading over shoulders too."

I chuckled, not realizing I'd been leaning to get a better look. "Sorry. I don't read a lot of comics. It really is beautiful."

"It is. And the stories … there's just something elemental about them. Good versus evil. Balance. Justice. And none of the characters are perfect. Sometimes the good guys lose and the bad guys win. But you keep turning the pages because they don't stop trying. Neither side gives up."

I bumped him in the shoulder. "You're a big ol' softy, Coop."

He smiled at me, eyes on my lips. "Don't tell anybody."

I smiled back. "Deal."

He leaned in for a kiss, and I backed away laughing. "Rules! You are *such* a liar. This is a date, which means I should go."

I tried to get up, but he grabbed me, pulling me back down. I fell, caught off balance, laughing when my back hit the ground. I was half in the grass, looking up at him. The sky was so blue behind him, the cherry blossom branches, heavy with flowers, framing his face.

"I'm sorry. I'll be good. It's not a date. Because what romantic date would involve books?"

"Uh, I'm thinking all of them should. I'm just saying. Books are sexy."

"Even comic books?"

"Sure. If you're fourteen."

He made a face. "How is Batman not sexy?"

I laughed, and so did he. He was propped on one arm, eyes soft as he reached for my hair. I might have stopped breathing. When his hand reappeared, there was a cherry blossom between his thumb and forefinger.

At that point, I was pretty ready to say fuck the rules myself.

But Cooper proved to be a man of his word. Behave himself, he did. He leaned away and turned his attention back to his book, and I lay next to him to open mine once more. I had to read the same page four times before I finally calmed down enough to actually absorb it.

Cooper was just being Cooper. I wasn't special — he was like this with everyone, I was sure. This was his normal, even if was my extraordinary.

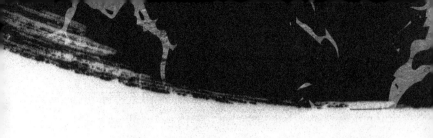

Hypnodick

COOPER

"**P**erfect, Cooper. hold it right there.*"

I hung off the ropes of my ship, staring off into the distance with Manhattan stretched up behind me. We were anchored just off Governor's Island in the middle of a gorgeous sunset. The sky had shifted from crisp blue to golds and pinks, exploding in color against the clouds.

Five women and one dude stood on the deck — the photographer, her assistant, a stylist, a makeup artist, and editor, and a journalist. I'd changed clothes twice, had my hair retouched half a dozen times, answered fifty questions, had about a kabillion photos taken of me, and was in desperate need of a drink.

The camera clicked away as the boat rocked gently. The photographer lowered her lens and smiled. "All right. Can you do that thing with the rope again? Like, undo it and redo it again."

I chuckled. "Sure." I grabbed the mainsail's halyard and pulled hand over hand to lower it.

The journalist, Elena, jotted in her notebook from where she sat on deck, leaning against the rope guardrail. "What are your favorite

vacation spots?"

I unhooked the halyard and untied the stop knot before reversing the process. "Greece and Istanbul. There's more culture and beauty in the Mediterranean than anywhere else in the world."

"Have you ever sailed there?"

"I've sailed the Mediterranean, yes, but I haven't crossed the Atlantic. Not yet, at least."

"Why not?"

I smiled at her over my shoulder. "Because I don't know if I'd ever come back."

Everyone chuckled. I retied the knot and slipped the halyard in the groove, then grabbed the rope and hoisted the sail again.

"You know," Elena said with a dramatic air, "you almost weren't considered because of your connection to Astrid Thomas."

"Is that so?" The sail hit the top of the mast, and I tacked it off. I hung my hands on my hips and looked up to make sure everything was right as the shutter clicked.

"It is. Our sources determined it wasn't serious, though."

I shot her a sardonic smile. "You'd know best, I'm sure."

"The tabloids love to speculate about the women you're seen with who *aren't* Miss Thomas. A bit of a player, are you?"

"That's what the gossip magazines say, so it must be true."

She looked a little embarrassed.

I smiled at her, shooting for comforting, but she pressed on.

"It's an easy assumption to make, wouldn't you say?"

I shrugged. "It's all about perspective, I suppose."

The photographer lowered her camera and looked back through a few pictures. "These are great. Can I get you to take your shirt off, please?"

"Yeah, sure." I reached behind me and grabbed the back of my shirt, pulling it over my head.

The camera clicked so many times, I didn't know how she had

any memory left on her card.

I tossed my shirt into the center of the deck and ran a hand through my hair. "Where do you want me now?"

The photographer's assistant wet her lips and pushed her glasses up her nose.

She glanced around, coming to rest on the cockpit. "Come over here and stand at the wheel."

I climbed off the deck and got behind the wheel, and the photographer lay in front of me.

Elena turned the page of her notebook. "So you received a degree from Columbia. Any plans for what's next, career-wise?"

"Not if I can help it."

She laughed and shook her head. "The heir to a billion-dollar fortune has no job aspirations? Your father doesn't have big plans for you at Moore & Co?"

"No plans for now. Would you be an investment banker if you didn't have to be?"

"No, but I'm terrible at math." She jotted in her notebook. "So, *are* things with Astrid Thomas serious?"

I bristled. "Astrid's a private woman, and I respect that. I'm sure you can imagine what it's like to live in the public eye."

She nodded, seeming to let it go. "Fair enough. So, what's stopped you from settling down for good?"

"I guess it's just never been the right time before, the right girl."

"But there have been a lot of girls."

I glanced over at her, smiling. "Yes, there have."

"I mean, with so much time on your hands, I'd guess you've had girlfriends all over the world. If those know-it-all gossip mags have any truth to them, you've got one in every major city on every continent."

"And a dozen kids, a secret Russian wedding, and a plastic surgery mishap."

She snickered and switched directions, seeming to take the hint.

"So, tell me about your dream girl."

I thought about my perfect girl as I stared absently at Manhattan in the distance, thought about all the women I'd been with, all the women I knew. The dial stopped on one in particular. "Unassuming, with a sense of humor. Kind, generous, trustworthy. Loyal." *About five-foot-four with curly blond hair, freckles, and a brother who would annihilate me if he knew our secret.*

The admission caught me off guard, and I kept my face still to mask it. There was no stopping my pulse, which ticked a bit faster and harder than it had been.

Elena nodded. "What are you looking for in a relationship?"

I hadn't really considered what I was looking for, since I hadn't really considered a *relationship* before. No one had inspired that for me — the want to just *be* with someone. There were women whose company I enjoyed, don't get me wrong. But I'd never needed any of them. It was always easy to walk away, so I did.

But in my life — The Life that was as lonely and separate as it was immersive and public — there was only one thing I wanted. Once I *did* think about it, the answer was simple.

"A best friend."

"It's that easy?"

"I don't see why it should be hard. Who better to share your life with than your best friend?"

The photographer got up and looked around. "Can I get you stretched out here on this front part?" She motioned toward the bow.

"Yeah." I hauled myself out of the cockpit and walked to the bow, lay down in the narrow space, and hung my arms in the ropes. One knee was up, my other leg stretched out in front of me in white linen pants, cuffed haphazardly

Her mouth hung open for a second before she disappeared behind the camera. "Oh, fuck — that's perfect. Don't move." The camera went nuts. "Jana, bring the reflector over here. Hurry."

Her assistant hustled over with a reflective panel.

"Yes, angle it a little more … there. Okay, Cooper, rub the back of your neck."

I smirked and did it.

"Oh, my God," she sang from behind the camera. "You're going to get half our readers pregnant just by pointing that smile at them. It should come with its own warning."

I full-on laughed at that. The camera went ballistic.

Elena had followed us up and was writing as she watched, smiling. "What are you going to do when you find your dream girl?"

"Who's to say I haven't already?"

She laughed. "All right, so what would you say to your dream girl, if you had the chance?"

I didn't know how to respond. Maggie's face was on my mind — she was the only inspiration I could find to formulate an answer. I thought about what she'd been through, thought about all the things I wanted to show her. To save her from and give her. The confession poured out of me.

"I've been around the world, and I thought I'd seen everything it had to offer until that night, until I saw you. In all my life, I've never seen anything so beautiful, not standing in the Blue Mosque or the Taj Mahal. Not in the streets of Rome or canals of Venice. Making you smile gives me life. Making you laugh gives me hope. Making you happy is all I want, other than to keep you."

The photographer had lowered her camera, and Elena's pen was still as everyone watched me. My chest ached — I felt raw, exposed.

So I threw The Smile at them.

"Hey, you asked." And then I stood, keeping my back to the water as they watched, still gaping. I jerked my chin at the photographer. "Heads up."

She snapped into action, raising her camera just as I backflipped off the bow with a whoop, hitting the chilly water feet first. I looked up as the bubbles dissipated and I could see the shape of my ship, the colors of the sky beautiful and distorted beyond the rippling surface, the sea around me wide and empty. And for a long moment, I stayed where I was in the solitude before swimming back to the air.

MAGGIE

y fingers flew on my keyboard that night, my brain tripping. I read over my response again to make sure I didn't sound like an idiot. Yes, I would be available for an interview tomorrow. No, the notice wasn't too short. That I was looking forward to meeting her, too.

I'd come home to a quiet apartment, all smiles. Went through my collection of delivery menus and ordered the best Thai curry I'd ever had. Freaked out when I'd gotten an interview request on a Sunday evening for an application I'd placed that morning.

Basically, I felt like I was standing on top of a mountain wearing a backpack full of hundred dollar bills.

I smiled and fired off the email before closing my laptop with a snap.

It was the job I wanted the most — Project Homestead. I'd need to put together a plan to prep, and I was grateful that the box of my teaching materials had already come from Jackson. I had my old textbooks and lesson plans and was ready to jump in, ready to get my head back in the game after so long off.

See, I'd only worked for a year out of college. When Jimmy and I got engaged over the summer, he urged me to quit so I could plan the wedding. Even before we were engaged, he made more than enough to

CHASER

cover our expenses, told me to hang onto whatever I earned teaching. That it was 'my money.' And thank God for that — I didn't know how else I would have made it on my own once everything fell apart.

I'd always thought he just wanted to take care of me. It made me feel safe and cared for that he didn't want me to worry about money. But looking back, I think he was just placating me, spoiling me like he would a child to keep me quiet and happy.

Everything looking back felt like a lie — I didn't trust that a single thing he'd ever said to me was genuine. That every look was with the knowledge that I wasn't his only girl, just his regular girl. That he'd been running around on me forever, and somehow, everyone knew except me. A spectacular show, that's what it was. Once I found out, they all said that it was none of their business, that they didn't want to intrude.

Southern manners, my ass.

In their defense, he seemed to have a regular set of girls — including my childhood best friend — and all of them knew about me. He never took them in public. It was all very discreet, nothing more than whispers and rumors. My best friend Brooke didn't even know. Because God knew if she did, she'd have told me in an instant.

No, Jimmy was smart about it. And I was a fool for never questioning a thing he did.

I sighed and climbed out of bed, trying to push my thoughts away and focus on now. Now was so much easier. Simpler.

Now was a sexy boy toy. Now was Manhattan and Central Park and a job interview. A job interview I needed to pick out an outfit for.

I was elbow deep in business casual when my phone rang on my bed. I smiled when I scooped it up and found a picture of Brooke giving me moose ears and a kissy face.

I answered and held the phone in place with my shoulder. "Hey, Brookie."

69

"Hey, Maggieboo. You free?"

"These days? Always. How are you?"

"Good. Just missing you. How's New York treating you?"

"Pretty brilliantly. I kind of had an amazing day." I held up a button-down to judge its worth. *You can do better.* I tossed it back in the pile.

"Tell me about your exciting adventures because I've got nothin' to report except that I ran into Richard Peck at Joe's bar. Remember how hot he used to be?"

"Uh, yeah. Everybody wanted some Dick."

She snickered. "With a name like Dick Peck, you'd think he would've had a hard time getting laid. But I'm not even sure if he can see his junk without a mirror, never mind use it for pleasuring the ladies."

A cackle shot out of me. "Oh, my God, Brooke."

"Seriously, I watched him eat a twenty-ounce ribeye, a basket of onion rings, a side of chili fries, a giant piece of chocolate cake, and I think he drank a case of beer. The guy's a mammoth."

I shook my head, still chuckling. "Guess nobody sent him the memo that you can't eat like a linebacker when you don't work out like one. When he was a senior and I was a sophomore, I dreamed about that boy. West used to give me so much crap for it. He always knew what douche Dickie was, even though none of the rest of us could see it. Around here, they call that douchesparkle, and Dick's was blinding." I sorted through the pile of tops.

"Oh, man. It's so true though," she said with a laugh. "So, tell me about your brilliant day? Did it have anything to do with Cooper Moore?"

"You don't always have to call him by his full name, you know?" I picked up a deep purple top with a little tie on the collar and eyed it.

"I can't help it. It's like calling Jared Leto just plain old 'Jared' or Michael Fassbender 'Mike.' I can't do it."

I laughed and tossed that one too. "He's just a person like

anybody else, Brooke."

"Whatever. Tell me the details of your bangin' sex life. Because Jackson is hot in every way aside from the kind that gets me laid."

"Things are good. I saw Cooper earlier today, after I finished applying to a handful of jobs. I have an interview tomorrow with one, which is part of why I'm feeling extra amazing right now."

"Ooh, that's awesome. I hope it goes well! Now, tell me the story of Cooper Moore's nakedness."

I picked up a peach blouse, but it was too sheer. Tossed it back in the pile. "His nakedness was definitely one of the highlights of my day."

She straight up giggled.

"I dunno, Brooke. He's just damn fine and knows exactly what he's doing. I mean, I've never been nailed so hard my knees go weak. Not before him."

Brooke sighed. "I am so jealous."

I shook my head, smiling as I picked up a cream blouse with a lace collar. *Perfect.* "It's nice to not have any strings, you know? I don't owe him anything, and he doesn't owe me anything. No pressure, and I get to have my vagina rocked on the regular, for a little bit longer at least."

"Right. The rules." I could almost hear her rolling her eyes.

My face scrunched up. "What the hell, Brooke? Don't you judge me."

"I'm only slightly judging you. And not just because you let him bareback."

I scoffed. "I've got an IUD, and he's clean. There's no reason to use condoms."

"So you trust him with your sexual health but not with your heart?"

"Basically. You think West would kill him if he found out we were having sex? Imagine what he'd do if he found out Cooper gave me the clap."

She chuckled. "I dunno, Mags. I think we should agree that one should never think twice about a gift such as Cooper Moore. I definitely don't think I'd ever tell him I didn't want to have meaningless sex with him anymore, or that he couldn't take me to fancy dinners and hoity-toity Manhattan restaurants that you have to book months in advance."

"Because then it could get serious, and I don't want to get serious."

"I'm just saying. You're basically telling one of the sexiest men ever exactly what to do."

"Sometimes he tells me what to do. In bed."

She laughed. "I bet he does. How much longer until time's up?"

"Two weeks." A little flash of sadness shot through me, but I ignored it, focusing instead on which pants to wear.

"So what happens if you want to keep something going? What if he does?"

"Doesn't matter if I want to or not. If I keep it going, there's a chance I could fall for him."

"You could fall for him anyway."

I rolled my eyes as I folded the rejected clothes. "People don't fall in love in a month."

"That's a pretty big presumption, Mags."

"I just don't get that sentiment. It's part of why I don't go bananas over romance novels. I mean, instant lust, that's fine. I get that. I've felt that at the laundromat. Imagined gettin' bent over a folding table by this gorgeous Persian guy. I might have propositioned him if he wasn't sorting G-strings."

"Were they his?"

"Wouldn't have even mattered, so long as they weren't his girlfriend's."

She laughed. "So you've experienced instalust, which makes it real. But since you haven't experienced instalove, it can't possibly be real. Sound right?"

"That about sums it up."

"Oh, Maggie." She sighed. "Instalust at the laundromat is way better than Dick Peck at Joe's. You're lucky you got out of here when you had the chance. You'd have been stuck here forever if you'd married Assface."

We had a pact not to speak his name unless absolutely necessary. "Don't remind me."

"Is he still texting you?"

"At least once a week. Haven't responded."

"I see him here and there. I swear, every time, he pumps me for information like penny slots. Pop a question in, pull the lever, watch as my eyes roll around and around. I haven't told him anything though other than to give it up. I maybe also threw my drink in his face on Friday night."

I laughed, hoping it burned like hell. "Oh, that makes me happy."

"I thought it might. So, what's after Cooper Moore?"

"I dunno." That sad feeling was back, and I brushed it away like a hornet. "I should just sleep around. Just be all about the D."

"You told your fuck buddy that he couldn't bang anybody else for a month. How the hell do you think you're gonna be okay banging randos you meet in bars? I mean, do people even go to bars alone in New York without getting mugged?"

"Depends on what part of town, but it's not like trying to run around Bangkok alone. Plus, West bought me a Taser, so I'm pretty sure between that and my lightning reflexes, I could fuck a sexual predator up."

"He bought you a Taser?"

"Of course he did."

"Well, at least you know he cares."

"Yeah, he doesn't exactly hide that light under a bush."

She giggled. "So, what did you cross off your list this week?"

"Well, I've done most of the touristy stuff — finally did the Statue of Liberty and went to the Met Cloisters — but I'm getting to the point where the tourists are actually starting to bug me."

"That's so snobby. You really are turning into a New Yorker."

"I know. But they'll stand in the middle of the sidewalk in packs trying to look at a map and figure out where to go. Or like you'll see groups all wearing matching T-shirts that just take up the entire sidewalk, and when they aren't standing still, they walk slow as hell."

"Eat any new weird stuff?"

I picked up the stack of tops and laid them back in the drawer. "Oh, we went to this one place called What the Kale where everything in the whole restaurant was made with kale. Like wraps in kale. Sandwiches, but instead of bread? Kale. Kale soup. Kale salad. Fried kale. Kale chips."

"Did it at least taste good?"

I snorted. "Are you kidding? Superfood my ass. Everything tasted like dirt. No amount of butter can save that level of funk."

"Damn hipsters."

"I just left wanting fried chicken and french fries, or a corn dog. Really, anything fried would have done. I would have even settled for that smelly mac and cheese with gruyere."

"Ew." She chucked.

"I don't really know what else. I've got this job interview tomorrow, and I've been doin' a whole lotta nothing otherwise."

"Liar. You've been doin' a whole lotta Cooper Moore."

I huffed and flopped back into bed, crossing my ankles as I adjusted the phone. "Call him Cooper, Brooke."

"I can't! Leave me alone!"

"It's weird. Stop it."

"Did you go to his fancy penthouse today?"

I smiled to myself. "Yeah, and then he came with me to read in the park."

"That's totally a date."

"No, it's not."

"Was there kissing?"

"Nope," I answered.

"Sensual touching?"

I laughed. "Not even a little."

"Boring, but still a date," she said flatly. "Do you think he's interested in you for more than a booty call?"

"We're talking about America's Playboy. Of course not."

"Okay, hypothetically, if he *was* into you, you really wouldn't extend the four week rule?"

I hated this conversation, and we had it almost every time we talked. "How could I? There's no universe that exists wherein I'm ready for a relationship, especially not with a sexy, rogue socialite."

"You wouldn't even be willing to try?"

"I don't know how else to explain it to you, Brooke. I don't trust myself or my feelings. I was a blind, naive fool with Jimmy. It's painfully clear that I don't know anything about relationships or love. How can I trust somebody else if I don't even trust myself?"

She paused. "I'm sorry. I don't mean to push. I just want you to be happy and okay."

I sighed. "So do I. But I'm happy, and I'm okay, okay?"

"Okay."

"Okay." I paused. "I miss you."

She sighed. "You too. It's just not the same with you gone."

I stared at my Passion Pink toes. "I just had to get out of there."

"I would have left too, honestly. Part of me wishes I had."

My heart sank. "You're doing the right thing, taking care of your grandma."

She let out a long breath. "I know. She's the only family I've got. But I still wish I could have come with you."

"Me too. There's so much to see and do, but I end up seeing and doing all by myself because everyone has real lives and real jobs."

"Everyone except Cooper Moore."

"Goddammit, Brooke."

She snickered. "You should sightsee with him."

"Have you not heard anything I've said? I'm not speaking German again, am I?"

"No comprende nada, Maggiecita!" she sang.

"No, you don't understand, do you? Pushy ass."

"I amuse you, don't lie."

I smiled. "Maybe a little."

"Well, I just got to work, so I've gotta run. I love you. I'm glad you're hanging in there like that cat on the poster in Mrs. Jensen's fifth grade class."

"Thanks, Brookie. I love you too. Make those tips."

"Waitress extraordinaire. Nothing makes you feel like a boss quite like getting yelled at over pickles and mustard."

"Just remember: Burgers and fries, nobody dies."

She laughed. "Exactly. Bye, Mags."

"Bye."

I hung up the phone, feeling bummed. I couldn't text Cooper again. I'd watched a million movies. My toes were already pretty, and I didn't feel like reading. I was tired of being all by myself, but Lily had a show. Maybe Rose was off. And if not, I could always go to Habits.

I opened my door, feeling a million times better when I found Rose on the couch watching TV. Her black hair was in a knot on top of her head, her hand was in a bowl of popcorn, and I think she was still in her pajamas — black spanky shorts, a gray V-neck, and dark purple knee socks.

"Hey, Mags," she said around a mouthful of popcorn.

"Thank God you're home." I plopped down on the couch next to her and smiled when I looked at the TV screen. "Oooh, *Clueless*. Good one, Rosie. Turn it up."

"You guys are all deaf." She grabbed the remote and adjusted the volume.

"You and Patrick have super senses or something."

She made a face. "This is why my room sounds like a wind tunnel ninety percent of the time."

I chuckled and grabbed a handful of popcorn. "You off tonight?"

She smiled happily and recrossed her ankles on the coffee table. "Sure am, which is why I won't be putting on a bra or makeup."

"Mind if I keep you company?"

"I'd love nothing more. *Bring It On* is up next, and then *Drop Dead Gorgeous*. I'm feeling the Kirsten Dunst tonight."

"*Drop Dead Gorgeous*?"

"Uh, hell yeah. You've never seen it?"

"I've never even heard of it."

She sat up a little straighter with her face lit up. "Oh, you are in for a treat. It's one of the most hilariously twisted movies I've ever seen, about a beauty pageant in Minnesota where all the contestants get offed one by one."

I grabbed a blanket off the back of the couch and settled in. "That sounds terrible. I can't wait."

"I've got chocolate and whiskey, too. Girl's night. Fuck yeah." She raised her hand for a high five, and I slapped it gratefully.

"Fuck yeah."

COOPER

Shelby poured us another round as West kicked his head back and laughed. Patrick and I sat on either side of him at Habits that night.

Lily was at a show, and Rose was off work, so when West said he wanted to have drinks, there was no way I'd refuse.

Everything was changing, shifting. Drifting. Not that it was a bad thing. I just knew that these moments would spread even further apart. I pushed away the thought that one day we wouldn't meet this way at all anymore — like it was normal, easy.

I raised my glass. "I feel like I haven't seen you in weeks, West."

"Alone, at least," Patrick added.

"I know," he conceded and picked up his whiskey. "But I'm not gonna apologize."

I shook my head and picked up the fresh scotch. "All in, huh?"

"I don't know how to operate any other way. Not when it comes to Lily."

Patrick leaned on the bar. "All settled down and grown up."

West looked into his drink and shook the ice around. "It's so strange, but it's the most natural thing. I've never been with anyone who I couldn't get enough of. I think I could spend every waking minute with her, sleeping ones too, and never get my fill."

I thought of Maggie, about how addicted I was to her. *Two more weeks.* The clocked ticked down, and all I could do was watch.

Patrick took a long pull of his drink and set it down. "I know the feeling."

We always tried to come on days we knew Rose wasn't there so he could speak freely — and so he'd pay attention. When Rose was around, he didn't always function at capacity.

They'd had a hot and heavy relationship, once they got together. Then Patrick flipped out. He'd been through enough in his life to know what it meant to be hurt, and when he realized how he really felt about Rose, he bailed. And then he blew the bridge up behind him. He'd never forgiven himself for it, either.

West shook his head. "Just talk to her, Trick."

He scratched his tattooed neck. "You know that doesn't do any good, man. She's done with me. I've got to find a way to let it go. I just don't know how."

West leaned on the bar. "Have you thought about, I don't know, avoiding her?"

His eyes were on his tattooed fingers as he spun his glass around. "I'd never leave the house. She's everywhere."

West nodded and turned to me. "Tell us some stories, Coop. There's comfort in that you're still out in the world, unaffected by matters of the heart while Tricky and I swoon and pine."

I shrugged, scrambling to think of a way out of the conversation. "Not much to report."

Both of them raised an eyebrow at me.

"Don't look so surprised."

"What's going on with Astrid?" West asked.

"The usual."

Patrick eyed me. "And you don't have any girls on the side?"

I took a drink, wishing I could tell them about Maggie, wishing she were a stranger to them.

"Ha." West looked at Patrick. "He does, but the question is, why doesn't he want to tell us?"

Patrick smirked. "Interesting."

"It's nothing. Just a fling."

West shifted to look at me full on. "Hang on, *a* fling? As in *one*?"

"It's not a big deal."

Patrick laughed. "Well, don't hold out. Who is she? A supermodel? Fuck, if they don't have the longest legs."

West nodded his respect.

"She's just a chick I know. It's just a hook up." *All part of the rules.*

"So, what's her deal? What's the draw?" West asked.

The list was long, but I rolled through it looking for points I could share that would be juicy enough get them off my back. "Well, she hasn't been with a lot of guys, so I've been *educating* her."

Patrick laughed. "Showing her the ropes."

"The ins and outs," West added with a snicker.

I laughed, mostly because he was snickering about his sister. "There's something about it that's like a drug. To just own her like that, to show her something she's never experienced. I never get sick of that look on her face. Like I blew her mind."

"Years of practice paying off," West said.

"What can I say. I'm a man of many talents."

Patrick shook his head. "I wish I could … I don't know. Give a fuck about another girl. I mean, I'm surrounded by hot chicks every day. Chicks I could take home with a word. Like Ronnie."

West and I made appreciative noises. Ronnie was a tattoo artist at Tonic, where Patrick worked — a smoking hot, cat-eyed, raven-haired badass, covered in tattoos, with piercings that were somehow light and feminine, gauges, lip ring. She even had her septum pierced, which I usually hated. But she wore it well. And she wanted a piece of Patrick, bad.

His mistake was … well, he'd made a lot of mistakes. After he dumped Rose like an idiot, he brought Ronnie to Habits in a display of next-level dumbfuckery. I don't know what he'd been thinking. But it was the final blow for Rose, and Ronnie hadn't ever given him up.

Patrick took a drink and continued. "I just can't, you know? It's like once I had a taste, nothing else will satisfy my thirst. I've been thirsty for six months, and I still can't think about being with anyone else. It's fucked up."

West picked up his drink. "Maybe one day you just meet a girl with a magical ass. Like she has some sorcery about her that renders every other ass null and void."

Patrick laughed. "Voodoo Pussy. No other pussy will do. It'll haunt you until you die."

West snorted. "Bewitching Box."

"Hexing Hole." I took a drink, and we all snickered like junior high kids. "Do you think there's a man-version of that? Like Incredicock."

"Witching Wang." Patrick shot.

"Jackhammer Juju." West added.

"Hypnodick. Dicknotize her with it," I said.

We laughed hard enough that Shelby shook her head at us from down the bar, smiling.

The idea made so much sense to me. "So instead of soul mates, you're fuck mates." I nodded and took a drink. "I can get behind this theory."

West smiled. "If Lily was the only woman I slept with for the rest of my life, I could die happy."

Patrick rolled his eyes. "Yeah, I hear about it. Like, every fucking night."

I shook my head at him. "You've got to get earplugs or something, Trick."

"Trust me, I've tried, but they bug me, or they fall out. Can't listen to music because I'll actually *listen* to it. And I keep getting these white noise machines, but I can't get one to work for more than twenty-four hours."

West made a face. "Weird, man. Maybe we should call an electrician."

"Whatever. It would just be nice if you could keep that shit between nine a.m. and eleven at night."

West shrugged. "Can't say I'm sorry."

Patrick sighed.

"It's so weird, you know? Being with Lily. All these years she's been such a big part of my life, and I had no idea what I was missing. Everything came together, and now it all makes sense. I hope I never stop feeling like I do. Like I know exactly what I'm doing and what I need. Like my life is completely full because of her." He emptied his drink and shook his head. "I'm sorry. I don't mean to get all sentimental. It's just that I've never felt like this. Like I can't see outside of what I'm experiencing because it's so overwhelmingly *good*."

Patrick and I shared a look, nodding as Shelby came around to get us another round, and our conversation turned to lighter topics, but I couldn't stop thinking about it. Patrick knew the feeling West described all too well, though he was even more familiar with the loss of it. And me? I realized distantly that I had an idea of what he meant myself.

Positions

MAGGIE

The next afternoon, I trotted up the stairs with a smile that wouldn't be stopped and blew through the front door of our apartment to find Rose at the table eating a bagel in her pajamas. She lit up when she saw me. "How did it go?" she asked hopefully.

I closed the door behind me. "I got the job!" I sang.

She threw her hands up and wiggled her fingers, smiling. "Oh, my God! Congrats, Maggie! Details."

I sat next to her and leaned on the table. "I was so excited — that job was at the top of my list, so I was super nervous. But the second the interview started, I was fine. The more we talked, the better I felt about it. Such a great fit. And they need someone to start immediately. She offered me the job on the spot, can you believe it? I start tomorrow!" I was so giddy, I almost felt like I was high.

"This is so amazing."

"I know!" I gushed. "I feel like I could run around doing the Flashdance right now." I let out a sigh. "I'm also really happy to actually have something productive to do. It's been a minute. Like, since the wedding."

Rose nodded as she took a bite. "It's gonna be great, Maggie. I bet you're so good with kids. Not like me. I make babies cry."

I laughed. "No, you don't."

"I totally do. Kids hate me. I think I'm scary and awkward with kids, like I expect them to burst into tears or explode or something. You, on the other hand, look like an adorable Disney character."

I shook my head and chuckled. "I'll believe babies are scared of you when I see it."

"You'll laugh at me when you see it, but that's all right too." She set down her breakfast and wiped her fingers on her napkin. "So you start tomorrow? That's so soon."

"I've got to start working on my lesson plans tonight, and tomorrow I'm getting a tour of the facility and working with the director on my lesson plans. Plus, it's not like I have anything else to do."

"Only Mr. M." She waggled her brows and picked up her coffee.

I laughed. "Yes, only him. But I'll still have plenty of time for him to tickle my fancy, even with a job."

Rose smiled. "We should definitely celebrate tonight. We can get everyone together and go to Habits, yeah?"

"Do you work?"

"Nope, I'm off again."

"You sure you want to go to work on your day off?"

She shrugged. "It's my home away from home. Plus, I didn't go in yesterday and had a pajama binge. My mascara's calling me."

My phone buzzed in my bag, and I reached into its depths, digging around before my fingers closed over it. I had a text from Mr. M.

How did it go?

I texted back, smiling. *Nailed it. They offered me a position!*

I knew they would. Can I offer you a position? You know, to celebrate.

My smile stretched wider. *I will accept all celebratory positions. After Habits tonight — we're going to have drinks if you want to come.*

I always want to come.

I giggled, and Rose watched me with an eyebrow up. *I guess I asked for that.*

I'll see you at Habits tonight. Wear those purple panties, the ones with the black lace. We'll go to my place after.

I bit my lip. *Anything you want.*

I love the sound of that.

My cheeks were hot as I set my phone face down on the table.

Rose shook her head. "You've got it bad."

My blush deepened. "It's nothing. We're just hooking up."

"Mmhmm. Sure."

My brow bent, and I crossed my arms. "I'm so tired of explaining this to everyone. It's like none of you trust me to handle my own decisions. Do you have any idea how frustrating that is?"

"I know. We're just worried about you is all."

"Well, I'm not blind."

"Do you really think you can keep your feelings out of it?"

"I have been so far."

"But you like him?" she prompted.

"I like him, and he rocks my ladybits."

"And he likes you?"

"He seems to. Sometimes he just … I don't know. He looks at me and I feel like he sees me. But Rose — he is seriously the worst idea ever. If you knew him, you would lose your shit and tell me I'm making a terrible mistake, and that's exactly why I agree. Getting *involved* would be a mistake."

"I mean, as long as you've got it under control."

"Whatever that is." I sighed and spun my phone around on the table absently. "Moving here was a clean start, all right. I can pretend nothing before I moved here ever happened. Like it was all a bad dream, or fiction. The story of a girl I used to know. Do you know what I mean?"

Rose's eyes were bright and open. "I do. Do you think about Jimmy a lot?"

"I think I'm somewhere between hurt and denial. Like, sometimes I'll see something or think of something I want to share with him before I remember what he did. The rest of the time, I just pretend like he doesn't exist. I don't quite know how to face it, and I wonder if I ever will."

"Facing it is probably inevitable. Something will happen, and the pressure valve will blow. It happens to the best of us, especially those of us who avoid, and it's never pretty."

I nodded, trying to imagine what would happen and dreading it. "It's gonna be bad, Rose."

"Probably. But you've always got us."

She smiled at me and picked up her bagel. I found comfort in knowing that it was true — Rose and Lily would be there if I fell apart. And I hung on to the hope that maybe, just maybe, enough time would pass that it would fade away into my past without enduring any more pain.

COOPER

Habits was packed for a Monday, and the drinks had been flowing for long enough that everyone was rosy-cheeked and laughing. Everyone had shuffled around to talk, leaving Maggie and me on the edge of the group, pretending to ignore each other.

Astrid hooked her arm in Maggie's and smiled, bringing a joke home with a punchline that had the girls all laughing. Astrid had gone way out of her way to talk to Maggie all night, hanging near her. I'd caught them nearly whispering to each other, Maggie nodding, Astrid with her hand on Maggie's arm, the two of them smiling. Between their truce and my cell phone purge, I hoped she wouldn't worry so much anymore.

I just wanted her to believe me. The thought that she didn't drove me crazy.

Something else that drove me crazy: the fact that almost every man in the bar was watching her.

There was one in particular, at a high table with his friends, almost directly in my line of sight. I watched him talk to his friends, the three of them eyeing the group, and I knew he was going to try to talk to her at some point. I caught his eye once and held it, hoping it was enough to keep him away. But I knew the chance was slim. There was no indicator that we were together — Maggie and I hadn't touched, had barely looked at each other, even though she was all I could think about.

I'd been almost silent all night. Everyone else was too drunk to notice, thankfully. But Maggie knew, and she knew why. And I knew she felt the same.

I was ready to drag her out of the bar the first minute I saw her. Her dress was simple — short, soft peach and loose with small lace detailing. The thin straps left much of her back exposed, the creamy skin begging to be touched, low enough to know she wasn't wearing a bra.

The knowledge didn't help my efforts to keep my hands off of her.

Her admirer stood up, and my eyes narrowed as he wove around everyone with his eyes on Maggie. I took a long sip of scotch and leaned back against the bar with my jaw ticking.

He was about my height and build, with blond hair and tan skin. A decent looking guy, so naturally, I wanted to hit him. He stopped next to her, and I resisted the urge to step between them.

I couldn't quite hear what he was saying, which somehow made it even more unbearable. When she laughed at something he said, I almost lost my shit. Astrid's eyes laughed as they bounced between Maggie, the intruder and me. I broke my gaze to glance at West, whose jaw was set as he watched.

She touched his shoulder, and I slammed my drink. Everyone else in the group was still talking, Rose and Lily giggling about something, though Patrick was watching West.

The intruder smiled before walking away, and Astrid leaned in to whisper in Maggie's ear. She laughed, her cheeks pink, eyes darting over to me. She nodded and whispered something back.

West seemed placated and turned back to Lily, and everyone was preoccupied again, talking amongst themselves. No one was watching us, and I couldn't take it anymore.

Maggie pressed against me as someone squeezed behind her to get to the bar, and her fingers curled against my leg like she wanted any reason to touch me.

I turned my head like I was looking behind her. "Meet me in the bathroom. Don't make me wait."

I stood and set my glass on the bar behind me, hitching a thumb over my shoulder when West jerked his chin at me in question. He smiled and turned back to Lily, and I looked down at Maggie. The small curve of her lips said she'd be right behind me.

I weaved my way through the bar and into the men's restroom to scope it out with my pulse thumping. The stalls were empty, and there was just one guy at a urinal, so I washed my hands and walked out, leaned against the wall in the hallway and waited. He left, and another guy walked back.

I put up a hand. "You may not want to go in there. It's flooded."

He eyed me. "That bad?"

"It looks look like somebody threw lamb vindaloo all over the walls."

He made a face.

"Yeah. You don't want naan of that."

"Thanks," he said, not even laughing at my pun before turning and leaving again.

Maggie rounded the corner a second later, and I smiled and jerked my head as I pushed the door open, laying a hand on the small of her back as we ducked into the bathroom. I grabbed her hand and pulled into the far stall, pressing her against the tiled wall in a breath, not giving her a moment to speak, needing her lips — lips I'd been thinking about every minute since I'd walked into Habits. Lips I was always thinking about.

I picked her up, keeping her back against the wall as she wrapped her legs around my waist. My hands slipped up her bare thighs to her ass, fingers splayed against the purple panties I'd ask her to wear.

She smiled up at me. I leaned back, pinning her against the wall with my hips as I lifted the hem of her dress to get a good look.

My fingers trailed up her thigh. "What did he say to you?" I rolled my hips, pressing my length against her.

Her voice was ragged. "He wanted to buy me a drink."

I cupped her cheek and ran my thumb across her bottom lip. "And what did you say?"

"I told him I wasn't thirsty."

"Good." I took her mouth, my lips crashing against hers as I slipped my tongue into her mouth, demanding her attention as my mind cycled a single word, over and over.

Mine.

The bathroom door opened, and I broke away when I heard West and Patrick.

Maggie's eyes were wide, swollen lips gaping. I laid a finger on them, mouthing *Shh* before laying kisses along her jaw and neck.

West was drunk, talking too loud, going on about the ramifications of power and ambition using *Macbeth* as an example.

Maggie was tense against me, but I just kept kissing her, soothing her, all while my heart raced, hoping to God they were too drunk to realize they weren't alone. Seconds later, they were washing their hands, and we heard the rise and fall of the crowd in the bar as the door closed behind them.

I kissed her hungry lips again. I thought about her talking to the intruder as I slipped my fingers in the leg of her panties and inside of her, pressing my hips against the back of my hand. Heard her laughing at what he'd said as she fumbled between our bodies for my zipper and freed me. I shifted my hips until my tip rested against the slick line of her, picturing her hand on his chest as I flexed and filled her to the hilt.

Mine.

I couldn't breathe as I pulled out and slammed back in.

"Harder," she breathed, and I gave her what she wanted.

My fingers gripped her thighs as I held her still, driving into her, flexing my hips until she tightened around me, her arms, her legs, her body. One thrust, then another, and she came — one more and I followed.

I held her against the wall with my body, and my hands cupped her cheeks, fingers in her hair as I covered her mouth with mine and kissed her deep.

When I broke away, she looked up at me with hot eyes. "I cannot believe we just did that," she said with a breathy laugh. "I've never done anything like that before." Her eyes widened. "And West ... oh, God, Cooper."

I thumbed her flushed cheeks. "Don't worry about West. He's too drunk on whiskey and Lily to notice us."

"We shouldn't have done this. Not here. We could have been caught so easily."

The door opened again, and someone went about their business. I brought my lips to her ear. "You're safe with me, Maggie."

"Am I?" she whispered, the question loaded, and my chest ached.

So of course, I made a joke. "I'd never risk the pants that I'm the boss of."

She stifled a laugh, and I kissed her again, hoping she could feel the truth as the door opened and closed again.

I put her feet on the ground and kissed her once more before we cleaned up quickly, and I moved to the door to check the hallway, which was clear. I motioned for her to follow.

She blew past me and down the hall, looking back over her shoulder at me with a smile before she disappeared.

I leaned against the wall again, my hands in my pockets, staring at the flyers stuck on the wall like wallpaper, layer after layer of them, trying to get a handle on the thoughts spinning through my brain.

I was jealous, I realized curiously. I was possessive of her. The feeling of ownership hadn't left me, though it was quieter than it had been, an undercurrent instead of a tsunami. It wasn't something I'd felt before — not at this level. And I had no idea what that meant. But until I figured it out, I'd play it cool, starting then.

And so, I put on The Smile and headed back into the bar, focusing instead on a plan to get Maggie to come home with me.

mr. M

MAGGIE

My heart chugged like a freight train as I walked through the bar and back to our friends, feeling like a sexy-ass criminal. Who knew sex in a public restroom could be so hot? And Cooper jealous? I mean, if that hadn't set off my libido, I might have thought about seeing a doctor.

Cooper was right about West — he was smiling with Lily in his arms, completely oblivious. Rose and Patrick laughed as Astrid told a story, and I sidled in, catching the tail end of it. I laughed when they laughed, half listening, my body still humming from Cooper.

He was beside me again a minute later, and I had to stop myself from looking at him. He brushed against me to take a seat, sending a shock through me.

I glanced at Lily, who stared at me with her brow quirked. She looked at Cooper, then at me once more, and her smile slowly fell, eyes widening.

I watched it all click like detonators going off behind her eyes, and I silently begged her not to say anything.

She threw on a fake smile and looked up at West, turning him so his back was to us.

CHASER

I glanced over at Cooper, and he met my eyes. And in that moment, I decided.

I was officially the queen of bad decisions.

I didn't know what to do, standing between Cooper and my brother, amongst my friends who I'd been lying to. Lying over a guy who I couldn't have, who I shouldn't want.

There was only one thing to do. I had to get the hell out of there.

I smiled. "Hey, y'all — I'm gonna head out."

Rose and Astrid whined and pouted.

"I know, I know. But it's late, and I've got a big day tomorrow. If I go in hungover and tired, I'll never make a good impression."

The girls conceded and gave me hugs, and West patted my head like I was a puppy, wishing me luck. Cooper gave me a long, lingering look, and Lily whispered something into West's ear. He smiled like an idiot and blushed a little, giving her a quick kiss.

"I'm out too, guys. Gotta be up early in the morning. I'll walk you home, Mags." She turned to me and grabbed my arm, hauling me out of Habits under the guise of a smile and a wave at our friends.

The second we hit the sidewalk, she spun around and let me have it. "Oh my fucking God, Maggie. Tell me that Mr. M is not Cooper. Please. Please, please, please." Her eyes pinched closed.

I bit my lip.

She cracked her lids. "*Please?*"

"I'm sorry, Lily."

She groaned and dropped her head back before taking a deep breath and letting it out slow. "Please tell me how the fuck this happened. From the beginning." She hooked her arm in mine, and we started walking toward our building.

I took a deep breath of my own. I hadn't told anyone besides Brooke, not a single soul. "Well, it all started on my wedding night."

She stopped dead, and I stumbled backward. "*What?*" Her eyes bugged.

93

I blushed. "God, don't make me say it again."

"Are you serious?" She looked me over. "Oh, my God. You're serious."

I had no idea how to explain myself. "I don't know how it happened. I was just so …"

Lily shook her head, fuming. "That son of a bitch took advantage of you. West is going to kill him."

I shook my head, blustering. "No. Really, Lily — he didn't take advantage. I wanted him. I needed him that night. I swear to you that he didn't have to convince me of anything. He promised me nothing. But if West finds out … well, West can't find out."

Lily ran a hand across her forehead. "No, you're right about that. I refuse to date a criminal." She sighed again, the sound heavy, and we started walking again. "Come on. We have an hour before West comes home, and you're about to tell me *everything*. If I'm going to keep this from him, there better be a damn good reason. And you'd better convince me that Cooper's not using you, because if he is, I'm telling West tonight, consequences be damned."

I nodded as we walked past the pizza counter. The smell normally made me salivate, but tonight, it only turned my stomach.

She watched me. "Do you need liquor or are you ready to spill the details?"

"Just promise me liquor at home and I'll start now."

"Deal. Start at the beginning. I think I can handle it this time."

I thought back to that night, the first night, my worst night. "Do you have any idea how hard the reception was, Lily?" I asked softly.

She turned to look me in the eye. "I can't even begin to imagine."

"I was okay for a lot of it, just smiling through, you know? Don't get me wrong — I wanted to have the reception — really. I felt like I needed it. Like I just wanted to throw that party and wear that dress and give Jimmy the big fuck-you. It was a *good* thing. But it was hard, Lily. It was so hard. And there was this moment when everyone else disappeared and I was alone for the first time since everything had fallen apart. I wasn't ready for that, to deal with that. I was scared, and I was alone, and Cooper was right there."

Lily didn't say anything, so after a second, I kept going. "For that moment, in his arms, everything was fine. He was a diversion, a distraction. That night, he was everything I needed."

"And then what happened?"

"The next morning he left, and I left, and I didn't see him again until he picked me up at the airport."

She paused, and I could almost hear her thinking. "Have you been together ever since?"

"Ever since Noir. Sneaking away from West and Patrick at the club wasn't hard. Astrid left on her own. I went home with Cooper."

"And what *about* Astrid? Is he banging her too?" Her voice was tight. "I never know what's going on with the two of them, and neither of them will talk about it."

"He says he's not."

"And you believe him? If he's stepping out on my sister for *West's* sister—"

"Lily, I believe him," I said earnestly. "Astrid is seeing someone else, but it's a secret ... he's, like, anti-media, so she and Cooper 'date' just as a cover so everyone would leave them alone."

Lily frowned. "But why wouldn't she have told me?"

"Sam is just so private, and apparently Astrid is really afraid she'll lose him if anyone finds out. Even you."

"I'm talking to her about this. I just don't know if I believe it."

"I've been having a hard time with it too. But I believe both of them," I said as we reached our building. It was the truth.

Lily pulled open the door. "I don't even know what to say, Maggie. I mean ... Cooper? I don't think he's ever had a serious relationship, and he's slept with every eligible woman in Manhattan — and most of Brooklyn. He's literally the opposite of boyfriend material."

We stepped inside and climbed the stairs. "Which is why I don't consider him my boyfriend."

"Cooper is Mr. M," she said half to herself. "You're having a no-strings affair with Cooper Moore. It seemed so much more relatable when it wasn't *him*. But I guess if there was one man who it might be safe to say feelings wouldn't be involved, it would be Cooper."

"I have fun with him. It's easy, aside from the whole sneaking around thing. He's *amazing* in bed."

She snickered as she dug in her bag for her keys. "I can't say I'm surprised, but ugh. Is he really not seeing anyone else? I don't think I've ever known him to only see one woman for any period of time, even Astrid. I mean, we all figured he was running around, but the fact that it's you is just crazy."

"I really don't think he is. Lily — he deleted all of his hookup contacts the other day."

She stopped in the hallway with her hand frozen in her bag. "No way."

"I know. And he did it smiling, like it was no big deal at all."

Lily blinked and shook her head, moving to unlock the door. "What in the world? Is this like a sign of the end times? Are we going to wake up tomorrow to zombie flu and flaming meteors?"

I chuckled and stepped into the apartment behind her. "He was trying to prove a point — that he was honoring the rules."

"Ah, the rules." She turned on the light and tossed her keys in the dish.

"I know everyone thinks they're dumb, but they make me feel safe."

She nodded, though I suspected she was keeping something to herself.

"There are only two weeks left before it's over, but in the meantime, it's a one day at a time kind of thing. I'm always free. He's always free. I'm lonely, and so is he. So we keep each other company. It's not all that complicated."

Lily shot me a look as she walked into the kitchen. "Except for West."

"Yes," I conceded. "Except for West."

Lily collected supplies for gin and tonics and set them on the table. "I just can't believe that Cooper would do this to West, you know? That he would risk his friendship for a fling."

I took a seat, feeling a hundred years old. "We're not doing it to hurt West."

"That doesn't mean it wouldn't still hurt him if he found out."

"It's another reason for the rules. Easier to hide it if it's brief, you know?"

She shook her head and poured us each a drink. "I really don't know what he would do. I don't like to think he would turn his back on Cooper, but I can't say that's not a real possibility. He'd be hurt, Maggie. Really hurt. Like, ultimate betrayal of the bro code. Especially if it's just for sport. But, if you two were serious …"

I picked up my glass and took a long drink. "I don't have it in me to be serious about anyone right now. I need somebody, and Cooper is safe … ish."

Lily guffed.

"No, but really. He's familiar. I know him well enough to know what to expect. I know he'll be careful with me because he loves West. It's safer than Tinder, anyway."

"Maybe."

I gave her a look.

She rolled her eyes. "All right. Marginally."

I looked down at my drink. "It just feels good to forget."

Lily shook her head and took a drink. "I just cannot believe Mr. M is Cooper." She sat up straighter. "Wait — tonight, when you both disappeared, did you …"

My cheeks were on fire. "Yeah. In the bathroom. West came in."

Her jaw was on the table. "Are you fucking kidding me?"

I dropped my head to my hands. "I know, Lily. I know! So, so stupid."

"You cannot do that again. And you can't hook up over here, either."

I looked up at her, hopeful. "Does that mean you're not going to tell West?"

She sighed, not looking happy about it. "No, I won't tell him." She picked up her drink. "This sucks."

"I'm sorry, Lily. I didn't want to drag you into this. But can I just tell you how relieved I am that you know? It's been so hard, keeping it a secret."

"No one knows?"

"Only you, Astrid, and my friend from back home, Brooke."

She watched me for a beat. "West is going to figure it out. You're his sister, and Cooper is his best friend. I saw you two together, and it was just so obvious all of a sudden that something was going on. The look on your face and his — it was written all over both of you. You've got to figure something out."

I chewed my lip. "There's nothing to figure out. It'll be over soon. Don't you think we can keep it a secret until it's over?"

"If you quit banging all over the place, maybe."

"Obviously. Two weeks. That's it." I looked down at my gin and swirled it around in my glass.

She watched me. "You look a little sad about that for this being 'easy' and 'no big deal.'"

It was the truth, though, and I knew it. I didn't really want it to end, even though I knew it was exactly what it had to do. "He's the one little bright spot in my life, and he's so bright that I almost can't see any of the bad."

"Why not date?"

I cackled. "Date? *Cooper Moore*? I mean, really, Lily. His last name literally means *excess*."

"I think it refers to a geographical feature—"

I gave her a flat look.

"—but I get your meaning."

I shook my head. "Cooper is like the chaser you slam after a shot of cheap vodka. He's there to wash the taste away after the pain." I didn't know how much I believed it, even though that was what I'd been telling myself for weeks. "Anyway, you even just said he's the opposite of boyfriend material."

She shrugged. "I'm just wondering if there's more to it than that."

"Regardless, I'm sure West would be pleased as punch if I dated Cooper."

"He'd be happier with a relationship than you guys just banging for fun, I'll tell you that for sure."

But I shook my head and dug in my heels. "I can't date. I can't. I'm not ready for that. Not to be serious. And not with Cooper. How could he be serious about me when he doesn't take *anything* seriously? I did that once, Lily. I did it once, and I will never, ever do it again. I don't want to fall in love. I don't want to date. I don't want expectations from Cooper, and I don't want to expect anything from him, either."

She reached for my hand on the table and squeezed it. "I get it. I'm sorry, Maggie."

I squeezed her fingers back. "It's not your fault that I have a type."

She gave me a comforting smile. "True. If things were different, do you think it could be more?"

"You mean if I weren't emotionally crippled, if Cooper weren't a slacker, and if West wouldn't club Cooper?"

She chuckled and picked up her drink. "Yes."

I sighed and picked mine up too. "Who knows. None of it's clear to me." I took a sip. "Growing up is dumb."

"The worst."

"Let's just make a blanket fort and hang out in there indefinitely."

She raised her glass. "If there are bacon burgers, I'm in."

"Bacon burgers and french fries and gin. And ice cream." My

phone vibrated in my purse on the table, and I dug around for it.

Lily's brow rose. "That's like the third time that's gone off."

It was Cooper. I sighed as I glanced at his messages. "He wants to know if I'm okay."

"Well," she said as she stood, "I'll leave you to it. I'm going to head to West's."

I looked up at her, hating that I'd dragged her into the mess. "I'm sorry to ask you to keep this secret."

"I get the necessity. Trust me. I don't know if I can lie to him if he asks me outright, though. And I can't save either of you if he finds out."

"I know. Do what you have to do. But I swear, you won't have to hide it from him because Cooper and I will just go underground. No more hanging out with everyone, no more being reckless. And if things get hairy, I promise, I'll end it. I don't want to put you out any worse than I already have."

She looked comforted by that. "All right. And I've got your back while I can."

"Thank you." I gave her a smile.

"You're welcome. Now go message pretty boy before he loses his mind." She bent to give me a hug, saying softly, "It'll be okay, Maggie."

"I hope so."

She pulled away. "It will. I promise. I'll see you tomorrow."

"My big day!" I cheered.

"Your big day! And it's going to be amazing." She grabbed her bag and slung it on. "Sleep tight."

"You too."

"Oh, I will." She leered at me.

I shooed her, laughing. "Get outta here with that."

"Bye," she chimed as she closed the door.

I let out a heavy sigh and picked up my phone. There were three texts from Cooper.

She knows, doesn't she? Are you all right?

I'm so sorry. This is my fault.

Really, I didn't expect murder from Lily. Hit me up when you can.

I texted him back. *I'm all right. She definitely knows. And this isn't your fault. Are you still at Habits?*

Not if I can see you.

Can you call me?

Give me five.

I peeled myself out of the chair and cleaned up the kitchen, then dragged myself into the bathroom to wash my face, thinking about what Lily had said. Having a confidant who knew West just as well as I did was comforting. I needed real advice, someone who knew Cooper and the situation. Astrid had cleared the air, but I didn't know if we were on the level that I could call her and talk to her about my love life.

I sighed and dried my face, then headed into our room to change into leggings and a tank before slipping into bed. I buried myself in the fluffy covers, pulling them up to my chin with a sigh, worn out from the whole ordeal.

At least I'd bought some time.

My phone rang, and I answered right away, not even caring if I looked desperate.

"Hey," I said.

"Hey."

I want you to come over. "I don't think I can see you tonight."

He was quiet for a beat. "I can't say I'm happy about that. Anything I can do to change your mind?"

I fiddled with the lace on my comforter. "Oh, just erase everything that happened to both of us before I moved here. Can you manage that?"

I must have caught him off guard because he didn't respond right away. "Possibly. I know a guy."

I chuckled. "I'm sure you do."

"What did she say?"

I rolled over to face the room. "She wasn't happy. She thought you took advantage of me."

"If she only knew that you were the mastermind behind the whole operation," he joked.

I laughed at the irony. Talking me into stuff was his best magic trick. "I can't help the fact that I have needs."

"Is she going to tell West?"

"She said she wouldn't."

"Good. We'll be more careful."

I sighed. "God, that was so dumb, Cooper."

"But so worth it. I couldn't stand it anymore."

"Me neither. Next time, let's just leave."

"I wish we had just so I'd have you for the night."

"It's probably for the best. I can't stay at your house until three, not when I've got to get up early. For work!"

"I wish I got that excited about working." I could hear him smiling.

"Never know if you don't try."

He laughed, and we sat in contented silence. "So you didn't call when you went to your interview today, which I can't say I'm not a little hurt about."

"Aww, is Giant Hammerhead Cooper pouty?"

"Nah. The beast has been fed and is content. For now, at least. I can wake him up, though — just say the word."

I laugh burst out of me. "Oh, my God, Coop. Never call it 'the beast' again. Like, ever."

"You and your rules. Ever think about just throwing them all out the window?"

"Nope, not really." I smiled. "Sorry I didn't call. I knew I'd see you tonight, and I didn't want to bother you."

"You're never a bother, Mags."

"You say that now, but wait until my brother's chasing you with a baseball bat and then let's talk."

It was his turn to laugh. "Are you sure I can't change your mind?"

"I'm sure. I'm already in bed."

"That's not a convincing reason. I'm right around the corner."

I pulled a pillow into my chest. "We've got to be smarter about this. Your face is too pretty to risk West's wrath."

"You think I'm pretty?" he asked.

"Ninety-eight percent of all humans who have seen your face think you're pretty."

"Only ninety-eight percent? My numbers have slipped."

"The other two percent just think 'tall, dark, and handsome' is passé."

He laughed again. "Text me tomorrow and let me know how your day is."

"I will."

"And Maggie?"

"Yes?"

"I really am sorry about tonight."

"I wouldn't take it back, but I don't want to put ourselves in this spot again." I squeezed the pillow a little tighter.

"I know. Me neither." He took a breath and let it out. "All right. I'll talk to you tomorrow. Sleep well, Mags."

"You too, Coop."

I hung up and laid my phone on the nightstand before clicking off the light. And then I lay in bed, the room in such deep shadows that I couldn't make out much, though I stared into the dark all the same, trying to make sense of what was right in front of me.

Two weeks. Really, it was twelve days before we'd end it. I was resolute, not willing to hurt anyone else for something I wanted, someone who I couldn't have in any real way, anyway. The thought gave me comfort. I ignored the niggling of dread.

Starving

MAGGIE

pulled open the door to Project Homestead the next morning armed with textbooks, my laptop, iron will, and a smile, ready to crush the day. I headed back to my new boss' office and found her sitting behind her desk. Her hair was a dark, rich gray, pulled back in a clip, her brown eyes shining from behind red-framed glasses.

She smiled up at me with rosy cheeks and stood.

"Good morning, Maggie." She extended a hand.

"Hi, Susan," I said as I took it. "Good to see you."

"Have a seat." She motioned to the chair, and I sat down. "Thank you so much for starting on such short notice. We're lucky to have you. Our benefactor is coming in tomorrow, and we've had a lot of trouble finding a qualified candidate to run the reading enrichment program."

"It's my pleasure, really." I set my bag down next to my chair and folded my hands in my lap.

She leaned on her desk. "Your credentials are just outstanding, and the references we spoke to had nothing but good things to say. We're feeling a bit like we've won the lottery," she said with a smile. "Today I'll need you to fill out some paperwork, and we'll be touring the facility. I want you to meet the kids, and then we'll need to sit down and talk through some curriculum points. I'd like to have a loose plan in place for the meeting tomorrow."

"I'm sure I can get something together in time."

Susan adjusted her glasses on her nose. "Perfect." She picked up a packet of papers from her desk and handed it over to me. "So, just to go into a bit more detail on what we touched on yesterday, your volunteer position will be three days per week for the kids in the shelter, similar to library programs. We want to bring reading into the children's lives in a way that shows them the magic of books and imagination. We'd also like to discuss an adult reading workshop, which we would schedule based on the interest we receive."

I flipped through the packet, a set of paperwork to fill out and some program overviews.

"This summer we'll have larger groups of kids than you'll have starting out, once all of the kids are out of school. It's when they need us the most, the time when they're unsupervised. Our shelters are mostly families trying to get back on their feet. Most have jobs, the kids in school, trying to maintain their lives even though they've lost their homes. It's a transitional place for them, a place for them to find solid ground again. Any questions so far?"

"No, ma'am."

She smiled and stood. "Great. Let's have a look around."

I gathered my things and followed her out of the office and through the building — through the kitchen and rooms, the common areas, the playroom where I met the kids who weren't old enough for school. We ended up in the common office, a room set up with a few older desktop computers, round tables and chairs, a wall of packed bookshelves, and one super hot guy.

He was a bit older than me, with blond hair and a killer smile that he shot at me like a laser beam.

Susan gestured to him, and I think his smile got even brighter. "Maggie, I'd like you to meet Brian, our illustrious chef and head of our kitchens."

He stood and extended a hand. "Nice to meet you, Maggie."

"Likewise," I answered, taking it with a smile. He gave it a solid squeeze.

"Maggie will be heading up our reading program."

He nodded amiably. "Great. Catherine will be glad to hear we finally found someone."

"Yes, she will." Susan sounded relieved and turned back to me. "You can store any supplies you have here and use the space for anything you may need. For the meeting tomorrow, if you could put together a proposal for your plan for the children's program as well as a general supply list, that would be a great start. And, no pressure, but if you have any ideas for the adult program, I'm sure Catherine would love to hear them."

"All right. I think can manage. I have some good ideas on where to start."

"Wonderful, Maggie. Let's plan on meeting this afternoon to go over what you come up with. I can't thank you enough for your help. Are you all right to set up here in the office? Do you have everything you need?"

"I do. Thank you, Susan." I adjusted my bag on my shoulder with my mind already turning over ideas.

"Just let me know if you have any questions or need any guidance."

"I will."

I moved to sit a table away from Hottie Von Chefpants as Susan left the room, feeling him watching me with his pencil hovering over his clipboard.

"You're welcome to sit over here, if you'd like."

I smiled politely, since refusing wasn't an option, not after he'd offered. "Sure." I set down my bag and took a seat across from him.

"What are you working on?"

He leaned back in his chair and ran a hand through his golden hair. "Menus for the next month and our grocery list for Catherine. She helps procure the donations we need to keep this place up and running."

I pulled a binder of lesson plans out of my bag and set it on the table. "How long have you worked here?"

"Two years. Doesn't pay much, in money at least." He smiled at me again — it really was a pretty smile, kind and genuine.

"Yeah, I hear that. I was a teacher in my past life."

"You're not from around here."

"Is it that obvious?"

He smirked. "A little hard to disguise that accent."

I dug around for a pen, wondering if I'd be able to get any work done in the office after all. "I just moved here from Mississippi."

"Small town girl in the big city, huh?"

I raised an eyebrow. "I don't know that I'd call Jackson a small town. Maybe compared to New York, but isn't everything?"

Brian laughed, his eyes twinkling. "Fair enough. Are you in the market for a tour guide? Because I know of a mean coffee shop around the corner that I think you'd love."

I raised a brow. "Already asking me on a coffee date?"

He shrugged. "I'm not known for passing up opportunities with beautiful, charitable Southern girls who are new to the city."

I smiled, shaking my head. "That's awfully sweet of you, but I've got to pass."

He nodded, unable to fully hide his disappointment behind a smile. "I should have known you'd already have a boyfriend."

"Who says I have a boyfriend?"

His smile fell. "I'm sorry, I—"

I waved him off with a sigh. "I'm sorry. It's not you, you seem perfectly nice, and I'm pretty sure that with a smile like that, you have no problems finding a date. It's just that I'm just getting out of a serious relationship, and things are … complicated for me."

"Bad timing. I get it," he conceded.

I smiled.

"Well, let me know if things change. You know where to find me. And in the meantime, we'll be friends?"

"Sounds more like my speed."

"And we'll have Folgers instead of the Sumatra blend."

I chuckled. "Deal."

He made to get up, smiling at me. "I'll go start a pot so we can get ready for Catherine. Cream and sugar?"

"Just sugar, thanks."

I watched him leave the room, shaking my head at myself. I hadn't thought twice about turning him down, even though he was … *safe*. He was the kind of guy I should be going after — a nice guy who worked in charity with a kind smile and a great body. I bet he gave back rubs and bought girls flowers before he took them on dates to hip coffee shops. But I wasn't interested at all. Not even a tiny little ovarian flutter.

It was so easy to say no to him, but somehow I couldn't deny Cooper when he set his mind to something. I wondered what in the hell that meant, other than I was apparently a glutton for punishment.

My phone buzzed on the table, and I picked it up to find a text from Cooper. Never mind speak of the devil — I couldn't even *think* of him or he'd appear.

How's work?

I texted him back. *So far, so good. Got a lot of work to do before tomorrow. What's up?*

Come by before you head home. I'll order dinner.

Ah, the old feed-and-fuck?

I mean, when you put it like that…

I smiled. *Sure. I'll text you when I'm on my way. I can't stay late though, okay?*

I'll take what I can get. See you tonight.

I set my phone down and flipped through my lesson plans, trying to clear my mind of boys and their pretty smiles, and before long, I'd buried myself in the task at hand, feeling productive for the first time in a very, very long time.

COOPER

My doorbell rang early that evening—it was either Chinese food or Maggie. I tried not to hurry to the door, imagining it was her, and when I opened it, I wasn't disappointed.

She stood in the entry, rosy cheeked and smiling up at me, wearing a sweet dress with tiny flowers all over it and white sneakers, unfussy and perfectly beautiful. "Hey."

"Hey." I wrapped my arms around her and laid a hot kiss on her lips.

She looked up at me dreamily when she broke away. "I was kinda hoping you'd already be naked."

"That would have been awkward if you'd actually been the delivery guy."

She chuckled.

"How was your day?" I closed the door and followed her into the apartment.

"Long," she said as she set down her bag. "I have a lot of work to do tonight. Our benefactor is coming tomorrow, and I'm supposed to put a proposal together for her."

I stiffened, smiling to cover my discomfort, hoping my decision to keep any details about her new boss to myself was wise.

Her eyes narrowed. "Why do you look weird?"

I grabbed her around the waist and dipped her. "I'm just hearing that you're not going to stay very long, and I don't like it. Not one bit." I kissed her deep, and her arms wound around my neck.

Her cheeks were flushed when I broke the kiss. "Well," she said, voice raspy, "better make the most of it while we can."

I wasn't one to argue.

I kissed her again with intention, contemplating just how I'd like to undress her when the doorbell rang. I didn't stop.

Her hands pressed my shoulders, and she broke away, smiling. "That's dinner."

"Fuck dinner. I'm ready for dessert."

She giggled and kissed me gently. "Well, I'm starving."

"Me too." I covered her mouth with mine, and she pulled away, laughing. "Answer it, Coop."

The doorbell rang again, and I set her down, grumbling before flying to the door and ripping it open, glad I'd already paid and tipped when I called it in. I swiped the bag of Chinese food and closed the door in one motion, leaving a stunned delivery man in my entryway. I tossed the bag on the island on my way back to her.

I scooped her into my arms.

She laughed into my neck. "Seriously, I'm so hungry. Can we eat first?"

"Nope." I pressed my lips to hers.

She pulled back, smiling. "If you feed me first, I'll last longer."

I sighed. "Well, in that case ..." I kissed her gently and let her go. "Thank you."

I made my way into the kitchen to grab plates. "Water or wine?"

"Water," she said as she sat down. "If I have wine tonight, I'll never get my work done."

I stacked up plates and napkins. "Meaning you'd stay longer? Because if so, I think you should reconsider."

"You are the worst influence."

"Thank you." I made my way to the island where she was already unpacking dinner.

She opened a carton and took a long whiff. "God, I could eat a horse."

"How about a Giant Hammerhead Cooper?"

A laugh shot out of her. "Why, did you get shark soup?"

I snorted.

She was still chuckling. "I've actually been thinking about The Hammerhead all day."

"Oh?" I sat down next to her, amused and very turned on.

She nodded. "Mmhmm. Sometimes I just need your dick in my face."

My brows shot up, and I smirked. "Keep talking like that and I'm not going to let you eat first."

Maggie pouted dramatically, though her eyes smoldered. "Aww. I *really* wanted some egg roll." She pulled one out of the paper envelope and inspected it. "They're so hot and fat." I watched as she opened her mouth and wrapped her pink lips around it, took a bite with a crunch and closed her eyes, moaning.

I couldn't tear my eyes away, and I realized distantly that my mouth was open. I wet my lips. "Mags …" The word was almost a warning.

She opened her eyes and blinked up at me innocently. "What?"

I turned and grabbed her stool, pulling her between my legs. "I thought you wanted to eat?"

She set down the egg roll and dusted off her hands. "I did say that, didn't I?" she asked as she slipped off the stool. "I'm hungry, Cooper." Her hands trailed down to my pants and tugged at my belt, her eyes wide as she looked into mine. My hands found her waist. "Will you feed me?"

I would have laughed if my raging boner wasn't straining against my underwear — I couldn't even answer. She unzipped my pants and wrapped her fingers around my shaft. Her gaze was locked on mine, but when I leaned into her for a kiss, she backed away smiling, teasing me.

She hooked her fingers in the elastic band of my underwear, eyes on her hands as they gripped me. I watched her tongue slip out to wet her lips, lips that smiled when I pulsed in her hand involuntarily.

She bent over, ass out, breath hot, lips wet as she closed them over me. I sucked in a breath, but I couldn't close my eyes, just slipped a hand into her curly hair and watched as I disappeared into her mouth. She pulled back and dropped down again, looking up at me, hand around my base as I hit the back of her throat.

"Fuck," I whispered, and her eyes smiled before her lids fluttered closed.

Her body moved in a figure eight as she backed away and dropped down again and again, sucking and rolling her tongue when she came to the tip. I reached for the back of her dress and gathered it with my fingers until the hem hung in the curve of her waist, ass exposed, my eyes on her black G-string.

My heart banged as I gripped her hair and pulled to stop her, and she popped off, lips swollen, lids heavy. In a breath, I was kissing her, our tongues rolling, lips a hard seam. I could have devoured her in that moment.

But instead, I turned her around and bent her over my kitchen table. She panted, forearms on the surface, as I lifted her dress and hooked my fingers in the string of her panties, dragged it over the curve of her ass and down her thighs. She shimmied until they were on the floor and spread her legs. I gripped my shaft in one hand and slipped the other around her waist, down her stomach until I reached the sensitive spot to trace letters with the pad of my finger.

F.

I guided my crown to the wet line. She turned to look behind her, sucking in a breath.

U.

I dragged it up the length of her.

C.

"Cooper," she moaned shifting her hips as I rested against the dip.

K.

"Are you hungry, Maggie?" I flexed my hips and filled her slowly.

Her mouth hung open, lids fluttering closed, and she gasped when I hit the end. *"Yes,"* she whispered, lowering her cheek to the surface, her fingers clenching and releasing against the wood, looking for something to hold on to. I arched over her and took her hand, guiding it over her head as I pulled out and slammed back in. She threaded her fingers in mine, her other hand grabbing on as she used the leverage to press back into me. I nuzzled into her neck as I thrust again and again, rolling my hips until her breath sped up, legs trembling against mine, fingers white-knuckle, and then she came with a cry, squeezing me, releasing me. And I couldn't wait, wouldn't wait. I pumped faster, the soft pat of skin against skin driving me, and seconds later I let go, eyes pinned shut, breathing her name.

I opened my eyes as our bodies slowed, and I wrapped her in my arms, lying against her back, still inside of her. I kissed her shoulder, and she hummed before mumbling something.

"Hmm?"

"Thatwasfuckinghot," she muttered, her cheek still resting on the surface of the table.

"You started it with your dirty egg roll."

She chuckled. "I told you. Sometimes I just need your dick in my face."

I kissed her shoulder once more. "Still hungry?"

"Kinda full right now." She shifted her hips, smiling.

I laughed. "I don't know what's gotten into you, but I like it."

"Oh, I think you know what's gotten into me."

I rolled my hips. "You're just going to keep going, aren't you?"

"Maybe."

"Let's eat and then maybe I can work this out of your system."

She twisted to look back at me. "Who's hungry now?"

I brushed her hair back and kissed just behind her ear. "Me," I whispered and pulled out.

She sighed and rolled onto her back, looking like she could take a nap on my table as I grabbed a fresh kitchen towel for me and one for Maggie. She took it lazily.

I cleaned up and tossed the towel in the general direction of the laundry room. I was washing my hands, still watching her with a smile as she made a half-assed attempt to get up.

"I'm too tired to eat," she said.

I dried my hands and made my way back to the take out cartons. "Hmm, too bad. There's lo mien, pork fried rice, orange chicken, beef with broccoli." I sniffed melodramatically. "Plus some hot, fat egg rolls."

She's perked up a little. "Damn you and your crispy fried goodness."

I was still smiling as I filled my plate with my chopsticks. She washed her hands and sat next to me, piling on even more food than I did. I gave her a look.

She raised her eyebrows. "What? I told you I was hungry. I don't mess around when it comes to food."

"I can see that you take it very seriously."

Maggie scooped up noodles with her chopsticks and stuffed them in her mouth, smiling at me with the lo mien hanging from between her lips for just a second before slurping them up.

I couldn't help but laugh. "How much more work did you have to do again? Because I really think you should stay."

"The night? Come on, buddy boy. You know the rules."

"A few more hours. The night. Whatever I can convince you of."

"I do wish I could stay a while. But ..." She sighed and fished around for some pork. "I have a lot to do. I mean, it's not that big of a deal, just three programs a week, but I need a plan of attack, sort of like a manifesto." She took a bite. "Mostly though, I'm worried about impressing our mysterious benefactor. I don't even know that much about her other than that she's a rich lady named Catherine who's been in working with the shelter on some level since the 90s."

"Don't worry about the meeting. You'll do fine. I promise." I hoped she did, at least. Knowing Catherine, Maggie would hit a home run.

She seemed reassured and smiled. "Thanks. I've got a lot to do for sure, but I'll get it done. Hopefully Lily is already at West's because I'm not quite ready to see her again after last night."

"Was it that bad?"

"No, not really. I just feel guilty for dragging her into the mess."

"I hear you on that." I picked up a piece of orange chicken and popped it into my mouth.

She sighed again. "At least we only have to sneak around for eleven more days. Then we'll both be on our way."

I almost inhaled the chicken and started coughing.

Maggie dropped her chopsticks and patted me on the back. "God, are you okay?"

I nodded and croaked. "Yeah, wrong pipe." I took a swig of my water.

She picked up her chopsticks again. "I'm just feeling really awful about it. I hate lying to West, knowing how upset he would be. It's selfish, us using each other, lying to everyone."

I watched her. "Maybe it's time you did something selfish for once."

She looked over at me, eyes wide and open.

"I'm just saying. Don't let anyone make you feel bad for doing something you want to do."

"Even if what I want hurts someone else?"

"No one's going to get hurt." I knew it was a lie as soon as it left my mouth.

She shook her head and looked down at her plate. "Maybe we should just end it now while we can, before anyone else finds out. Before things get any more complicated."

Anxiety ripped through me at the thought of ending it now. I wasn't ready — that was one thing I knew without a doubt. A very alarmed part of me wondered if I'd ever be ready.

In a heartbeat, I was off my stool and holding her. I looked down at her, smiling to hide. "Let's just enjoy it while we can. We'll be more careful. We'll be smarter about it. Because I'm not ready to stop yet. Are you?"

Those eyes. Those eyes would be the end of me.

She shook her head.

"Then it's decided." I placed a soft kiss on her lips and sat back down, picking up my chopsticks like everything was normal, like my heart wasn't hammering against my ribs. I glanced back at her. She was still watching me, though I couldn't quite place the look on her face.

I shot her The Smile. "You'd better eat that dirty egg roll before I do."

She picked it up, making a show of taking another bite, and I laughed, trying not to sweat the bullet I'd dodged.

The Surface

COOPER

Bobby pulled up in front of Astrid's building that night, and I climbed out to greet her.

She smiled and made her way out from under the awning, her high, black studded heels clicking on the sidewalk. She was dressed in black — tight jeans and a tank, black leather jacket — even her blue eyes were lined in kohl, which made them shades brighter than usual. The only light was her blond hair and creamy skin.

She pressed her cheek to mine as we embraced. "Hey."

"Hey." I helped her into the backseat and slipped in behind her. "Take us to Church, Bobby."

"You got it, Coop."

"You ready for tonight?" she asked as Bobby pulled away from the curb.

"How can I not be ready to go to a bar called *Church*?"

She snickered. "I heard it's all Gothic, and they have these amazing stained glass displays."

"I love concept clubs, if I have to go out." I sighed and leaned back. "Is it just me or is this getting harder and harder to bullshit?"

"It's definitely not you. Think Ash is already there?"

"He's probably doing body shots off willing girls as we speak."

She laughed. "Ash is never going to grow up."

I raised an eyebrow. "He'd say the same about us."

"Yeah, well, we know better, don't we?"

I shrugged. "Maybe he's faking it too."

We shared a look and burst out laughing.

Astrid shook her head. "Yeah, okay, Ash is definitely not faking it." She angled toward me in the seat with an accusatory look on her face. "So Lily had an interesting story to tell me today."

I shifted in my seat, knowing exactly what she was going to say and playing dumb anyway. "What'd she say?"

"Oh, just that you banged Maggie in the bathroom at Habits last night."

I propped my elbow on the door. "Don't look at me like that. Do you have any idea how … *intense* it is to be around her when no one knows we're together?"

"No, how about you tell me about it."

"I wish I could. There aren't words."

"Lily also said Maggie told her about you and me. I had to explain Sam and everything just to calm her down."

"I'm sorry, Astrid."

She sighed and adjusted her bag in her lap. "It's fine. It actually felt really good to tell her what was going on, even though she was pissed at me for not telling her about him. I think she gets it though. And plus, now she believes all of us."

"Maggie said she agreed to keep it from West."

"For now. She's not going to lie to him. In fact, if he ever finds out about you two, he's probably going to be pissed at her too."

"Thanks for piling that on."

"I'm just saying," she continued. "This isn't the simple, easy thing the two of you like to pretend it is. More and more people are getting dragged into it."

"I know."

"So what are you going to do? Because you're eventually going to have to do something."

"If Maggie has her way, we'll be through in a couple of weeks." I sniffed and ran a hand down my tie, feeling uncomfortable.

Her eyebrow raised. "And if you have your way?"

"I don't know. She suggested ending it tonight, and I didn't want to."

She shook her head. "Am I hearing you right? You want to date Maggie? Publicly?"

"That's not what I said."

"It's what you implied."

"I don't know, Astrid. I'm not ready to walk away, not just yet. But I won't hang you out to dry with Sam."

She put up a hand. "Listen, if we have to end the charade, it's fine. I don't want to stand in the way of something you want just because of my own fucked-up relationship. But I'm just surprised to hear you say you want that much more from Maggie."

I frowned. "Me too."

She watched me for a breath. "So what are you going to do? Ride it out the next couple of weeks and then decide? Talk to West?"

I laughed wholeheartedly. "There's no talking to West. But I might be able to feel him out, see if I can figure out how bad it will be. But I don't know exactly what to do about Maggie."

"What are your options?"

"Do nothing. Wait and see. Talk to her. It's just that I don't know what to say."

"You better watch out — you're gonna spook her."

I looked down my nose at her, smiling. "You doubt my skills of persuasion? I'm as adept at navigating social situations as I am sea charts and Prague. Which is to say, very good."

STACI HART

She rolled her eyes and laughed. "Easy for you to say. You weren't just cheated on at the altar."

I frowned. "It's been three months. I mean, she *seems* fine. She never talks about him, doesn't act like she's bothered by it."

Astrid looked at me like I was an idiot. "And you don't think that's a front? It seems pretty obvious that her rules are just something for her to hide behind."

"Of course they are. It's not like I'm asking her to get married, Astrid. I just don't want to walk away, but that means we can't hide. And if we're going to agree to tell West, then she has to admit that she wants me for more than just a fuck buddy. And then … well, we can just take it day by day. I don't know what the fuck I'm doing otherwise anyway."

She chuckled. "Isn't that the truth?" We pulled up to the club, and her smile fell as she looked beyond the window at the people and paparazzi. She took a deep breath and said half to herself, "Here we go."

Astrid threw open the door and slid out, and I did the same, hurrying around the car to meet her as we were flanked by photographers. Flashes strobed, and Astrid hung on to me as we barreled toward the entrance, though I couldn't see anything, just followed one of the bouncers toward the door as the rest pushed the paparazzi back.

We stopped just inside the door to adjust to the dark after the visual assault, the bass from the club thumping. I glanced into the club, nodding in appreciation as we walked in.

The vaulted ceiling swept up in pointed arches, the dance floor lined with columns. At the end of the long space was the DJ, the tables standing in front of a massive stained glass display in a seemingly random pattern. But as I watched, I realized it was changing, moving slowly. It was a screen. I shook my head, smiling.

Astrid pulled me toward the bar in the main club.

"Where are we going?" I yelled over the music.

She pointed to the bar. "Bastian."

I glanced over to find Bastian leaning against the bar, dark and muscular, smiling bright and looking dapper as fuck in slate pants and a white tailored shirt. He smoothed his tie and pushed off the bar to greet us. He was one of Astrid's closest friends and a dancer with Lily at the New York City Ballet.

"Hey, bitch." He kissed Astrid on the cheek.

"Hey, whore." She kissed him back. "I'm glad you came."

"I'm glad you invited me. How are you, Mr. Moore?"

I smiled. "Living the dream."

He looked me up and down. "Yeah you are. Is Lily with you?"

Astrid laughed. "That's funny, Bas."

He shrugged. "I had to ask. I wish she'd come out more often. We only see each other at work, which is a sad, sad thing."

"None of us see her much these days. She's holed up with West."

"Well, at least she's got that. I wouldn't be complaining about being holed anywhere by him."

A laugh shot out of me.

"Let's go get drinks," Astrid said and hooked her arm in his. "Really, what would I have done if you hadn't come?"

"I dunno, maybe you would have hung out with your date? I know that's what I'd be doing. I mean, have you seen him?"

I snorted.

We headed up the stairs to VIP, and Ash caught sight of me from across the room, smiling as he threw his hand up in the air to greet me. It was the same boyish grin he'd had ever since we we'd met at age five. I couldn't help but smile back. The asshole was the closest thing to a brother I had.

He met us halfway and went in for a hug, clapping me on the

shoulder as we bumped chests. "Coop, you made it. What's up, man?"

I shook my head, still smiling. "Oh, you know. The usual."

He jerked his chiseled chin at Astrid. "'Sup, Astrid?" He leaned in to kiss her cheek.

"Hey, Ash." She pressed her cheek to his. "How long have you guys been here?"

He ran a hand through his blond hair just as a giggling brunette came out of nowhere and nearly fell into him. He hung an arm on her shoulder, smiling wide at me. "Not nearly long enough. Come on, let's get you guys drinks." He swung an arm in invitation, and we followed him through the club to his table, which was packed with people. His entourage was hanging around, mostly friends we'd had since high school, each with a girl or two I'd never seen before draped over them.

Ash poured Astrid a gin and tonic, then a scotch for me and Bastian. I nearly emptied mine on the first sip. Everyone was drunk and laughing, all carefree smiles and general not-giving-a-fuck. It was their specialty. It was mine, too, in a way.

He laughed and hooked his arm around my neck, his drink in his free hand. "Fuck, man, we were just talking about Bikini Girl in Ibiza."

"You can't put sunscreen there!" Ash and a couple of the guys yelled, and we all broke out laughing.

Ash shook his head and let me go. "We haven't been back in, what, three years? It's time, man. Way past time. Let's do it this summer."

"Only if you wear the hat."

He clinked his glass to mine. "Oh, fuck yeah. I'll wear the hat to Bocca Scopare if it'll get you to Ibiza."

Bastian raised an eyebrow. "What's so terrible about 'the hat' that it takes bribery to get one to wear it?" He took a sip of his drink.

I shook my head. "We found this hat in Turkey that looks like the head of a giant dick. With a baseball rim."

Bastian nodded, amused. "I approve. Seems appropriate to wear to a restaurant called Mouth Fuck."

I laughed. "I just want to see him try to make it through the front door of Scopare with that hat on. It's got veins and everything."

He raised his glass. "And it was worth every penny I paid for it, too."

I shook my head. "He walked up and down the nude beaches asking girls if they knew any dickheads."

Astrid laughed. "Oh, my God. You would, Ash."

"I have no fear."

"Or shame," she added.

"Same thing." He took a drink.

Astrid killed her drink and patted him on the shoulder. "Oh, Ash. Come with me to get a drink, Bas. Don't make me brave the wildlife alone."

She took his arm as they headed to the table, and Astrid rolled her eyes at the giggling girls hanging all over the guys, stepping over legs and stripper heels to get to the liquor.

Ash jerked his chin at me. "What's up, man? Haven't seen you much the last couple of weeks." He took a drink.

"Not much."

"Then where the hell have you been?"

I played up whatever I could to assuage him. "Had a photoshoot the other day with *W*."

"Oh? Fashion or something else?"

I smirked. "Eligible bachelors."

A laugh burst out of him. "Of course you did. So, that was one day. And how about the rest of the time?"

I shrugged, not knowing what else to add because there wasn't anything except the truth. "I've got a new girl."

Ash smiled mischievously. "Now we're getting somewhere. How hot is she?"

"I can't judge her on that scale. She's a good girl."

"Oh, fuck man. I love the corruption of a good girl," he said knowingly. "What's her story?"

"She just moved here. Needed someone to show her around."

"Yeah, I bet she did." He chuckled. "Astrid doesn't suspect, does she?"

"You know she doesn't care. I've told her all about it."

He shook his head. "Astrid Thomas *and* all the side ass you want? It's the dream."

His dream, maybe. I shook my head, amused as I sipped my scotch.

His eyebrow raised with one corner of his mouth in a smile as he looked behind me. "Don't look now, but Ali Banks is currently strutting this way with mischief on her mind. And by mischief, I mean blow jobs."

I laughed, even though I was annoyed. I'd hooked up with the actress a few times, which was plenty. Let's just say that some actresses are *always* acting. I hadn't called her in months, but for some reason, she hadn't gotten the hint.

"Hey there, handsome." Her voice was silky, and she slipped her arm around mine.

I turned to her, plastering on The Smile. At least Batman got a legit mask. "Hey, Ali." I kissed her cheek, and she smiled up at me.

She was gorgeous — long, copper hair in shiny finger waves, ivory skin, big, green eyes, and a wide, sexy smile. She really was a fantasy on legs, a model before she started acting. But that smile was just as plastic as mine.

Her fingers gripped my bicep. "Where've you been, Coop? I haven't seen you in forever."

Ash raised his glass. "Hey, Ali. No, I'm good too. Great to see you."

Ali shot him a flat look. "Hey, Ash," she said, sounding bored, but when she looked back at me, she lit up. "Really, though. I've missed seeing you. Have you been in New York or on vacation?" She didn't wait for an answer, just kept talking. "I've been dreaming of Italy.

As soon as we're finished filming, I think I'll †
Maybe you could come meet me for a week‹
her was suggestive — her eyes on me, the cu⁞
pressed into my side — even if her words ha⁞

"Sounds refreshing."

Ali smiled, her eyes on my lips. "I'll text you about it." She got even closer. "So, what are you doing tonight?"

I looked her over. Even with her breasts against my arm, her long thigh against mine, those big, green eyes of hers looking up at me hopefully, I wasn't interested at all. She looked too polished. Too perfect. I thought of Maggie's wild hair, the peppering of freckles across her cheeks and bridge of her nose. She didn't even have to try — Maggie was effortlessly beautiful, unlike Ali, who looked like she'd had a makeup artist and a stylist put her together, which I was certain was the truth.

Even more appealing: Maggie would never throw herself at a man the way Ali did.

I smiled apologetically. "Ali, I'm here with Astrid."

"Oh." She blinked and let me go, putting a little space between us just as Astrid walked up, smirking.

"Hey, Ali."

Ali threw on the brightest smile in her repertoire, I was sure. "Oh, hey, Astrid. I didn't see you were here."

"Obviously."

She lasered her charm on Astrid, touching her arm as she beamed. "I saw your Barney's ad in Times Square. So hot."

Astrid gave her a flat, bullshit smile. "Thanks. Jean-Pierre does amazing things with a camera."

Ali laughed, the sound practiced. "Please. You're so gorgeous. I bet you even look good with the front camera on your phone." She waved a hand at Astrid and turned back to me. "I've got to head back, good to see you, Coop."

I motioned to her with my drink. "You too, Ali."

Her smile curled a little in the corners. "I'll see you around." She turned to walk away, hips swaying.

"Bye, Ali," Ash called, too loud, laughing when she didn't turn around.

Astrid shook her head. "Shameless."

Truth or Dare

MAGGIE

The next morning, I found myself standing in the entry of the shelter between Susan and Brian, amongst a handful of volunteers and residents as our benefactor walked through the front door with her assistant by her side. And the second I saw her, my heart took a swan dive out of my chest and hit my shoes with a splat.

She was tall and beautiful, with thick, jet black hair cut just above her shoulders, eyes sparkling and blue, just as I remembered. Her shirt and pencil skirt were tailored, lips red as she smiled warmly at us. It was a smile I was very, very familiar with.

It looked exactly like her son's.

Cooper's mom blinked at me, her smile stretching wider with recognition. "Maggie! It's been years, how are you?"

I smiled back, stunned as she embraced me. We'd met when Cooper and West graduated from Columbia, had dinner together. "I'm well, Mrs. Moore. It's good to see you."

"Please, call me Catherine. It's been too long. Cooper told me you were in town and looking for a job."

everyone was staring at me as I stood in front of my new boss —
my booty call's mother — smiling like an idiot as my thoughts spun
around like they were on the Tilt-A-Whirl.

"Oh, did he?"

"He did. We're so lucky to have you. Between Cooper and
Susan's glowing recommendations, I'm just so thrilled that you've
landed in our laps." She turned her attention to Susan. "Lovely to see
you, Susan."

"Hello, Catherine. We're so happy to see you, too."

"I'm glad to be here. Hello, Brian, and everyone."

I was still smiling, barely listening as she said her hellos, feeling
like a deer in headlights. Cooper had something to do with me being
hired. I was all of a sudden certain of it.

She turned to everyone after a moment. "Let's head to the
kitchen and get started."

I followed them into the kitchen and sat down, listening to
everyone discuss their updates with my mind on Cooper, my
discomfort waning as my anger blazed. I didn't need his help to find a
job — I didn't ask for it, and I didn't want it, but he did it anyway. He
told his mother about me, maybe even called Susan. The thought that
I hadn't gotten the job on my own filled me with fury.

Part of the reason I'd wanted the job was to get away from
Cooper, and now I found myself working for his mother.

It came to my turn, and I stood in front of a group that included
my fuck buddy's super rich mother and a very hot chef who was
eyeing me like an *amuse-bouche*. I did my best to ignore all that and
smiled through my plans for the program in a short presentation,
outlining my philosophy and means to teach the range of readers I'd
be working with. I hoped it was enough, hoped I'd make a difference
for the children, maybe bring some sunshine into their lives after
enduring so much hardship.

Catherine was pleased, which was a relief. I realized as I sat down that I wanted her approval, badly. I tried to convince myself that it was just because she was so important to the shelter, to my new position. It had nothing to do with Cooper. Cooper who would be seeing a very pissed-off me in a few hours when I left work.

When the meeting was over, Catherine and Susan left for a walk through while I worked on my craft supply list for the majority of the day, jaw set and fingers flying on my keyboard. I didn't even see Brian until he pulled up a chair and set a cup of coffee next to me.

I looked up and sighed, grateful and a little embarrassed.

He sat back in his chair and smiled. "You were working a little hard, so I brought you some fuel."

I picked up the coffee. "Thanks, Brian. Is there a chance there's liquor in this? Because that would be fantastic."

He chuckled. "Not this time, but I'll see what I can do for the next round." He took a sip of his own coffee, watching me over the rim. "So you know Cooper Moore?"

My smile fell. "He's my brother's best friend. They went to Columbia together."

I couldn't quite read his expression. "Interesting."

"Listen," I bristled. "I didn't know Cooper's mother was our benefactor, and as far as I know, that fact had nothing to do with me getting this job." I hoped, at least.

He put up a hand in surrender. "I'm not judging or accusing. I know you've got the muscle to handle it."

My brow was low. "Damn straight, I do."

"I'm sorry, I didn't mean to upset you."

I let out a breath and tried to relax. "I'm sorry to snap at you. I just don't like the idea of not being taken seriously or that I got here any way but by my own merit."

"I get it. I mean, this is a highly competitive field full of sharks, the old charity game. Wouldn't want anyone to do you any favors."

I smiled, feeling sheepish. "Well, when you say it like that, it does sound pretty silly."

"Nah, not silly," he said with a comforting smile. "You work hard and want that to be your legacy, not who you know."

"I really had no idea about Catherine's involvement with the shelter. I knew she did charity work, but I really only met her a few times, years ago. She's been here since the nineties?"

He nodded. "She's done so much for the city, for the people who live here. It wasn't until she took over that the shelter really took off, expanded its reach. I've seen how much the people who come through here are touched, and that's largely thanks to Catherine's efforts." He was so earnest, so heartfelt.

"You really love it, don't you?"

"I do. It's definitely more rewarding than being a sous chef. That was nothing but low pay, long hours, and loads of backstabbing. And let me tell you — they've got sharp knives."

"Hurts less going in, at least," I said with a chuckle.

He smiled, watching me for a second. "Let me take you to dinner."

"Man, you don't quit, do you?" I shook my head at him, amused.

"Not when I want something."

I sighed, still shaking my head. "I'm sorry, Brian. You seem like a really nice guy …"

He sucked in a breath through his teeth and laid a hand on his heart. "Ouch."

I smiled. "Just friends. Okay?"

Brian pushed his chair back and stood, smiling back playfully. "All right, all right. Duly noted." He hitched a thumb over his shoulder. "I'd better get back to my spaghetti sauce. I'll see you later."

"Bye, Brian."

He left me alone in the office, and I took a breath, sitting up a little straighter and laying my fingers back on the keyboard with my mind a mess. Not about Brian — once again, I didn't feel a single thing, even as he threw his charm all over me with the subtlety of a busted fire hydrant. I swear, my brain was broken, hijacked by hormones or pheromones or some other invasive mone that wanted to ruin my life.

I checked the time. Two hours until I would head over to Cooper's and give him a piece of my mind. I'd been lied to, and he'd betrayed my trust — two things I wouldn't stand for. My heart lurched when I thought this might be the end. Because I couldn't stand for this.

There was no way for him to talk his way out of it, not this time.

COOPER

Music played softly as I stretched out on my leather recliner in my favorite room in the entire world, reading *Watchmen* for the ten thousandth time.

Some rich guys had a red room of pain. I had a black room of nerd.

Shelves lined one wall completely, lit to display collector action figures, graphic novels, comics. The other three walls were covered in framed artwork with gallery lights — Gambit and Rogue's first kiss signed by Stan Lee, the original *Batman* movie poster signed by Tim Burton and Michael Keaton. Art made from my favorite comic frames, one floor to ceiling piece from *V for Vendetta* with a note from Alan Moore along the bottom.

And in the corner, in a standing case, was my very own custom-made Batman suit.

Seriously, don't look at me like that.

My defense is this: I really, *really* wanted to go to ComicCon. My addiction is my dirty secret. No one knows, and I don't want them to. If I went to ComicCon as Cooper Moore, everyone would find out. But if I went as *Batman*, my secret would be safe, even if a hundred people took pictures with me that day.

I smiled to myself. It was maybe the most epic day of my life.

My doorbell rang, and my brow dropped when I looked at my watch. It was six, and I wondered who it could be as I hauled myself out of my chair and made my way to the door. There were only a handful of people on the list of visitors who could come up unannounced, and I hoped I knew which one it was.

I opened the door to find a very angry, very adorable Maggie in my entryway.

"When were you planning on telling me that your *mother* runs Project Homestead?"

I had good reason for keeping it from her, and I opened my mouth to defend myself. "Mags, I—"

"Don't you *Mags* me, Cooper. You told her about me. Did you call Susan? Did you get me that job? I don't need your goddamn help. I'm a grown-ass woman with the ability to get a job I want without your help." She poked me in the shoulder.

"Maggie—"

"I'm not finished!"

I smirked and leaned on the doorframe, folding my arms, waiting for her to get it out of her system.

Her eyes narrowed even more. "Don't you gimme that smile, you son of a bitch. I'm sure you pull strings all the time to get what you want, but that's not how I do things. You had no right to interfere."

"I didn't."

Her lips twisted in a scowl. "Don't lie to me, Cooper. Your mother told me you spoke to her about me."

"I did, but not about your application."

She tilted her head, confused. "But she said …"

I watched her. "Did she say I had anything to do with it?"

Her brow dropped. "Well, no, not exactly … but you knew I was applying there. Why didn't you tell me your mother was a benefactor?"

"Because I knew that was the job you wanted, and I wanted you to apply. I had a feeling you wouldn't if you knew I was connected. Looks like I was right." I gave her a smile as her face softened.

"You really didn't say anything?" Her eyes were wide, her voice apologetic.

"I really didn't."

"God, Cooper. I just … when I saw her … and she said … and I just thought …" Her shoulders slumped as she let out a breath and turned. "I'm sorry. I should go."

I reached for her wrist, chuckling as I pulled her into me. "No, you shouldn't."

Her cheek pressed against my chest. "The way she said it just sounded like you had something to do with it. I didn't even ask you, just came here and started yellin'. I'd just been thinking about it all day and had myself convinced. I'm an ass."

"Maybe a little." I laughed.

She groaned. "Aren't you mad at me?"

"Of course not — I might have made the same assumption. But if you really feel inclined to make it up to me, I can think of a few things you could do."

She smiled and looked up at me. "Oh, I'm sure you could. I'm sorry, Cooper."

"Quit apologizing." I kissed her cheek. "As long as you believe me, we're fine."

"I believe you."

"Then we're fine." I brushed her hair back from her face. "You hungry? I was just about to make dinner."

She raised an eyebrow. "As in, cook?"

"That surprises you?"

"I just figured your kitchen was for show."

"You can only order takeout so many times before you're over it, and I'm not busy enough to warrant having someone to cook every night for me."

"No, but you're rich enough to."

I chuckled. "Come on. Let me introduce you to another on one of my many talents." I dragged her inside and into the kitchen where she sat at my island bar. I fired up the stovetop grill built into my gourmet kitchen.

"Is that a real grill? Inside?"

I smiled at her over my shoulder. "Sure is."

"That is swanky."

"See? I can't have this kitchen and not use it."

"Oh, don't get me wrong. I was sure it was being used, just not by you."

I pulled out chicken I'd been marinating from the fridge and set it on the counter. "Think you've got me all figured out, do you?"

"No, actually. Just when I think I do, you surprise me."

I smiled and grabbed the chicken breasts with tongs, setting them on the grates with a hiss. "To be fair, I don't clean. I don't grocery shop, either."

She laughed. "Oh, God. I can just see you walking through the produce, sniffing cantaloupe."

"I *am* very picky about my melons."

She snickered. "Do you need any help?"

"Just with this." I grabbed a bottle of wine and gave it a little shake.

"All right. I'll do my best," she joked.

I opened it and poured her a glass. "Let's play a game."

"What kind of game."

"Truth or dare." I smiled and handed her the wine.

"Maybe we should wait until after dinner."

I poured myself a glass. "Oh, I've got plans for dessert already."

She smiled and took a sip. "So, who goes first?"

I smirked and took a drink. "Truth or dare?"

"I feel like I owe you a dare after yelling at you."

"I was hoping you'd say that."

"Shit," she muttered.

"I dare you to wear nothing but this apron for the rest of dinner." I opened a drawer, grabbed an apron, and tossed it to her.

She picked it up curiously, laughing when she opened it up. "Really, Coop?"

I just smiled.

She stood and held it up to her body. It was a replica of Botticelli's Venus, made to look like the wearer was the goddess of love herself, fingers on her bare breast. "Where the hell did you get this?" she asked with a laugh.

I leaned against the counter and crossed my arms. "Florence. I have David, too."

"Of course you do." She sighed. "Well, a dare's a dare." She set the apron on the counter and smiled at me as she kicked off her shoes. I leaned against the counter, folding my arms across my chest as I watched her strip. The apron hit her mid-thigh, and she tied it around her waist, blushing. "There you go."

"Give us a spin."

She spun around, and I caught a glimpse of her pert ass. "Happy?"

"You have no idea."

Maggie took a seat and picked up her wine again. "My turn. Truth or dare?"

"Truth."

"Boring. Okay, um …" She looked up at the ceiling. "Most outrageous place you've ever had sex."

I didn't miss a beat. "Confessional booth in Barcelona."

Her jaw hung open, and a surprised laugh slipped out of her.

"Her name was Vivica. It was also the only time I've been propositioned in a church. I doubt it was the first time she'd made the offer, but I couldn't pass it up."

"Was there a priest there? I mean …"

I chuckled. "No, it was empty. My turn. Truth or dare?"

She blinked and shook her head. "Ah … okay. Dare."

I raised an eyebrow and turned flipped the chicken. "Not feeling like sharing today, huh?"

She gave me a look. "All right, bossy. Truth."

"Too late." I grabbed a wooden spoon and handed it to her. "Sing me happy birthday like Marilyn Monroe."

Maggie laughed as she stood and made her way over to me. "Dammit, Cooper." She snatched the spoon and tried to stop giggling as she bent over, exaggerating the pucker in her lips, breathing the words as she stepped closer and ran her hands up my chest.

"…Happy birthday, Mr. Sexypants." Her hands slipped lower, trailing between my legs. "Happy birthday to you."

Her face was tilted up to mine, and I smiled as I pressed my lips to hers. Her body was flush against mine, the thin fabric of the apron all that separated me from her naked breasts.

I broke the kiss while I could, taking the spoon and popping her bare ass with it. She squealed and giggled, and it was the most glorious sound I'd ever heard.

"Truth or dare?" she asked.

I watched her ass as she made her way back to her wine. "Dare."

She pointed to the drawer where the aprons were. "If I have to be Venus, you'll have to be David."

"I knew I shouldn't have told you I had it."

She smiled.

I made a show of taking off my clothes, tossing my shirt in her face as she cheered and cat-called me. I tied the apron and held up my hands in display.

"Give us a spin," she said slyly.

I spun around and smiled.

"Now, flip the chicken."

"You want me to touch the breasts while you watch?"

"Give them a good fondling. They need to be hot before we eat them." Her brow was up as she took a sip of her wine.

I laughed and made lewd noises while I poked at the chicken, knowing she was staring at my naked ass.

"All right," I said when the show was over. "Truth or dare?"

She hesitated before answering, "Truth."

I thought carefully, turning to lean on the counter again. Her eyes fell between my legs at David's cock, and she giggled.

"I don't know if I can take you seriously in that."

I didn't miss a beat. "What would it take for you to date me?" I threw the question at her knowing full well I'd catch her off guard.

Her smile fell. "Cooper …"

I shot her The Smile. "Don't wimp out on me now, Williams."

But her face was tight, unamused. "All right. It would take a time machine, a peace treaty with my brother, and proof that you were serious about something. Anything. Truth or dare?" she shot, closing the conversation.

I nodded and wet my lips, letting it go like I knew I should, even though I wouldn't forget it so easily. I turned and took the chicken off the grill. "Truth."

"What's your deepest, darkest secret?" The question was pointed, and I turned to look at her.

You. I raised an eyebrow. "Wow, this escalated quickly."

"You started it." She took a sip of her wine.

I pushed off from the counter, part of me not believing what I was about to do. But she'd asked, and I found that as nervous as it made me to answer, I wanted her to know. "Come here and I'll show you." I extended a hand.

Her eyes widened as she took it and slipped off the stool. "Why am I a little scared?"

I chuckled and dragged her through my apartment to the door of my nerd sanctuary. I leaned against the wall, feeling more than a little scared myself. But I wanted her to know everything about me. I wanted to share all of myself with her simply because it felt good to do it.

"Go ahead. Open it."

She clasped her hands in front of her, fingers threading together. She looked tentative, eyeing the door with uncertainty. "If there are whips and chains and butt plugs in there, I'm probably going to freak out."

I smiled. "Just open it, Mags."

She took a breath and turned the handle, gasping when she saw what was inside. "Oh, my God." She spun around, gaping. "Are you for real?"

I wasn't sure if her reaction was good or bad, but I stepped into the room and around her to explain. "I've been collecting ever since I was a kid, obsessively, really. I've just always loved comics and sci-fi, my dad too. You should see *his* collection."

"Holy shit," she breathed and wandered around the room, awestruck, stopping in front of my *The Empire Strikes Back* movie poster. "How do you have Stephen Spielberg's autograph?"

I relaxed, smiling at the wonder on her face. "My dad's firm manages his finances."

"This is amazing, Cooper." She moved to the shelves. "First

edition Harry Potter … are these signed too?"

"They are. They were the first novels I ever read."

She blinked. "I think I just had a bookgasm." She reached for one. "May I?"

I nodded, and she pulled out the first book reverently, opening it to the inscription.

"Wow," she breathed. "You are officially the most hardcore geek I've ever met."

I laughed, relieved, feeling the unfamiliar comfort of sharing myself with someone else. Someone I trusted. "Now you know my deepest, darkest secret."

She set the book back down and turned to me, her eyes soft. "No one knows?"

I shook my head.

"Not even West? How were you able to hide … *this*?" She motioned to the room.

"He knows a little. I've always collected comics, but he doesn't know how serious it is."

"Yeah, because this is pretty fucking serious, Coop." She smiled, wandering past me and over to the Batman costume.

My eyes were glued to the apron string that swayed back and forth as she walked. She turned to me, and my eyes snapped up to hers.

She shook her head, smiling. "Please tell me you're not *actually* Batman."

I walked up behind her and wrapped my arms around her waist. "No, I'm not actually Batman."

She leaned back into me. "Is it from a movie? You didn't have it made, did you?"

I paused. "Maybe."

"For Halloween?"

"ComicCon."

A laugh bubbled out of her. "Put it on."

"Can't. We need one more person to assist."

She laughed even harder. "I bet you look amazing in it."

"I do. Have I scared you off yet?"

She turned in my arms. "Um, no — one look at the Harry Potter books has me *seriously* hot and bothered."

"Just wait until I show you my Tolkien collection."

She smiled, lips parted as she angled her face to mine. There were maybe two millimeters of slinky fabric between us, and I could feel the warmth of her body just on the other side. When I brought my lips to hers, she wrapped herself around me and tightened her arms until I was as close as I could be.

My hands roamed down her back and to her bare ass. I squeezed, and she laid her hands on my chest, pushing gently, moving us back to the only piece of furniture in the room, my black leather recliner. The backs of my knees hit the seat, and I sat down, but she didn't follow right away, just stood in front of me, smiling. My hands were on her hips, fingers on bare skin.

She touched my face as my hand moved down her thighs and under the apron, trailed up the inside of her thigh and between her legs to cup her, squeeze her. My middle finger rested against the line of her, and I ran the pad down the length before slipping inside. She leaned into me, eyes closed, her face soft and relaxed as I stroked her.

Her arms rested on my shoulders, and she bent down to kiss me, a slow kiss, a heady kiss. She slipped a knee next to me, and I leaned back as she climbed onto my lap, reaching behind her to pull the apron string with a zip. I yanked it off and tossed it, her curly hair bouncing as it passed through the neck. Her hand skated down my stomach to the hem of my apron, her eyes down as she moved it out of her way and wrapped her fingers around my base, lifting me. She licked her lips as her hips rose, and I watched her lower her body onto me with a sigh. Our bodies met in a seam, no space between us, her hands on my chest, arms pushing her breasts together. The sight of her naked body straddling mine, her hair in her face, her hands on my chest as she rocked gently — I committed the moment to memory.

My hand found her breast, and I traced the curve and squeezed. The other hand rested on her hip, riding along as her body rolled in waves. Her fingers clenched against my chest, and her brows came together, the softness in her face shifting as she came closer. I knew her body so well that I could almost count down the seconds. A shallow breath she took — three — a small moan passed her lips — two — her nails dug into my skin — one. She came with a cry, grinding against me, pulsing around me.

After a moment, she slowed, lifting a hand to move her hair from her face, smiling at me lazily as she leaned back. She reached behind her, resting her hands on my thighs as she rolled her body, lifting her hips every time she rocked back. I watched our bodies meet and separate, my hands on her hips as I flexed into her, pulling her down faster with each motion until I couldn't hold on. Her name was on my lips, my heart stopping for a long moment when I came, my body thrumming inside of her.

When I finally opened my eyes, she was smiling at me, lip between her teeth as she shifted to lie on top of me. Her lips found mine, soft and sweet, and my fingers tangled in her hair, not wanting to separate.

But she broke away, smiling down at me as her hand found my jaw. "Do you bring all the girls in here to impress them with your collection?"

"No one else has been in here besides you and my maid," I answered quietly.

She watched me for a moment. "Why me?"

I smiled and touched her cheek. "Because we were playing a

game, and I trust you."

Some emotion passed across her face in a flash, too fast for me to catch it before she kissed me again. But the kiss was different, laced with longing, burning hot.

When she backed away, she seemed fine, just smiled at me once more and said, "I'm still hungry."

And I let it go, because that was what she wanted. "Well, put that apron back on and let's get you fed."

She climbed off of me and grabbed the apron from the ground. "I'll meet you in the kitchen."

"I'll be waiting."

She headed to my room, and I cleaned up in the hall bathroom with every thought on her. And then, I made my way back to the kitchen to finish dinner, feeling lost and found, together and broken, all at the same time.

I had the bread and bacon on the flat top and was busy slicing tomatoes, grateful for the mundane distraction, feeling a little more together by the time that Maggie returned looking fresh as a magnolia blossom. She snickered, her eyes on my ass.

"I kinda forgot you were wearing that."

I smiled as I set the bread on plates and smeared garlic aioli mayo on them, then laid the chicken breasts on the top.

She took a seat and sipped her wine. "Oooh, fancy sandwiches."

I topped them with tomatoes, spring mix, and bacon. "I can't help it. I'm just a fancy guy." I made my way over to the bar and set her plate in front of her. "*Bon appétite, Madame.*"

"*Merci beaucoup, monsieur.*"

I took a seat next to her, my ass sticking to the leather.

She picked up her sandwich and adjusted her grip. "So what are you up to tonight?" She took a bite.

"Actually, West and Patrick are coming over in about an hour."

Her eyes widened, and she froze mid-chew.

"You have an hour. Don't worry."

She made a face and started chewing again.

"I'll call Bobby to take you home.

"I don't need—"

I shook my head and picked up my own sandwich. "I'm not letting you walk through the park in the dark."

"I can take a cab."

"Maggie. Just let me call Bobby."

She sighed. "Fine. What are you guys doing tonight?"

"Playing video games. You?" I took a bite.

"Well, I don't have work tomorrow, so I'm not sure."

I wiped my lips with my napkin and laid it back in my lap. "What's left on your sightseeing list?"

"Chelsea Piers, Brooklyn Bridge, Coney Island, off the top of my head."

I smiled and shifted the sandwich. "Let's go to Coney Island tomorrow." I took another bite.

She raised an eyebrow. "Who invited you?"

I shrugged and swallowed. "You shouldn't go by yourself. Plus, when it gets dark, that place looks like where survivors of the zombie apocalypse go for group meetings."

She laughed.

"Seriously. I once saw a guy beating a bench with a cane, laughing like a maniac."

Her smile fell. "Maybe I don't want to go after all."

"It's fine during the day, and with muscle."

Maggie eyed me. "You're telling me that you and I going to Coney Island wouldn't be a date? How do you figure?"

"I won't buy you a single thing, not even a hot dog or a soda. I won't even try to win you a giant pink gorilla. I could, just to be clear. But I won't. I'll be good. But the second we're back here tomorrow night, I make no promises."

She laughed. "Sounds fun, but it's a bad idea." She seemed stalwart, but I pressed her anyway. I wanted to spend the day with her. I wanted to know if it would be everything I thought it would be.

"Give me one good reason why we can't go to Coney Island."

"Because …" Her face scrunched up. "Well, I don't know. It just feels like a date."

"I already covered that one. What else?" I took another bite, playing it off, watching her.

She was still trying to think of something, and I knew I had her. I went in for the kill.

I swallowed and set down my sandwich. "You want to go to Coney Island. We're both free tomorrow. There will be no making of moves, buying of cotton candy, or any otherwise sinister, predatory shenanigans. Come on, Mags."

Boom.

She rolled her eyes with a sigh. "All right. It's not a date, though."

A smile stretched across my lips. "Of course it's not."

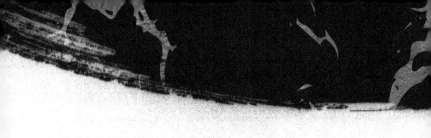

Sore Loser

MAGGIE

Half an hour later, I skipped out of Cooper's apartment feeling high. Constant surprises, that's what being with him boiled down to. Just when I thought I had him pegged, he'd hit me with something that would send the dial spinning again. But as Bobby drove me home, I came down, and the second guessing began. I'd agreed to another not-date, this time at an amusement park.

I had almost zero willpower when it came to Cooper.

Coney Island on a spring afternoon with Cooper Moore. I sighed, feeling like an indecisive fool, needing to talk to somebody, but Lily was at the theater. I couldn't call Brooke — it was too late on a Thursday when I know she had to wake up early. That only left Rose. I'd just have to play it off, be as vague as possible. No details, no names. Relief settled in at the thought of talking through it. She'd help me decide.

Bobby dropped me off around the corner from Habits, and I thanked him before climbing out, feeling like I should have tipped him or something, even though I knew he'd never take it. A driver. So freaking weird.

The night was cool and a little breezy as I walked the stretch to Habits and pulled open the door. Rose's face swung toward the door, and she smiled when she saw me. Her black hair was in a high ponytail, her long neck exposed, cleavage bangin' without looking overdone or showy.

I waved and headed down to the end.

She tossed a coaster on the bar, looking glad to see me. The feeling was mutual. "I didn't expect to see you tonight, Mags. What are you up to?"

I took a seat and pulled my bag off, hanging it on a hook under the bar. "Not much. I was out, but … I don't know. I wasn't quite ready to go home to an empty apartment."

She smiled. "I know the feeling. Maker's and ginger?"

"That sounds like heaven. Thanks, Rose."

"No prob." She grabbed a glass and tossed in a scoop of ice. "How was your day?"

"Weird. Today at work, I met Cooper's mom."

Rose looked like something had exploded in her brain. "Oh, my God. *That's* the charity she works for? You even told me the name and everything. I can't believe I didn't put that together."

"It's fine. I mean, how often do you talk about Cooper's mom?"

She chuckled and poured whiskey into the glass. "True."

"So that was weird. And then I went over to Mr. M's. We got into a little … kerfuffle."

Rose smirked and grabbed the soda gun to top my drink off. "Is that a euphemism?"

I laughed. "No, although I got some of that too."

"At least one of us got laid." She handed the glass over.

"How long's it been?"

Rose sighed. "Too long."

"Have you thought about dating?"

She leaned on the bar. "Of course. Just haven't met anyone worth the risk."

I nodded and took a sip, knowing exactly what she meant. "What about a dating site?"

"I'm not that desperate yet." She leaned on the bar. "So what was the kerfuffle about?"

"Oh, it was silly — a misunderstanding. I'm just paranoid, I think. I'm afraid to trust him, you know? I don't want to trust anyone."

"I get that. I'm glad you guys worked it out, though. How long before his time is up?"

"A week and a couple of days. He wants to go with me to Coney Island tomorrow."

She raised an eyebrow. "Sounds like a date."

"That's what I said. I just don't know if it's a good idea. But he swore it was friends only, nothing datey like holding hands or kissing."

"Are you going to go?"

"I told him I would, but now I'm not so sure." I looked into her eyes and begged her to just decide for me.

She nodded thoughtfully. "Coney Island is on your list, right?"

"Yeah. I just … I don't know. I'm only supposed to be banging him, you know?"

"Right. What about upgrading from fuck buddy to friends with benefits?"

I considered it. "I mean, we *are* friends at this point."

"And theoretically, you're going to cut this all off in a week or so anyway, right?"

"Right."

She shrugged. "I don't see a problem here. Go on the not-date and have a good time. Then let him rock your junk out and feed you again. That sounds like a cycle I can get behind."

I laughed, feeling better. "Can I just have you make all of my decisions for me?"

A laugh burst out of her. "I don't know how well that would work out for you, but as long as you don't get pissed at me when your life blows up like mine, then sure."

"Thanks, Rose. I'm having a hell of a time with this, which sucks considering it was supposed to be easy."

"You've been through a lot over the last few months, including a move to Manhattan. Don't beat yourself up too much."

I took a drink and did just that — cut myself some slack. She was right. I wanted to go to Coney Island, and I'd have fun with Cooper like I always did. I could handle it. Friends with benefits. Easy.

COOPER

A *couple of hours later, I* was sitting in my media room with the lights out, flanked by Patrick and West as Scorpion and SubZero beat the shit out of each other in Mortal Kombat style digital surround sound. We each had our own leather recliner with built in speakers, and the ninety-inch TV was close enough to us that it took up our entire field of vision.

The sound boomed as West's player, Scorpion, yelled, "*Come here!*" then a splat as he stabbed SubZero in the face with his grappling hook and pulled, ripping his head off. We all groaned, laughing as blood splattered everywhere and the announcer said, "*Scorpion wins!*"

West crowed. "Bring it on, Coop."

I grabbed the controller from Patrick and shook my head. "You may beat me on the basketball court, but this is my turf."

I joined in as Raiden and squared off against Scorpion. The round started, and we went nuts on each other. I dodged as he tried to spear me, shooting him with lightning before I flipped over him and kicked him the back.

The click of the buttons punctuated hisses and swear words from West as we fought, but I just smiled, taking it easy on him to make him feel like he had a shot.

"177 IQ and you play Mortal Kombat like that?" West snickered.

I zapped him with electricity and made him explode.

"Dammit, Cooper!"

"Fatality," I crowed along with the announcer.

West eyeballed me.

I shook my head, laughing. "You're such a sore loser, dude."

Patrick snorted.

"I am not. Fuck you guys."

We laughed even harder.

"Y'all suck," he tossed the controller at Patrick, who barely caught it.

He sat back in the seat, smirking. "You're so mad. Like Blaingry-mad or don't-touch-my-sister mad."

"Well," West huffed, "Blaine was a punk-ass fuck who hurt Lily, and if either of you touch my sister, I will beat your ass."

Patrick laughed and held up his hands. "Yeah, yeah."

I tried to play it cool, smiling crooked. "You know, some day she'll meet a guy she really cares about, and you'll have to find a way to accept it."

"I can accept whomever she chooses, as long as it's not one of you two."

Patrick raised a dark brow. "That's not what you said earlier about that guy Maggie works with."

Outwardly, I was still smiling. Inwardly, I was nuclear. "What's the story there?"

West scowled from behind his dark beard. "Apparently the chef at the shelter won't stop asking her out."

"She told you that?" I asked, disbelieving that she'd offer up any information about a guy who was hitting on her to her brother.

"Sorta. She told Lily."

Patrick chuckled. "You should have heard him asking Lily questions about the guy like he was a criminal. He works at a homeless shelter for chrissake."

I made a mental note to ask my mom about him, and Maggie too. For the sake of the rules, of course. "So did she agree?"

"No. She keeps shooting him down."

Relief slipped over me, and I took the opening to press my point. "So you don't want Maggie to date someone you don't know, but you don't want her to date someone you *do* know, either? Who exactly fits into that criteria?"

West's brow was low, his face pinched as he tried to explain himself. "Who would meet my expectations? It's not all that complicated. A man who's got his shit together. Someone who will love her and treat her like the goddamn queen she is. Jimmy squandered the gift he'd been given, and she's not over it. I don't care how much she pretends like she's fine and dandy. She's hurting and alone, and I won't see her go through that again, so until she meets a man who will protect her and care for her, who won't drag her down with him, I'll keep being a picky, overbearing son of a bitch." His jaw was set, eyes hard as he stood. "I need a drink. Y'all want one?"

We nodded and muttered our agreement, subdued, and West blew out of the room.

The second he was gone, Patrick spun his chair around to face me. "Do you have a thing for Maggie?"

My face froze, along with my heart and my breath. "I don't know what you're talking about."

But his eyes were wide. He leaned back in the chair and ran a hand over his mouth. "You're *seeing* her." His eyes bugged even more.

"Wait. You're *educating* her. Jesus fucking Christ, Coop."

"Seriously, where is this coming from?" I feigned confusion, apparently poorly.

"I'm not gonna tell West," he said, and I believed him. "It's so obvious, I can't believe I didn't see it before."

I glared at him. "There's nothing going on." It was worth a final shot.

He gave me a flat look. "Just fess up. How long has it been going on?"

I rubbed my face and sighed, knowing I couldn't avoid the conversation. "A long time, and not long enough."

He frowned. "What are you going to do? Is it serious?"

"I don't know, Tricky. I really don't. She gave me all these rules, put a time limit on me. It's supposed to be over soon, and even though I don't know if I want it to end, I may not be able to convince her to agree to more than this, whatever this is. And even if we did want to, you heard what West said. He wants her to be with the exact opposite of me, on top of telling me for the fifty thousandth time to never even think about seeing her."

"That's what West wants, but what does Maggie want?"

I looked away. "I don't know that either. What she says and what she does tell me two different stories."

"You're the first guy she's been with since Jimmy, and that was just three months ago. It's risky, man. She's not ready. And you're serious about her." He scanned my face like he could read me, shaking his head. "Wow, Cooper."

"Wow, what?" West asked as he entered the room carrying scotch for all of us.

Patrick smiled and spun his chair to face the TV again. "Cooper was just telling me about this girl he's banging."

West raised a brow and handed me a drink. "The one you're educating?"

Patrick snickered, and I nodded as I took it, avoiding eye contact, contemplating the ways I'd murder Patrick Mortal Kombat-style.

"What the story there?" he asked and took his seat.

"Not sure. Taking it one day at a time." I took a drink and set my glass in the cup holder in the arm rest. "Come on, Trick. Time to die."

He smirked and picked up his controller, and I played the game without thinking, my mind on Maggie and the mess we were making. The mess I'd rather kick under the bed than clean up.

That night, after everyone had gone, I lay alone in the dark with the mess still on my mind, trying to untangle it knot by knot. For a moment, I wondered if it was worth it — the risk of West's friendship — and for what? I didn't even know if she really wanted me for more than just a distraction.

But I pictured her face, thought of her smile, of those moments when she looked at me and saw more than I meant to show her. She felt more than she let on.

I didn't want to let her go, not for the bro code. And I knew that West would find a way to forgive me, if I could convince him I wouldn't hurt her. That I wouldn't treat her like I had every other woman in my life. If I could convince him of that, everything would be fine.

The only other person who I needed to convince was Maggie.

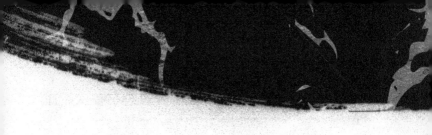

Not Date

COOPER

I **leaned against the Mercedes the** next morning, hands in my pockets, smiling like a fool as Maggie approached. Her blue V-neck made her eyes a shade brighter than usual, and I marveled at her for a moment — golden curls, rosy cheeks, pretty legs in denim shorts and white canvas sneakers that looked like they'd been loved. She was beautiful.

"Hey." The flush in her cheeks deepened.

I pushed off the car and opened the door for her. "Hey, Mags."

She slipped in and smiled up at me, and I climbed in behind her. "How'd it go last night?" she asked as Bobby took off.

"We played a lot of Mortal Kombat and drank scotch, so … perfect."

She chuckled and looked out the window. I wanted to reach for her, kiss her. Touch her. Anything. But, I'd promised not to like an idiot.

"What'd you end up doing last night?" I asked, trying to keep my mind off of the fact.

"Not much. Went to Habits to hang with Rosie for a bit and then headed home and crashed. I didn't even read, which is weird. I've just been so tired lately. It's hard going from doing nothing to having a ton to do."

"I can only imagine."

She rolled her eyes, amused.

"Tell me how you like work. I feel like we've barely talked about it."

"Truth or Dare didn't leave much time for idle chit chat." She smiled at me knowingly.

I smirked back. "Guess not."

She settled back into her seat. "Work is great, although now I have the added pressure of impressing your mother."

I laughed. "I really wouldn't worry about her too much."

"Easy for you to say."

I thought about the guy who had been hitting on her. In fact, I'd been thinking a lot about him ever since Patrick brought him up. I smiled, hoping I wasn't being too obvious. "Meet anyone else at the shelter?"

"Oh, sure, almost everyone. Why?"

I shrugged, realizing I had no idea how to handle jealousy. "No reason."

She narrowed her eyes, though she was clearly entertained. "What's your angle, Mr. Moore?"

"No angle."

"Liar. Are you asking about Brian?"

"Who's Brian?"

Maggie laughed at me. "Wow, Coop. Who told you about him?"

There was probably no way out unscathed, but I threw West under the bus anyway. "Your brother."

"Ugh. I knew Lily would end up telling him, but I didn't think he'd blab it to you."

"To be fair, Patrick brought it up."

"Dammit, he knows too?" She rolled her eyes. "I don't know how y'all ever keep secrets."

"It's not easy. So, what's the deal with him?"

"Nothin'. He asked me out, and I shot him down. Twice."

I smiled. "Good."

"Why, you jealous again? Like the harmless boy at Habits who was devastated that I wasn't thirsty?"

"Nah. Just, you know, *the rules*. If I'm not allowed to see anyone else, neither are you."

She shook her head. "Throwing the rules at me, just like that."

"Paybacks."

"Now I know how you feel."

I smiled, wondering just how true the statement was.

I'd woken up that morning feeling determined. There was something deeply satisfying about testing Maggie's boundaries. I'd persuaded her to come on a date with me under the guise that it wasn't really a date. I had to believe that she knew what I was doing, but she'd come with me anyway.

Every time I nudged her closer to the edge, she'd move with barely any resistance. And if I could keep nudging her, I could make her fall for me.

That is, if she hadn't already.

But I kept my promises. I'd keep my hands to myself and my money in my wallet for the day, if that was what it would take to prove it to her. It took every ounce of willpower I had not to kiss her in the Soopk-A-Rama that afternoon, but I just kept reminding myself that the anticipation of not touching her for an entire day would pay off when I took her home with me.

I was so right.

MAGGIE

he afternoon was gorgeous, clouds high in the sky, the ocean breeze crisp. We'd already ridden the big wooden roller coaster and went through the Spook-A-Rama, which was so over-the-top campy, with giant animatronic rats eating plastic

STACI HART

entrails, or the robot serial killer in the electric chair. He'd kept his promise — he hadn't offered to buy me a single thing or even tried to so much as hold my hand. I'll admit I was a little disappointed that he didn't try to kiss me in the spook house, but I'd never admit it to him.

We found ourselves walking up the boardwalk, eating our Nathan's Famous chili cheese dogs.

"Mmm," I hummed as I took another bite. The wind blew my hair across the chili and stuck in the cheese, and I groaned, glancing at my full hands.

Cooper chuckled, setting down his dog in the paper tray before he reached for my hair and wiped it off, his fingers barely grazing my cheek. He winked at me.

I shook my head, smiling.

"So," he said, "what do you think so far?"

I looked around at all the people, the long, wide boardwalk, the big Ferris wheel as it spun around. "I like it," I answered definitively.

"You should see it for the Mermaid Parade." He smiled and looked down the boardwalk like he was imagining it. "It's insane — people everywhere, a complete madhouse — but it's a riot. Everyone drinks all day and dresses up like sailors, mermaids, fish. I once saw a guy dressed as a sea cucumber."

"Oh?"

"He was basically naked and painted green, head to toe."

A laugh burst out of me.

He smirked. "The parade itself is great, and they have an art festival, shows, big fireworks. Definitely worth seeing at least once."

I imagined the park packed with mermaids and smiled. "Sounds like it. What's next?" I took another bite, being sure to turn my face to the wind.

"The Wonder Wheel. Not gonna lie, it's a little terrifying."

I swallowed and shook my head. "It's a Ferris wheel, you wuss."

He jerked a chin at it with an eyebrow up. "Look at it."

I took a good look, watching one of the cars near the top as the wheel spun. It was on a track, and when it hit the tipping point, it careened toward the edge and rocked out past the end just shy of horizontal.

"Oh."

Cooper smiled. "Don't worry. It's safe. And anyway, there are stationary cars, if you're scared."

I made a face at him. "I'm not scared. Death cars it is."

We finished our dogs and bought our tickets — Dutch, per the rules — and made our way to the line, under a creepy-ass sign with a clown on it that said THIS WAY. There was almost no line, and before long we were climbing into a red swinging car with bright yellow doors. I might have been second guessing things as I took a seat in the front bench — there were two rows that faced out, and I assumed he would sit in the back. But of course he slid in next to me, because Cooper Moore. I raised a brow, and he shot that crooked smile at me.

"What? This is the good seat. How else am I going to watch us plummet to our deaths?"

"Funny." I elbowed him, which took almost no effort, since we were sitting arm to arm. The attendant closed the door, and within a few seconds, we were moving.

Once we were out of the dock and the wind was against our faces, I sighed, feeling lighter as I looked out across the island and into Brooklyn, then to Manhattan off in the distance. It was peaceful, quiet. We were all of a sudden very alone. I resisted the urge to lean into him, threading my fingers in my lap instead to keep my attention anywhere but on him. It was pretty much pointless.

The day with Cooper had been easy and fun, just like being with him always was. He was like a kid sometimes, so excited to show you things you hadn't seen before. He'd watch you experience the thing for the first time, full of satisfaction. Pride, almost. Like it was a way for him to connect.

It was infectious. It made me *want* to experience it just for him. It made me feel carefree and lovely and alive.

Nine days left.

Nine days, and we would just be friends. I told myself I could be just-friends with Cooper. I mean, we were already close, and I definitely didn't want to lose that. So I was attracted to him. After a little space, it wouldn't be a big deal. I was certain that would fizzle away after a little time and distance.

Surely we'd both be able to walk away from that part of the relationship. No one had to get hurt. Then, maybe I could date someone else. He would too, probably the night that we ended things. The thought of him with another woman made me squirmy, but I took a breath and talked myself down. We didn't belong to each other. We were just having fun. That was it. And we'd walk away and be buddies after all this. Hooking up wasn't necessary. I pictured us hanging out just like this. Just as friends.

I smiled at the simplicity of it. We were adults. We could totally do this.

The car above us slid down the track to the squeals of the girls inside, swinging violently when it hit the end.

My heart beat a little faster, realizing we were next. "So, how old is this thing?"

He was trying not to laugh, that ass. "Almost a hundred."

I felt the car shift as we climbed higher, the tilt of the track lowering until gravity took hold and the car took off. My stomach flipped, and I grabbed his hand, screaming as we raced down the track and swung out when we hit the curve.

We laughed breathlessly. "Holy shit!" I yelled.

Cooper smiled bright. "Told you."

I didn't let go of his hand, you know, because of the height, and I settled back into the seat as he squeezed my fingers.

"It's so pretty up here," I said, looking out as the wind rushed through the grated cage, blowing my hair across my face as we climbed higher.

"It is." There was a strange quality to his voice, and I turned to find him watching me.

I was hypnotized, looking into his eyes like I could see all of him, if I looked deep enough. We were near the top, the city stretched out in one direction, the ocean in the other. And when we reached the pinnacle, he slipped a hand in my hair and kissed me. I couldn't even be mad. Couldn't defend the rules or put up a fight. In fact, I couldn't say a word. Because in that moment, his lips were all I'd ever wanted.

The Rules

COOPER

I *watched the city out the* window of the car the next night with a smile on my face. The day before was what I'd thought it would be — everything. I pictured her face on the carousel when she'd turned to me laughing, and we rose and fell as the world whirled around us. Thought about the kiss on the Wonder Wheel. Taking her home last night. All of it.

It was almost too much.

I didn't know what my next move was. All I knew was that I wanted more. I just had to show her that she felt the same, and I only had a week left to do it.

Bobby pulled up in front of the restaurant, and I thanked him as I climbed out and made my way inside. The hostess didn't need to ask my name, just smiled and asked me to follow her, which I did, through the restaurant. I spotted my parents across the room. My mother leaned into my father, her hand on his forearm that rested on the table, the two of them smiling at each other as they talked.

I couldn't help but smile myself. They stood when they saw me approach, and I reached for my mom first, pulling her into a hug.

"Hi, Coop." She pressed her cheek to mine, and when I pulled away, Dad extended a hand.

I clasped it. "Hey, Dad."

"Good to see you, kid. What's new?" he asked, adjusting his suit coat as we took our seats. He smiled at me as he leaned back in his chair, picking up his scotch.

"Not much." I reached for a glass of water on the table and took a sip.

Dad smirked. "Jillian from *W* said your shoot went really well."

"Of course she did." I chuckled. The waitress approached and asked me what I'd like to drink. "I'll have what he's having." She nodded and disappeared.

He shook his head, amused. "I can't believe you didn't tell me."

I snickered. "Yeah, I'm sure it's a real shock that I didn't tell anyone."

"I don't know if I'm supposed to tell you, but Jillian's considering putting you on the cover."

I thought about West seeing it at the grocery store and sighed.

Mom laughed at me and propped her elbow on the table. "Why in the world did you agree to it if you didn't want anyone to know?"

"How does one turn down an offer of that sort? I was surprised and flattered. Just didn't think it all the way through, I guess. Apparently their definition of 'eligible' has little to do with actual drive and motivation."

"Oh, I don't know, Coop," Dad said. "You're driven and motivated when you have purpose. Like sailing, or chess, or building Lego models when you were a kid. Purpose, driven by something that fulfills you. That's really what it boils down to."

"Is it that simple?" I asked genuinely.

Mom shrugged and picked up her glass of wine. "It's that simple and that impossible." She took a sip.

I shook my head, feeling out of place. It was a more and more common feeling these days. "I don't know why you let me do this."

Mom's brow quirked. "Do what?"

"Nothing. Do nothing, all day."

Dad shifted and hung his arm on the back of Mom's chair. "Because you're smart. You have respect for others, and you want more from life than what you're living. So we're giving you room to grow."

She patted his hand that rested on the table, smiling at me. "Don't get your father wrong. We want you to figure out what you're going to do with your life. But we've seen our friends try to browbeat their kids into submission. It doesn't work, and they all end up hating each other in the end. We can't force your hand, not when you can't even see your own cards."

Dad nodded. "Honestly, we don't care what you end up doing, Coop. You could make pottery or give surf lessons in Cancun to spring breakers, if that's what you really want."

I laughed, and Mom smiled at me. "We were pretty sure that might be a legitimate career path for you, at one point."

He was smirking again, his long face amiable. "The point is that as long as you're happy, we're happy. I'd love nothing more than for you to come and work with me. You've got the brains for it, and you'd be good at it — when you interned at Moore & Co in college, we all saw it. You enjoyed it, even though I knew then that you weren't ready to commit. My father built something powerful, and he passed that on to me. I want to pass it on to you, but I'm not going to force feed you. You'll figure it out. Just see if you can do it before you're forty, all right?"

I chuckled, feeling relieved and more pressured somehow all at once. "I'll see what I can do."

The waitress brought my drink, and we ordered dinner. Mom leaned on the table as the waitress left. "Oh, I meant to tell you — Maggie Williams is running our reading program at the shelter."

My heart jolted at the mention of her name, and I smiled. "I heard."

"She's fantastic, Cooper. Her program is going to help engage the kids, show them how much joy reading can bring them. She's only been with us for a few days, and Susan has just been raving about her. We've wanted someone for this spot for a long time, and now that we have her, I don't know how we ever survived without her."

I knew the feeling.

"I'm campaigning for Susan to offer her a permanent paid position. And, God, if she's not the most adorable little thing. All that hair, and that smile. I think she had the entire male residency trying to make sure she was comfortable, even Brian, our chef. That boy is usually unflappable, but she had him swooning."

I took a long sip of my drink, feeling twitchy. "What's his story?"

Her eyes narrowed, though her smile was still in place. "Why do you ask?"

Dad was eyeballing me too.

I wondered if I'd completely lost my touch or if it was only in matters related to Maggie in which I couldn't keep my shit together. "No reason. I heard he'd been hitting on her is all." I didn't sound nearly as casual as I'd wanted.

"Are you seeing her?" he asked curiously.

I huffed and made a face, scrambling for an answer.

"You are," Mom said simply.

"Or he wants to," Dad added.

My ears were hot. "Why are we talking about Maggie and me?"

"Oh, he *really* wants to." She nudged him.

"What's the story, Coop?"

I ran a hand over my mouth and picked up my drink. "I'm seeing her, and it's complicated."

"Because of West?" he asked.

"And because of Maggie. She's been through a lot. The wedding was only a few months ago, and I think she's just skittish. She says not ready for anything serious."

Dad's eyebrow rose. "And you are?"

I took a sip, following the burn as it dove through my chest. "I don't know."

"What do you know?" Mom asked.

I was overcome with honesty, sitting across from my parents, whom I trusted more than anyone. And so I answered the question I'd been avoiding at all costs. "All I know is that I can't stop thinking about her or wanting to be with her. She makes me laugh, makes me happy. But she said the other day that I couldn't be serious about anything, and I think that she believes that if I'm not serious, *we* can't be serious. Maybe she's right."

Dad shook his head. "Purpose, Cooper. When you find purpose, it changes everything."

"I've never felt this way, Dad. I have no idea what I'm doing or what to do next."

He smiled. "None of us ever do. Here's the secret to life: figure out what you want and then go get it. Everything falls in line with that."

"You make it sound so simple."

Mom smiled. "That simple, and that impossible."

Servers appeared with our food, and the conversation veered to topics less invasive. My mind was on Maggie.

Purpose. A reason. A spark to light up my gray life, make me want more.

Was it her?

I wanted to show her everything, give her everything. I wanted to prove to her that what I said was true. I wanted her to believe me, believe in me. I needed her to.

When I thought back over the past few weeks, I realized that she wasn't a spark. She was a wildfire.

I excused myself, my chest burning as I made my way to the restroom. I leaned over the sink and splashed cold water on my face, closed my eyes with my palms on the granite, listening to the slow drop of water from my nose as it hit the porcelain sink.

I wanted her. She needed to know that I was serious. So I needed to show her.

When I looked back up at my reflection, there were no more questions. There was no more indecision. I knew exactly what to do.

Maggie had better watch out. Because I was coming for her.

MAGGIE

My face was half-smushed into a pillow as I tried to catch my breath that night. Cooper kissed a trail down my back, and I blinked slow, smiling.

"I dunno how you do that to me," I said mostly into the pillow.

"Hmm?"

I shifted, and he moved so I could roll over — when I saw his smile, I couldn't stop my own. "Nothin.'"

He climbed up my body and lay on top of me. "Have any plans this weekend?" He brushed my crazy hair out of my face.

"No, why?"

"Come sailing with me."

I blinked, not knowing what to say. "What will I tell West?"

"The truth. Tell him you have a date."

I gave him a flat look. "Cooper."

He gave me one right back. "Maggie."

"Doesn't that break the rules?"

He shrugged and traced my bottom lip with his index finger.

"You said you wanted to see New York. Well, I can show you New York in a way you can't see anywhere else. We can sail up the coast to the Hamptons, spend the night, and sail back on Sunday."

Butterflies flitted around in my stomach, those traitorous bastards. "Sounds like something couples would do."

"Listen, we only have one week left. Can we just say fuck the rules for thirty-six hours?" He kissed the bottom lip his finger had just been on. "Plus, just think of all the rope I have on that boat. And I know *a lot* of knots."

I laughed. "God, Cooper."

He smiled back at me, contented. "Call it whatever you want. I just thought you might like to sail. Would it make you feel better if I promise to keep conversation and clothing to a minimum?"

"Maybe a little."

"Consider it done." His smile softened, and his eyes locked on mine, voice a little lower as he cupped my cheek. "Say yes."

My resolve was about as sturdy as a bridge made out of Pixy Stix. The rules. Fucking rules. Could I agree to thirty-six hours, rule-free? That wasn't even two full days, and he was right. It was almost over, and what better way to spend our last weekend but together?

I didn't know how I could refuse with him looking at me like that, with his fingers against my skin and my pulse fluttering. It was a terrible idea. The worst. *I should definitely say no.*

"All right."

God damn that smile of his. "Meet me at the dock at nine. Pack a swimsuit and a dress for dinner."

"And purple panties?"

"Underwear is entirely up to you."

I laughed.

"Stay the night, Maggie."

His voice commanded me — his eyes held me still. My smile

slipped as I looked up at him, hypnotized out of nowhere. I wanted to say yes, so badly. But I'd already given too much.

I blinked and took a breath, dragging my smile back out. "The rules are in place as long as we're on Manhattan soil. Plus, I've got to get my rest for our big weekend. I should pack now if I've got to meet you all the way on the south side by nine."

He sighed. "I'll let you have that, but only because I get you all to myself for the weekend." His lips met mine in a smoldering kiss.

I could barely open my eyes when he broke away, and I thought real hard about staying. Real, real hard. When I finally peeled my eyelids open, I smiled up at him. "It's late. I should get going."

He brushed his lips against mine once more. "All right."

Cooper rolled off of me, and I grabbed my clothes, heading to the bathroom to get cleaned up and dressed before I changed my mind.

When I came out, he was waiting for me with a smile, took my hand as we walked to his door.

"Bobby's downstairs waiting for you."

"Thank you."

He raised an eyebrow. "You're not going to fight me on it?"

"Would it do any good?"

"No."

I smiled. "Exactly."

He smiled back. "Want me to send him to get you in the morning?"

"Nah, I'll take the subway."

"I'll text you the address." His hand slipped into the crook of my neck, and he kissed me once more, reverently. "I'll see you tomorrow, Mags."

"'Night, Cooper."

I stepped into the elevator feeling giddy as I leaned against the rail, my eyes still on him until he disappeared behind the elevator doors.

My mind skipped around, daydreaming about sailing to the beach house. But every second brought with it a little bit of doubt and confusion.

The getaway was a date. A weekend long romantic *sailing to the Hamptons* date where I'd be alone with Cooper for thirty-six hours. Nowhere to run. No getting away from him. The thought excited me just as much as it freaked me out. Which was to say, a lot.

I looked back over the last week, not sure how I'd gotten to the point where the rules had been called off, even just temporarily. Reading in the park had been a bad idea. Truth or Dare had been even worse. Coney Island just proved that I was a raging dumbass for convincing myself we were only banging. And now, a weekend getaway.

It was impossible to pretend that whatever was happening between us was nothing. It was all too clear that we were more than nothing.

I was in much deeper than I thought.

The elevator doors opened, and I nodded at the doorman as I headed to the back entrance. Bobby was waiting for me and opened the car door for me to climb in.

"Thank you, Bobby."

"No problem, Maggie."

He closed my door and walked around the car to climb into the driver's seat. My thoughts didn't stop spinning as we made our way up 5th and to the traverse through the park.

I watched the trees out of the window, trying to think my way out of it. I could still back out. Just text him and tell him no. He might be hurt, but what would I risk if I went with him?

Maybe he wouldn't care at all. Maybe it was just a game to him, and he just liked to push my buttons, get his way.

But I knew as soon as I thought it that it was a lie. And that thought scared me worse than anything.

Bobby stopped a block away from the apartment, and I thanked him before slipping out and walking home. I trudged up the stairs and unlocked the door to find Lily and Rose at the kitchen table.

"Hey." I tried to smile and apparently wasn't very convincing. "What are you doing here, Lily?"

Her brow dropped, worried. "I just got home from the theater, was about to head over to West's. You okay?"

I made a face and took a seat, my eyes darting to Rose. "Mr. M is getting serious."

Lily sighed. "Shit."

Rose's brow quirked. "That's a bad thing?"

I leaned on the table, trying to be vague. "It just complicates a situation that's already sticky."

Rose shrugged. "What's so sticky about it? Do you like him?"

"I'm not ready to like anyone."

"You seem like you're fine," she said.

"I feel like I'm fine, but I don't trust myself."

"Then just use him until the time's up and walk away."

I shook my head, frustrated. "There is no walking away, Rose."

"What do you mean?"

Lily watched me with her arms folded across her chest, and Rose's eyes bounced between us.

"What's the story?" Rose asked, edging on impatient.

Lily sighed again. "Just tell her, Maggie."

I chewed on my lip.

"Tell me what? What the hell is going on?"

I took a deep breath. "Mr. M is …"

Rose leaned forward. I couldn't even say it.

Lily blurted, "Cooper. She's banging *Cooper*."

Rose's eyes bugged, her mouth hanging open. "No fucking way."

I nodded, feeling guilty. "Since my wedding night."

"Jesus fucking Christ, Maggie." Rose blinked.

Lily shook her head. "You've got to figure out a better way to break that to people, Mags. No one is ever prepared for Cooper wedding night fuckery."

I dropped my face into my palms. "I know. Please, don't judge me."

Rose put up a hand in surrender. "I'm not one to judge people for who they sleep with or when. I'm just shocked. What about Astrid?"

Lily answered for me. "It's a sham, Cooper and Astrid."

Rose ran her fingers through her bangs. "What the fuck."

"What happened?" Lily asked me.

"He wants to take me sailing this weekend, to the Hamptons."

Lily sighed again and fiddled with the placemat in front of her. "Oh, man. That's a dream date, Maggie."

"I don't know. I mean he's pushed past every boundary I've defined."

"Sounds like Cooper, all right," Rose said.

"What am I supposed to do?"

"Do you want to go?" she asked, brows up.

"Of course I want to go. But it's a horrible idea."

"Why?" she asked simply.

"Because I don't want to *date* Cooper. I don't want to have feelings for him."

"I feel like it may be too late for that."

"I feel like maybe you're right." I felt panicky. "I should end it. I should end it now before it goes any further." The thought of cutting it off made me feel sick. "It's gone on long enough. One more week isn't going to help anyone at this point."

"Is that really what you want?" Rose asked.

I couldn't stop shaking my head. "I don't know what I want. The timing is so bad."

"Is it though?"

I paused. "The wedding was only three months ago."

"But what does that have to do with anything?" Rose said it like all the answers were a straight line, simple and easy.

I stammered. "I ... well, I don't know. I don't feel like it's responsible to jump into something yet, especially not with *Cooper*. This was supposed to just be for fun, no feelings. I thought it would be easy to keep it casual with him while I figure myself out. But the problem is that I haven't figured *anything* out. I feel like I'm split in two. Before New York and After New York. Maggie with Jimmy and Maggie without Jimmy. Like the old me is a mirage. I don't even know her anymore, but I don't know the new me either." My nose burned, and I sniffed to stave off the tears. "I'm a mess, see? A tangled-up mess. I cannot get involved with Cooper any deeper than I already am."

Rose looked straight through me. "But what if he's good for you?"

I looked at her like she'd sprouted an extra head.

"Hear me out." She leaned forward. "Cooper wouldn't be asking you on a weekend trip if he was only interested in a booty call. It's too intimate. And if Cooper cares about you like that, then this is huge for him. What if he could be what you needed? What if he could give you all the things Jimmy couldn't?"

"Maybe I could consider it if we were a year from now. It's too soon."

"Well, we're not a year from now. We're exactly where we are. Look, if you're really not ready, then you're not ready. But you want to be with him, and he makes you feel good, right?"

"Yes," I answered quietly.

"Then I think the answer is much easier than you want to believe." She sat back in her chair and brought her knee up. "I say go. Go and pretend like nothing before this weekend ever happened. Pretend just for the course of the trip, and if there's something more to it, then you'll know. If there's not, then walk away." She sighed. "There's no set mourning period when you break up with someone. It takes however long it takes. Maybe moving here just sped up the process, and you're more okay than you realize. Maybe you never really loved Jimmy at all. Maybe old Maggie and new Maggie are the same person. Maybe if you walk away from Cooper now, you miss an opportunity that you won't have again."

My eyes rested on a spot on the table. "Is it wrong to put Cooper through this if I end up walking away?"

"Do you think he'd miss the chance to find out?"

I thought about it for a moment before answering honestly. "No."

She hung her arm on her knee, looking satisfied. "Then there it is. Just go. See what happens."

I turned to Lily. "Do you think it's possible that I'm whole enough to get into something so soon? What if I'm just rebounding?"

"I think you won't know until you try. I also think if Cooper really cares about you, he'll understand if you're not ready."

I didn't respond, just considered it all. On paper, it looked ridiculous, me and Cooper. But in my heart, I knew it wasn't as crazy as it seemed. "I've been talking myself out of Cooper for weeks, and now I'm trying to talk myself *into* him."

Rose smirked. "I don't think you need all that much convincing."

I took a deep breath. "Go and pretend like nothing else happened. Just forget about everything else for thirty-six hours." I shook my head. "I've been living in denial for long enough that I'm pretty sure ignoring my problems for a couple more days will be a piece of cake."

Lily laughed.

"Leave the decisions for when you get back. Lily and I will be here on Sunday if you need to trip out. We're excellent ledge talkers."

"We'll have bourbon, too," Lily added.

I chuckled, feeling nervous and excited. "All right. I'm gonna do it."

"Yeah, you are." Rose said with a nod and a smile.

"I should pack and try to sleep."

Lily sighed. "I'm so jealous you're going sailing. It's going to be amazing, Maggie."

I smiled, my heart fluttering in my rib cage. "I hope so."

Fly

MAGGIE

The morning was bright and golden, and my heart was full of promise and nerves as I walked down the dock with my duffle bag on my shoulder.

Fourth dock down, second slip on the left, the gate attendant had told me, and I counted them. I spotted *Midnight Caller* as she bobbed in the water, and a small but very loud part of my brain made its final plea to talk me out of the whole thing. I could walk away. It was the last chance.

But I took a breath and kept going, ready to leave life behind for a moment. Ready for what the weekend held in store.

The ship was a deep navy, the wooden deck stretching around the cabin to the bow. My eyes followed the ropes up the mast, and butterflies took off in my stomach, imagining what it would look like when the sails were raised. I stopped when I reached the boat, scanning the deck for Cooper. I found him kneeling in the cockpit — white shorts and deck shoes, navy sweater with white stripes, sleeves pushed up his forearms. My eyes lingered on his hands as he ran a rope through his fingers, that that little voice that had been so loud a moment before shut up mid-sentence.

I shifted and hung a hand on my hip, smiling. "Well, hello there, sailor."

He looked up, and that crooked smile of his lit up his face as he stood and extended a hand. I took it to steady myself as I stepped into the boat, and he pulled me into him the second my feet hit the deck.

"Morning," he said, his lips inches from mine.

"Morning," I breathed.

"Are you ready for this?"

Anxiety blew through my chest, flipping my heart around. "I think so."

He gave me a kiss and took my bag. "Then let me show you around so we can get going."

My cheeks flushed, and I looked over the deck again. "This is so amazing, Cooper."

"Glad you approve." He took my hand, and we stepped into the space where the wheel and benches were. "This is the cockpit, where we'll be most of the day. Come on down and I'll show you the cabin."

We climbed below deck, and I glanced around, taking everything in. The space was all dark wood, granite counters, dark leather seats. Art hung on the walls, and the table was littered with sea charts and compasses. It looked comfortable, livable, *rich.*

Cooper waved a hand across the room, smiling. "Welcome aboard."

I shook my head, amazed. "I don't know what I expected, but it wasn't *this.* You could actually live on this boat."

He smiled and walked through the main room. "So this is the galley," he said as he gestured to the fancy, stainless steel kitchen, "and back here are the extra bedrooms." I followed him down a narrow hallway, and he opened another door. "Here's the head, and back here is the master bedroom."

The room was almost entirely bed, but there were nightstands and lamps, a small walk-in closet, and a standing shower with sleek tile and a glass door. He set my bag down on the bed.

"Are we sleeping here tonight?" I asked hopefully.

"No, we'll stay at the Hampton house tonight."

My face fell, and he chuckled.

"Don't worry. You'll be much more comfortable there."

I was still looking around in awe. "How do you not just sail away in this?"

"Well, I can't sail her overnight without at least one other person. You can't go on autopilot for any long period of time, definitely not long enough to sleep."

My eyes widened a little. "Am I going to be enough help for you? I've never sailed before."

He grabbed my hand, and I followed him out. "You'll be plenty of help, if you're interested. And if not, I can sail her by myself." He smiled at me over his shoulder.

"How often do you take her out?" I asked as we entered the main room again.

He stopped next to the table and laid his hands on the surface. "A lot more in the summer when everyone is free. I have crew on staff too, for when I want to go on longer trips." I followed the line of his body — his strong shoulders, the curves of the muscles in his arms and forearms. A book was open in front of him, a map with complex sets of lines, numbers, and markings that I didn't understand. "These are sea charts, like a key map for the ocean."

I took a seat and pored over them. "They're really beautiful. But I have no idea what any of this means. What's this big compass?"

"That's the magnetic field for the area."

"Why on earth would you need to know the magnetic fields?"

"Because the compass doesn't always point true north. These charts help you navigate the local waters if you're using a magnetic compass."

I folded my arms on the table. "How do you know where you're supposed to be?"

He dragged his finger along the map, stopping at points. "These numbers mark the water depth, and these lines mark the channels. Getting out of the harbor is the hardest part — a lot of traffic and rules to keep everything in order. But once we're out, we can pretty much go wherever we want."

I looked over the maps. "This is a little overwhelming."

He smirked. "That's why we're using GPS."

I laughed. "Wow, Coop. Did you just put all this here for show?"

"Maybe."

I propped my chin in my hand and smiled up at him. "You're something else, you know that?"

He stacked up the charts and compasses, taking them around the corner to back them in the small desk built into the wall. "I thought you'd find it interesting. I'm here to show you a good time, which would be complicated by sea charts and math."

"Yuck. Nobody wants to do math on a Saturday."

"My point exactly." He smiled. "The bar, pantry, and fridge are stocked, so help yourself. You ready to go?"

I nodded and slipped out of the bench as he picked up the CB to get clearance from the harbor master, listening to his easy confidence, wondering how many times he'd sailed. He hung up the receiver when he'd gotten word, and we climbed back out into the cockpit.

"Give me just a minute. Make yourself comfortable." He smiled as he turned the key and pressed the ignition, and the motor came alive with a rumble.

I took a seat as he jumped onto the deck and made his way around the boat with purpose, casting off all the boat lines except the ones in the front and back. He pulled in the bumpers and stowed them before casting off the line in the back, then hopped back on the boat and let the final rope loose, rolling it up and putting it away as he did the others. I watched, fascinated.

I'd found something that Cooper was very serious about.

He gave me a smile, slipping on his sunglasses as he stood behind the wheel and pulled out of the slip, then out of the marina. He turned on music, and I stretched out on the bench, taking it all in. The city passed by us as he navigated through the harbor, past cruise ships and big party yachts, tug boats and towering shipping boats stacked with cargo crates, talking all the while.

"How do you know where to go?" I asked, curious.

"See those buoys? We want to keep the green ones on our starboard — right side — when we're heading out, just like on the road. When you're coming in, you keep the red ones on your starboard."

"How often do you sail?"

I watched the wind ruffle his dark hair. "Whenever I can. A couple of times a month, at least. Even in the winter."

"Did you have to take classes to learn? Or…"

He smiled at me before looking back to the water. "I've been sailing since I was a kid, first with my dad and then sailing school. I was on a team in high school and college, too. There's just something infinitely satisfying about earning the freedom of the wind in my hair with burning muscles and salt on my lips. It's addictive."

"You really love it, don't you?"

"I really do."

My heart was all fluttery, thinking about the countless hours he'd spent sailing, thinking about how he was sharing something he was passionate about with me.

He kept talking, and I listened, captivated by the deep timbre of his voice. "This ship is easy to sail, in the way of sailboats. It's big enough that I can bring people with me, small enough that I can handle it on my own. I have an even smaller one with no automation for when I really want to work for it."

"So this is your party boat?"

Cooper laughed. "Yeah, this is my party boat. But I sail it alone most of the time."

"*Always* alone?"

He smirked at me. "Are you asking if I've brought girls onto my boat?"

"Maybe." I shrugged, pretending to be indifferent.

"A time or two. But like I said, I'm usually alone."

I knew he meant it in more ways than one. I changed the subject. "So, do you have to chart a course or something? I don't know what you call it." I chuckled awkwardly. "Or do you know where to go? Or … I don't know how any of this works."

"I've sailed to the Hamptons hundreds of times — my dad and I have been making the trip as long as I can remember. But I did chart the course in my GPS. It's hooked into the autopilot, but otherwise I can watch the screen to stay on track. Just makes it a little easier, less work. So I can enjoy your company."

I tried to suppress my smile and looked up at the mast. "When can you put the sails up?"

"Not until we're out of the harbor. It's not really safe with all the traffic, so we'll use the engine to get us out into open water and move out of the shipping channel to hoist sail. And then the trip really begins." His smile sent a rush of adrenaline through me.

I settled back in the seat, hanging my arms on the back of the bench, chin tilted up as we rode past the towering skyscrapers. I watched them all, thinking about the people inside, thinking about who built them, marveling over this city composed of concrete and steel, constructed by millions of men and women over hundreds of years, with sweat and blood and mountains of money. And Cooper and I floated by, just a little speck on the river passing by for a quiet moment in time.

Cooper turned up the radio, and I watched him inconspicuously behind the shade of my sunglasses. His legs were planted firmly on the deck — he was more solid than I'd ever seen him on dry land. I watched his forearms as he turned the wheel, the flutter of tendons and muscles under his tan skin almost hypnotic. The wind blew through his hair, the black shock that somehow stayed out of his face, his jaw under perfectly neglected stubble, set without looking hard. My eyes rested on his mouth, the bow of his upper lip, the swell of the bottom. I knew those lips.

A flash of possession washed over me.

Forget everything from before. Pretend that this is everything there is or ever will be. What do I want?

In that moment, the answer was simple. If you stripped everything away, I wanted him.

Emotion washed over me, and I looked away, pushing away the anxiety as questions filled my head, questions I couldn't answer. I didn't know what any of it meant. And for this weekend, I would accept that as all I needed to know.

We passed under the Verrazano bridge, and the bay opened up. I spotted Coney Island in the distance, the Wonder Wheel spinning as we rounded out into open water. Cooper smiled and pulled the boat around into the wind.

He locked the wheel and reached for my hand. "All right. Here we go, Mags."

I followed him up to the front of the boat where he silently slipped the rope in the halyard and hooked it into the mast, then hoisted the mainsail, pulling the rope hand over hand, face tilted up to the sun until it hit the end. He wrapped the end in a figure eight around a cleat and we moved to the next. He tied the halyard to the second sail the same way and hooked it into the jib, then he shot me that beautiful smile of his again.

"Together?" He extended the rope, his eyes shining so brilliantly, I could barely breathe.

The boat rocked under our feet, and I smiled back before taking the rope. We raised the sail together until it hit the top, and he cleated the rope as the sails snapped and flapped, the ship rocking against the waves as we hurried back to the wheel.

I knelt on the bench, face turned to the wind, heart hammering against my ribs.

"Hang on," he called, and my heart beat faster, adrenaline pumping as he turned off the motor and turned the wheel. The wind caught the sails with a heavy thump of canvas, and we began to move, slowly at first, then faster until we were racing across the waves.

It was like nothing I could have imagined. I had no idea ships could fly.

COOPER

She hung on to the handle on the back of the bench, her eyes on the horizon, cheeks flushed as a laugh shot out of her. The sound was wild, full of abandon and wonder.

I knew the feeling. It was why I sailed.

We rode in silence, the only sounds the rushing wind and crash of the water against the hull, both of us taking the time to appreciate the day, the moment, each other as I tacked toward the shore.

She shook her head and turned to me after a long while. "This is incredible, Cooper."

I gave her a smile with my hands on the wheel and the wind in my hair.

She looked toward the shore as we passed Coney Island. "Why

aren't we going straight?"

"You can't sail directly into the wind … you have to skate across it at an angle, then switch back. It's called tacking, like a zig-zag."

"So, you just turn the other direction?"

I smiled. "You have to adjust the sail when you tack, catch it from the other direction of the sail. Tacking is when you really do work."

"How often do you tack?"

I shrugged. "Shorter tacks would get us there faster, but they're more exhausting. We're not in a hurry, and I'm not trying to expend all my energy sailing. Not when I've got you for a whole night to myself."

She laughed. "Long tack it is. How long until we reach the Hamptons?"

"About five hours. I made reservations for dinner, but we should have plenty of time to shower and get settled in at the beach house."

"I'm so excited right now!" she bubbled, and I laughed, leaning over to kiss her.

"Good."

The day was perfect — clear skies, steady wind, and Maggie on my boat with a smile that rivaled the sun.

"Can I walk around?" she asked. "I'm not going to get knocked off the boat or anything, right?"

"No, you'll be fine. I'll let you know before I tack the other direction. This," I pointed at the bottom of the sail in front of us, "is the boom. It'll swing around when I jib — turn — but I'll let you know before that happens, every thirty or forty-five minutes."

"Ooh, I'll wait. I want to watch you do that."

I smiled, feeling larger than life.

"We're close enough." I reached over to the jib's rope and unwound it, hanging on as the boat drifted through the wind in a lurch.

Maggie sat down, watching me.

The boom swung over our heads as the sail changed directions and caught with a snap, and the boat turned sharp, angling the deck as I held on, pulling tight to secure the sheet on the opposite side of the boat. Maggie gasped, hanging on with her eyes on the ocean as we straightened out. I grabbed the wheel, adjusting the angle until the wind hit the sail in the sweet spot.

Her eyes were huge, cheeks flushed as she gaped at me. "That was fucking awesome!"

I laughed. "Keep an eye on the boom, okay? The wind could shift and move it, but you're fine once you move up to the mainsail."

"I'll be careful," she said with a smile and climbed out of the cockpit.

I watched her walk along the deck, hanging onto the rope guardrail until she reached the bow and stood in the wide space made by the angle of the mainsail, hanging onto the rope, hair flying.

I wished I could see her face.

She sat after a moment, watching the ocean, and I stood at the helm of my ship with the wind rushing past me, feeling like everything was right. As if everything was exactly what it should be, where it should be. And when she looked back over her shoulder at me, I knew it was true.

MAGGIE

Hours later, I felt wind whipped and sun worn and absolutely amazing. I'd never experienced anything quite like it.

Cooper Moore — nautical badass. Who knew.

I sat next to him in the cockpit and watched him, talked to him, laughed with him. I sat on the bow of the ship where the wind was the strongest, feeling free, full of hope. For a little while, I sat in his lap, steering the boat under his direction as he told me what we were looking for — the fullness of the sails, the direction of the wind against them. And the rest of the time, I watched him navigate his ship, the attention to every small detail as deliberate as it was second nature.

By the time we reached Shinnecock Bay, I wasn't ready for the ride to end. I took comfort in that we'd do it all again in the morning, and after watching him handle his ship all day, I was ready to have him to myself, with no distractions.

He pulled into a slip in a marina in the north of the bay that he'd reserved, and he called for his car service before showing me how to close up the boat. We grabbed our things, and I felt so unbelievably *good* as we walked out of the marina and slipped into the backseat of the car waiting for us. I was tucked into his side, watching out the window as we rose up the coast, past a few subdivisions until the driver turned down a long driveway.

You wouldn't have known it was there if you weren't looking for it — the unimposing entry with a gate just past what you could see from the road. The driver pulled up to the box where Cooper punched in a code, and once the gate opened, we drove over the hill.

My mouth dropped open when I saw the Hampton house at the bottom.

It was a beachy Cape Cod with dark wooden slats and white trim, a massive home, but somehow it didn't feel pretentious at all. It looked homey, sitting there on the beach without another house in sight, the ocean stretched out forever beyond. Like a safe haven, secluded from everything.

It was a bubble I had a feeling I may never want to leave.

The driver pulled around the circular driveway, and we climbed out. Cooper picked up our bags, smiling at me over his shoulder as he unlocked the door. And when he pushed it open, I stepped inside, holding my breath.

The quiet house looked like it came straight out of a design magazine. Everything was crisp and clean, modern and simple, as unassuming as the exterior of the house in whites and grays and dark wood. The furniture looked comfortable and simple, and my eyes followed the exposed beams across the ceiling.

I'd never seen anything so perfect.

"I can't even believe this is real." I was still looking around in awe as he stepped up behind me and took off his sunglasses.

"Welcome to the Hampton house." He kissed my hair, close enough that his chest was against my back.

"Why would you ever leave this place?"

I felt him shrug. "This is where we come to get away from life. Everything else is in New York. It's only a matter of time before it drags you back."

I shook my head, looking out the wall of windows at the ocean. "Nope. Never leaving."

He laughed and wrapped an arm around my shoulders. "Fine by me." He pressed a kiss to my temple and grabbed my hand. "Come on, let me show you around."

We walked through the house — through the living room, the massive library and media room, the gourmet kitchen — then down the hallway where the bedrooms were. The master bedroom was more than half the width of the house with a bathroom that was bigger than my bedroom in Manhattan. I gaped at the giant soaker tub.

"I'm getting in that at some point."

He chuckled and set our bags down. "Still want to sleep on the boat?"

"Absolutely not."

Cooper walked up behind me and slipped his hands around my waist. I leaned back into him, feeling his solid body behind me, and he rested his chin on the top of my head. I caught sight of our reflection in the bathroom mirror and couldn't tear my eyes away.

We looked carefree and full of life, windblown and young and alive. And in that moment, everything shifted, moving forward in a jolt without having moved at all.

He looked down at me, and I looked up at him, and when he kissed me, I knew nothing would ever be what it was before.

Stay

COOPER

adjusted my tie in the mirror over the dresser, smiling at my reflection that evening.

Maggie. All day, all night, in my dreams and in my arms.

I looked at the man in the mirror, barely recognizing who I saw looking back. I was me, the same me I'd always been — same nose, same eyes — but somehow, everything had changed.

The feeling of certainty, of rightness, overwhelmed me again. I was high off of it, off of her. Off the perfect day and her lips and her laugh.

I realized that the man I saw in the mirror looked different because I was hers.

It was a feeling I could get used to.

Purpose.

Maggie stepped out of the bathroom but stopped in the threshold, hanging on to the doorframe as she lifted her foot to adjust her heel. Her dress was simple and black, the neck scooped low, her black suede heels dainty and sexy all at once. She stood and looked up at me with eyes bright and blue, scanning my body.

When she made her way over to me, she laid her hands on my chest, slipping her fingers under my lapels. "I can't handle you in this suit."

My hands trailed down her waist to her hips. "I can't handle you in this dress."

She smiled and kissed me gently.

"We'll never leave, Mags."

"There's food here, right?"

"I'm not letting my 'no rules night with Maggie' go to waste. I'm going to feed you, take you on a real date like I can't in New York."

She chuckled. "West would approve."

My smile slipped, and I cupped her cheek. "Would he?"

She didn't answer, only sighed.

"I have to believe that if we were honest with him—"

But she shook her head, her eyes on my lips. "Not tonight. Okay? Today … today's been one of the most perfect days of my life. I don't want to think about what happens tomorrow or what happened before. I just want right now. Can you give that to me?" Her eyes met mine.

My throat was tight — I couldn't speak. So I nodded.

"Thank you. Now, let's go eat shellfish until we can't move."

I laughed, though the tension never left me as I grabbed her hand and took her down to the garage. She shook her head, hand on her hip when I turned on the light.

"A Porsche? That's so predictable."

I shrugged and walked over to the black Boxster. "It's my beach car."

She followed, the beat of her heels against the concrete echoing in the room. "I don't think I've ever actually ridden in a Porsche before."

I smiled. "Well, allow me to introduce you." I opened the door for her, and she slipped in, looking around, wide eyed.

"Swanky, Coop."

I chuckled and closed her door, walking around to climb into the driver's seat. She perked up when I started the engine.

"Oh, that sound."

"Just wait." I took a second to appreciate Maggie dressed like she was, sitting in my Porsche, looking like an absolute fantasy. I smirked and backed out of the garage, taking off up the driveway with the chirp of my tires.

She giggled. "Okay, I guess I see the appeal."

I laughed.

We drove into town and parked on the main drag in front of the bistro. I helped her out of the car and offered her my arm.

I was king of the universe with Maggie on my arm.

We stepped into the quiet restaurant, following the host through the dim dining room and to a table for two with crisp white linens. I pulled out her chair, and she smiled at me sweetly as she set down her clutch and took a seat.

The restaurant was dark enough that the only light seemed to come from the cluster of candles on the table. I glanced around to see the faces of other patrons like islands in the dark around us. Our waiter materialized next to the table with a smile and poured our water, introducing himself and giving us a brief rundown of the menu before disappearing again, leaving us alone.

I sat back in my seat watching her look over the small menu, her brow creased just enough to know she wasn't quite sure of herself.

"This all sounds delicious, but why aren't there prices?"

I smiled. "The price is per meal. Just pick three courses."

She raised an eyebrow. "Do I want to know how much it costs?"

"Probably not."

She sighed and shook her head, red lips curved into a smile as she glanced back at her menu. "I don't know that I've ever eaten dandelion before. And oxtail … is that actually …"

I chuckled. "Yes, it's exactly what it sounds like."

"Oh. Maybe I'll stick to lobster, then."

I glanced at my menu. "They'll pair our wine, if that works for you?"

"I'm sure they'd do a much better job than I would." She looked up at me. "I'm a little intimidated."

I gave her a reassuring smile. "Well, here's a tip. Everything here is amazing. It really doesn't matter what you choose."

She seemed comforted. "I suppose that makes sense, what with the unspeakable price tag and all." She laid her menu back on her plate and reached across the table for my hand. "Thank you, Cooper."

I took her hand and ran my thumb across her knuckles. "You don't have to thank me. I'm just glad you're here. This has been …"

Her face softened. "I know," she said quietly.

I put on The Smile, skirting the topic like I'd promised. "Not that either of us doubted I could convince you to come."

Maggie laughed and squeezed my hand. "No, I'm just a sucker for you. I'm generally much more fastidious in my decisions."

"Oh, I know. We're old buddies, the rules and me."

"Never stops you from trying to break them though, does it?"

One week. This is it. Don't let her go. I pushed down my rambling thoughts and shrugged. "I didn't break them. Just bent them a little."

The waiter appeared again and took our order, removing our menus with a smile and a quiet whoosh before he was gone once more.

I steered the conversation away from us and sat across from her, hanging on every word, every smile, as a small part of me held its breath, not knowing how long our moment would last. I watched her face when our food came, as she took each bite and moaned ever so softly, the light in her eyes sparking with adventure.

It was too perfect, too good. The taste of reality she'd given me before we'd left the beach house had shaken my confidence, the reminder that our lives were waiting for us back home — West, her rules, her past. It was a reminder that I didn't know how she felt, didn't know what she wanted.

I didn't know if I was ready to find out.

I wasn't ready for the day to end, but it would. The clock would tick and tick until the seconds piled up and turned into minutes, into hours. And then it would be tomorrow.

I didn't want tomorrow at all.

I hung on to the hope that I would be enough for her. That she'd take a chance on me. I knew she felt what I did. I just needed her to *want* to feel it. I needed her to say yes.

I wasn't prepared for anything other than yes. I couldn't fathom it. I couldn't imagine a universe in which Maggie wasn't sitting across from me looking like everything I've ever wanted.

If no was the answer, I'd keep trying because I couldn't walk away from her. Especially not now.

We walked to the ice cream shop after dinner, eating our cones in my Porsche like the irresponsible youths that we were. I took her hand and towed her out of the house and down the trail to the ocean. Her shoes hung on her fingers with the moonlight in her hair, on her skin, in her eyes as we walked along the shore, letting the waves wash over our feet.

She held my hand, shifting her fingers against mine as if she were paying just as much attention to the places where we touched as she was anything else, which was a lot. Maggie just experienced life that way — she was an open vessel, pouring the world into herself as if she'd never fill up.

I pulled her to a stop on the beach, and she looked back, confused for only the blink of an eye before she smiled and stepped toward me, reaching up to cup my face and kiss me. She breathed me in, and I breathed her, our lips tender and insistent.

My arms were around her. Her body was against mine. My heart was in her hands, and I knew.

There would never be anyone else.

She smiled up at me, turning to walk away without breaking her gaze as she tossed her shoes up the beach and reached for the hem of her dress. Her fingers hooked under it, and she pulled it up over her hips, over her ribs, over her head. She had nothing else on.

I tossed my shoes in the direction of hers and tugged at my tie, unable to get my clothes off fast enough as I watched her step into the ocean in the moonlight. I followed her in, reaching her once she stopped past the breaks where it was calm.

She turned to face me, and I reached for her, slipped a hand around her waist and pulled until our bodies met, her soft skin against mine. Her legs wrapped around me, and as she dragged her hands through the water, a soft glow trailed through her fingers. She did it again, and we watched in wonder at the magic of it all. When she looked up at me, her eyes were too open, too much.

I love you. Don't leave me.

But I couldn't speak. Not with words. So I told her the story of my love with the rest of me. With my lips and my hands. With a touch and a sigh. I loved her, and I didn't know if I could keep her. But I would try.

I would never stop trying.

I made the silent promise with the ocean in my ears and her arms around my neck. And when I slipped inside of her and took her mouth, took her body, I could feel her heart, feel her soul. I only hoped she could feel mine too.

MAGGIE

My face was buried in his neck, my body humming as he pulsed inside of me. We were wrapped in each other, cradled in each other's arms in the moonlight, my body his completely. My heart reached for him with every beat.

I closed my lips over the salty skin of his neck, eyes closed and heart open. The day had been a dream, but the night — the night had shown me something I hadn't even realized I'd been hoping for. It gave me a glimpse into what it would be like to be with Cooper. What it would be like to love him. What it would be like if he loved me, too.

I didn't want to let him go.

His hands slipped into my hair, his lips finding my shoulder, and I leaned back so I could see him. The shadows cast half of his face into the dark, his blue eyes so full of moonlight that they almost glowed. Those eyes were full of adoration. I knew mine said the same.

His eyes disappeared behind a flutter of dark lashes as he leaned forward to kiss me, a kiss full of devotion and quiet worship, and I gave him the same, this beautiful man who showed me what it meant to be cherished.

He carried me back to the shore, setting me down once we were waist deep. I took his hand and followed him out of the ocean to the pile of clothes we'd thrown on the beach, gathering them with smiles on our faces.

Neither of us spoke. We'd already said it all.

My thoughts circled as we walked up to the house. I'd denied him, denied myself the chance to be with him, and why? The reasons that seemed so concrete a few days before had dissipated like fog in the sunshine.

I wanted Cooper, and he wanted me. It was that simple.

We climbed the stairs to the back patio and made our way into the dark house. He paused to kiss my hair.

"Mmm," I hummed. "I think I want to take a bath."

His hand skimmed down my back. "I'll make us a drink. Bourbon?"

"Yes, please." I turned and slipped my hands up his chest to his jaw, pulling him down to kiss me once more.

When he broke away, he trailed his nose against the bridge of mine, and we breathed for just a moment before he smiled and turned for the kitchen, taking my breath with him.

I couldn't stop smiling. Not as I dimmed the bathroom lights and ran the bath or as I sank into the steaming water. Definitely not when he came in, still naked, carrying a scotch for himself and a bourbon for me. I took it graciously and sighed, sinking a little further into the massive tub.

He smirked and moved to the shower.

"No bath for you?" I pouted.

That rogue corner of his crooked lips climbed a little higher. "You look so comfortable. Wouldn't want to disturb you." He opened the glass door and reached in to turn on the shower, taking a sip of his drink while he waited for the water to heat up.

My eyes roamed up and down his body. "Oh, it'd be no bother. Really."

He laughed and set his drink on the counter before stepping into the steaming stream.

I sighed again, my chest so full of emotions that I felt as if I didn't exhale, I'd cracked open and they would spill out.

I'd told him earlier that I wanted to wait to talk. I saw the hurt and fear flit behind his eyes when he'd agreed. But in the ocean, in the moment when we were as close as we'd ever been, I'd looked into his eyes, and I knew there was no going back. I didn't want to lose the feeling. I didn't want it to end. I wanted to be with him.

I wanted to try.

The second I thought it, my heart and stomach switched places. Doubt flew through me as I worried I wasn't ready, worried he would hurt me. But it was gone just as quickly.

When I looked beyond our past, the answer was clear. I wanted to be with him. Everything else was just details.

I watched him through the glass as he ran his hands through his hair, face upturned to the light, eyes closed as the water ran down his body. I'd cared for him all along, I realized. Since the very first night.

I'd used everything that had happened to me as an excuse because I was scared. But deep down, I knew Cooper wouldn't hurt me. I'd always known.

He turned off the shower and grabbed a towel, and I watched as he took a moment to dry himself off, running the towel over his hair before wrapping it around his waist. The second he stepped out of the shower and his eyes met mine, he shot me that smile that made my uterus do flip-flops. My gaze wandered down his chest, coming to rest on his hips where the towel was wrapped around that V that pointed straight to the Promised Land.

Cooper smirked at me and whipped that towel off like a goddamn stripper. The next thing I knew, the towel was flying at my face, and I laughed when it hit me, the sound muffled by the thick terrycloth as the ends sank in the water around me.

By the time I looked up, I only caught sight of his bare ass as he walked into the bedroom.

"Don't make me wait, Mags."

My cheeks flushed as I fished the wet ends of his towel out of the water and wrung them out.

I wouldn't make him wait anymore. Not a second longer.

A few minutes later, I slipped in bed with him, naked as he was. He lay on his side, head propped on his hand, and as soon as I was under the covers, he pulled me into him. My head rested against the mattress, and I looked up, smiling.

He moved my hair from my face and traced my jaw. "Thank you."

"For what?"

"For agreeing to come with me here. For letting me show you all of this."

"I had no idea. You kinda blew my mind." I made an explosion sound with my mouth, and he laughed.

"Then we're even."

We watched each other for a moment as his hand slipped down my shoulder and arm.

"Maggie," the word was tight, and he looked down to his thumb shifting against my skin.

I laid a hand on his solid chest, feeling his heart beat under my palm. "To hell with the rules."

His eyes darted to mine, and he watched me, his hand moving to cover my own. "Do you mean that?" It was almost a whisper.

"I don't want this to end, you and me. You make me feel good and true and … *right*. I don't want to lose this feeling."

"You want me?"

I laughed, the sound tight as I held back tears. "I want you, Cooper. Do you want me?"

His eyes searched mine. "More than anything."

"Then everything else will be all right," I said simply. "Just be patient with me."

"I'll do whatever I have to do, Maggie." His hand found my cheek, fingers in my hair. "Just tell me what you need."

"You," I whispered. "Just you."

He didn't speak, just closed his eyes and kissed me, touched me, gave himself to me as I'd asked. I could feel the echo of my past buried somewhere in the back of my mind, but I wouldn't be swayed to listen, not in Cooper's arms. There was nowhere I'd rather be but surrounded by him where nothing could touch me. No one could hurt me.

The weight of his body, the softness of his skin against mine, was everything. The sweetness of his lips, the hardness of his body as he slipped inside of me, stealing my breath, stealing my heart. His eyes were on mine, the emotion written on the planes of his face as he thumbed my cheek. I turned into his hand and pressed my lips to his palm as he dropped his forehead to mine.

My legs wound around his waist, and the sheets slipped away as our hips rolled against each other faster. And when I looked up at him, I understood what I'd been missing for so long. I understood what I'd always been missing, what I'd misunderstood for all my life.

I let my heart go, let my body go, and he was right behind me, breathing my name like the word was sacred.

Our bodies slowed, and he wrapped his arms around me, shifting to his side, holding me to his chest with his fingers in my hair.

We lay that way in the moonlight for a long time, not moving, just breathing until our breaths finally slowed, leaving us hanging on the edge of sleep. His warmth left me for the briefest, coldest of moments before returning to me. He placed a towel in my hand that I used to lazily clean up before tossing it away, and then I slipped back into his arms.

I felt everything — the heat of his skin against my cheek, the beat of his heart thundering through me until mine matched its pace, the length of his body entwined with mine. His strong arms held me like he'd never let me go, and that was exactly how I drifted off to sleep.

Pieces of Me

MAGGIE

shifted against him, feeling his arms around me, wanting nothing more than to stay in that bed all day. Forever. His arms tightened as he stirred, pulling me into his chest.

He kissed my bare shoulder, and I rolled over to face him with my heart fluttering. The sandy stretch of beach and rolling ocean beyond the windows framed him, and when he smiled at me … well, I knew it was a moment I wouldn't forget.

"Good morning," he said, his voice rough from disuse.

"Morning." He was so warm, and I nestled into his chest. "I don't want to leave."

"Then let's stay."

I sighed. "I wish we could."

"There's not much that could stop us."

The ache in my chest was deep, but I smiled, making light. "But I'll never prove my worth to your mom if I quit showing up."

He chuckled. "Oh, your work there is done."

"Why does that terrify me to think that you've been talking to your mother about me?"

Cooper backed up so he could see me. "She brought you up the other night at dinner. She kind of went on about you."

"So she likes me?"

"She definitely likes you."

"I hope she didn't think I was weird the other day. I was just so surprised your *mother* was our benefactor. And also super pissed at you for interfering."

"I know what it's like to be controlled. I'd never do that to you."

I curled back into his chest, and his arms squeezed a little tighter. "What are we going to do about West?"

Cooper's chest rose and fell as he sighed. "I don't know. He's not going to take it well, but I have to believe that if he knows I won't hurt you, he'll be all right."

Worry over their friendship wriggled through my brain. "I hope so."

He stretched to look at the clock and sighed again. "We should probably get going."

I groaned.

"Hungry?"

I piped down. "Actually, yes."

"Let's go get breakfast and get back on the water."

I let out a breath. "Food and sailing. Those are maybe the only two things that could drag me out of bed, besides you. But you're here, so …"

He laughed, squeezing me once more before we rolled out of bed, got dressed, and packed up our things. The car service sent a driver to take us back to the harbor. I watched the Hampton house disappear behind us and I sighed, missing the magic of the place within seconds.

The diner was somehow cozy and upper crust all at once, and my omelet was incredible, stuffed with bacon, tomatoes, avocados, and buttery crab meat. And an hour later, we were climbing back onto

Midnight Caller.

We readied the ship, cast off the lines, pulled in the fenders, and then we rode out of the harbor, back to the ocean and down the coast. The day passed too quickly, and every minute took us closer to the real world. Our reality was so much more complicated than the last twenty-four hours had been. All I could do was hope that if we just held onto each other, we'd be all right.

It was almost dusk by the time we made it back into the marina in Manhattan, the sun dropping down in the sky too quickly. He pulled the boat into the slip and hopped onto the dock to tie us up.

He smiled at me as he climbed back in and stepped into the cockpit. "Come home with me."

I stood. "I wish I could, but I should get back and get cleaned up. I have some work to do before tomorrow. It's my first day with the kids."

He wrapped his arms around me. "Well, I've got about an hour's worth of closing down the boat to do. Did you want to hang out? Bobby's here. He can give you a ride if you don't want to wait."

"Nah, that's all right. I'll just take the subway."

"You sure?"

I smiled up at him. "I'm sure. Thank you, Cooper. For everything."

"Don't thank me. This won't be the last time. Maybe we can take a week or two this summer, just you and me and the Hamptons."

I sighed, imagining we were back there already. "That sounds glorious."

He smiled. "Can I see you tomorrow?"

"Absolutely. I'll come by after work."

"Seems like a million years from now, after having you all to myself." He kissed me sweetly.

A big part of me didn't want to leave his side for even a minute. "I know. I'll text you, okay? And I'll see you tomorrow."

"All right." Cooper helped me out of the boat and handed me

my bag, then stepped onto the pier. He threaded his fingers through mine before kissing me once more. "Be careful. I'll talk to you later."

I hesitated, almost afraid to leave. Like the minute I walked off the dock, the magic would disappear. But I tried to have faith. As scared as I was, I had to trust that we would be all right. That everything would work out.

I smiled, looking forward to that time as I stretched up on my tiptoes to wind my arms around Cooper's neck and kiss him deep. He picked me up, and my sneakers dangled off the ground.

I broke away, smiling at his lips.

"Tomorrow."

His lips brushed mine once more. "Tomorrow."

He set me down, and I turned to leave, looking back over my shoulder at him. He stood on the dock with his hands in his pockets and the most brilliant smile on his face, watching me as I walked away.

My heart skipped as I walked out of the marina and toward the train station. But when I turned on my phone and it connected for the first time since the morning before, my notifications went nuts. Texts rolled in, piled on top of each other, and I pulled them open, wondering what the hell was going on.

West: *Hope your date is nice and that you have a good reason from hiding him from me. Text me if he turns into a creep.*

Lily: *Dude, a package came for you like five seconds after you left.*

There was a picture of a box sitting on our kitchen table. I stopped in the middle of the sidewalk when I saw the hand addressed label.

It was from Jimmy. I held my breath as I scrolled through her texts.

Lily: *WTF could Jimmy have sent you? Rose and I are dying. Tell me I can open it.*

Lily: *Just kidding, that was really forward, but text me and freak out with me.*

Lily: *Okay, you're obviously super busy getting your junk rocked, but Rose and I have been staring at this for twelve hours and we're dying.*

Lily: *Do you guys really have zero service? This is balls!*

Jimmy: *Hey. I sent you something, my tracking says it was delivered yesterday. Let me know if you got it and call me, if you want. I'm around.*

I felt like hurling as I picked up my feet and pulled up Lily's messages. *Just got back. On my way.*

My phone dinged within seconds. *THANK GOD. I hope it was amazing. Hurry up.*

My mind spun around in circles, and I headed down the stairs of the subway station, through the turnstile, and stepped onto the train. The tables had turned, tilting my world sideways. New Maggie was nowhere to be found — Old Maggie had taken her place and found herself sitting scared and alone on the train, wondering how she'd gotten there.

I barreled out of the 86th St. station and to our building, up the stairs and into the apartment. The door opened with a whoosh that sucked all of the air out of the room. Lily and Rose sat at the table, their faces turned to mine. No one spoke.

All I saw was that box.

Inside that box was everything I was trying to forget.

I dropped my bag and stepped toward the table in slow motion, picked up the scissors and sliced through the seam, through my name on the label, splitting it in half. My eyes locked on the dark crack, not wanting to know what was inside and knowing I couldn't avoid it. Not anymore.

I took a breath and opened the box with trembling hands.

It was like a time capsule straight out of my past. Jimmy had assembled the package with care, choosing things that he knew I would understand, that would remind me. Our prom picture. A photo of us at a football game, me in my cheerleader uniform and him a sweaty, smiling, hulking mess, football helmet in hand, our smiles bright and carefree. Movie ticket stubs. A velvet box full of dried rose petals. A picture of us in the Bahamas after he asked me to marry him. And when I picked that up, what lay beneath stopped my heart.

I knew that black satin box. I knew what was inside without looking, but I picked it up anyway with quaking hands, the hinges squeaking softly when I opened it. The light caught the two-carat diamond inside, the ring I'd worn every day for a year until the day when I was supposed to wear it forever.

I closed the box with a snap, my fingers numb as I picked up the letter in the bottom of the cardboard box with my name on the front. I opened the envelope and unfolded the paper inside, sinking into a chair as I read.

Maggie —

These months without you have been the worst of my life. I found all of this in our closet, the box full of our memories, and it was too much. I've been giving you space, but I can't stay quiet anymore.

Tell me what I have to do to get you back. Tell me what to say. I love you, and I always have. Come home, Maggie. Because my life doesn't make sense without you in it.

—Jimmy

Tears spilled down my cheeks, hot and fat, so fast I could barely see. I closed my eyes, ribs aching as I dragged in a skipping breath, letting it out with a sob. And my past rushed back to me, overwhelming me. It wasn't what was in the box. It was the deluge of my memories, the ghost come back to haunt me. To push me over the edge.

"Oh, God, Maggie," Lily whispered and reached for me.

I shook my head, hands clasped over my mouth. Beaten. Broken.

My eyes found the picture from the football game again, what felt like a million years ago and yesterday. We looked so happy. I thought we were happy.

Everything about him was constructed, manufactured to make me feel safe and wanted, and it was all a lie. I didn't believe that he cared about anyone but himself. But for years, for my entire adult life and even before, Jimmy was all I'd ever known.

The memory of him, of seven years of loving him — it all crashed into me.

Everything I'd been hiding from, everything I'd been running from had found me.

I couldn't breathe, though the tears still fell, my heart beating so hard in my chest that I felt like I'd been shot. My fingers tingled, black spots swimming in my vision.

Rose turned my chair. "Maggie? Breathe, Maggie."

I tried. I tried to slow down, closed my eyes and held my lungs still, but they sucked in another frantic breath, sobs shuddering through me until the black spots spread.

And then they were gone.

Gravity

MAGGIE

The children's faces were turned up to mine, eyes full of hope and wonder as I read to them the next morning, feeling like I'd been hit by a steam roller. Which was to say that I felt nothing. I was stretched out and flattened.

Numb.

I'd opened my eyes after passing out the night before to find Lily and Rose leaning over me, looking terrified. And the tears fell. They fell in the shower, mingling with the scalding water that beat down on me like a fiery baptism. They slipped down my cheeks and into my ears, onto my pillow as I lay in bed, alone.

Lily wanted to stay with me, but I didn't want to see anyone. I didn't want anyone to see me.

I wanted to disappear.

I'd woken up feeling nothing. Got dressed and left the apartment in a daze, came to the shelter and did my job. I didn't check my phone until the morning, and when I finally did, I found texts from Cooper, saying he hoped I was asleep and had gotten some rest. Said he couldn't wait to see me.

My chest was hollow as I messaged him back, telling him I was busy and that I'd be over after work. And then I put my phone in my bag, unable to check it again. I just couldn't.

The one thing I'd learned after all was said and done: I wasn't ready. I hadn't even been close to being ready. What I had been doing was fooling myself. Pretending. I was too broken, so broken that I'd been walking around, stuck together with duct tape and bubblegum, acting like I was fine.

I didn't trust myself to make decisions about Cooper. He gave me his heart, and I took it too soon. And now, I was about to drop it. Break it. Shatter it.

So stupid. So careless.

Maybe it was for the best.

I hadn't been enough for Jimmy — how could I ever be enough for *Cooper Moore*? I believed that he wanted to try, that he'd do the best he could to only be with me. I wanted to think he could do it. But the only other boy I'd ever given my heart to didn't care for it. He just wasn't equipped, and I couldn't be sure that Cooper was, either.

But the scariest thing of all — my feelings for Jimmy were back, buzzing around my head, around my heart, reminding me of everything I'd lost. The love I'd never had to start with.

I could see a dozen ways out of my mess, and no path was easy. In my favorite one, time healed my wounds, Cooper earned my trust, and we could be together. But every other path ended up in heartache, mine or his. Or both.

I couldn't risk any more than I already had.

I turned the page of Cinderella, the version by Hilary Knight with the most lovely illustrations. It was the same one my mom read to me as a girl, the one I always used in class. The kids sat at my feet, leaning forward as I read. I didn't need to look at the words. I knew them by heart.

For so long, I believed in fairy tales. That Jimmy was my prince, and I was living my happily ever after. But the reality was that my life was the opposite of a fairy tale. My prince lied. My happily ever after didn't exist.

No, if my life were a fairy tale, it would go something like this.

Once upon a time, there was a girl named Maggie who was honest and true, who danced her way through life with sunshine in her eyes and a smiling heart.

One day she met a beautiful boy with a beautiful smile who showed her what it meant to love, and her gravity shifted until her whole world revolved around him, her sun, the middle of her little universe that he filled with laughter and happiness.

But then the sun went out, and in the darkness, she found the truth.

That beautiful boy had lied. His smile was plastic — the truth cracked it until it crumbled, like sunshine cracks thirsty earth. And her little universe blew apart, sending her spinning, flying into the darkness with nothing to grab onto, nothing to stop her.

She closed her eyes to hide until she felt the warmth of a new sun, a bigger sun, a sun brighter than she'd ever seen before. But he pulled her in too fast. She couldn't trust his smile, couldn't let herself believe. And as she spun around him, he pulled her closer, spinning her faster and faster until she couldn't hold on.

And so she flew away once more into the dark, feeling free and lost in equal measure.

I read the last page of Cinderella and closed the book. The kids smiled up at me, and I smiled back against the hollow in my chest. We moved to the table where strips of orange construction paper and yarn waited for their tiny fingers, and I sat them all down and began to help them assemble paper pumpkins.

I felt a little like Cinderella, like I'd gotten to live a dream life for just a moment before I had to face reality again. The carriage smashed into pumpkin bits. The shoe was lost. And now I had to tell the prince that I couldn't be with him after all.

So the clock ticked on, counting down the moments before the magic would end. And when the time came, I packed up my things and walked the blocks to his apartment. Rode up the elevator and knocked on his door. And if my heart could have felt, it would have broken.

COOPER

An entire day of elation, a weekend that changed my life, a month that had opened my heart — it was all washed away when I opened my door and saw Maggie.

She looked small, grey and dull everywhere except her eyes. Her eyes were on fire.

Alarms rang as I watched the curves of her face, looking for answers, knowing what she felt without her needing to say a word. But I asked her anyway, afraid to move.

"What's wrong?" My voice was tight. My heart was tighter.

"Can I come in?"

"Of course." I pulled open the door and stepped out of the way, and she walked past me, into my apartment.

I closed the door, barely able to hear over my pulse rushing in my ears. Her hands were clasped in front of her, fingers twisted together, flexing like they did when she was nervous or scared. I didn't speak, just waited until she was ready.

I was the king of waiting.

Her words were soft — she wouldn't look at me. "I'm sorry, Cooper."

My heart stopped, starting again like a kick drum. "Why are you sorry? What happened?"

She shook her head. "I … I came home to a package from Jimmy. A letter. I thought I was ready to do this, but I'm not, and I'm sorry. I'm sorry I was careless, I just … this weekend … I was just so caught up in you. But Jimmy's not gone. And that's not fair to you."

"Do you still love him?" My voice was rough.

The honesty in her eyes hurt almost as bad as the words themselves. "I don't know. I don't know how to let go of him … I've never even really tried. I just ran away. But I can't run away anymore."

I couldn't speak.

"I'm broken, Cooper. I thought I was ready, but I'm not. I don't want to hurt you, and I don't want to get hurt. I don't know what else to do but take some time to sort through it all."

I hung onto a sliver of hope. I could give her time. I'd give her anything she wanted. "I'm here, Maggie, and I'm not going anywhere. Whatever you need, whenever you need it, I'm here."

She took a shuddering breath with her eyes on the ground. All I wanted in the universe was to pull her into my arms and hold her. I just loved her too much to do it.

She shook her head, her eyes on her fingers. "Cooper, I'm sorry."

"Don't be sorry. You didn't do anything wrong."

A tear slipped down her face, and I stepped toward her, chest aching as I cupped her cheek, urging her to look at me.

"Hey," I whispered. "Maggie, you didn't do anything wrong. Do you hear me?"

Her eyes were bright and open when she met mine. "I wanted to be okay. I wanted everything to be fine. I thought it was, but it's not."

"It will be. I promise." I kissed her forehead, and she leaned into me.

"I should go," she said softly.

I knew she didn't want to, but I stepped back anyway, let her go. Watched her walk away, not knowing if she'd ever come back to me.

MAGGIE

T*he only time I'd felt* alive all day was when I was there, with him.

I'd wanted to stay. I'd wanted to fall into his arms where I was safe. But he wasn't safe with me. I'd been selfish enough.

The second I walked away, the fire in my heart turned to ash, blowing through me. Empty.

Time was stretched out and strange as I made my way home through the park at dusk, the sky golden, the trees green and rustling from the wind. Fallen blossoms skated and spun across the path in whirls and currents before flying away.

My mind was everywhere and nowhere as I walked the path, then the blocks to my building and up the stairs. And when I opened the door, I found Rose and Lily waiting for me, sitting at the kitchen table with drinks.

Lily's blond hair was loose, her blue eyes soft. "Hey. You okay?"

I set down my bag. "No."

"As suspected. Whiskey or gin?"

I cracked a smile. "Whiskey."

Lily motioned to the Maker's on the table. "You heard the woman, Rosie."

I felt the slightest bit better and took a seat as Rose poured drinks.

"So, here's the deal," Lily said with a smile. "We can talk about it, or we can not talk about it. We can get piss drunk, or we can stay sober. You're the boss."

I took a deep breath, thinking about it. "Let's start with this and see where we end up."

Rose passed the drinks out and raised her glass. "Fuck it."

"Fuck it." Lily and I added and clinked our glasses together.

We all took drinks, and Lily and Rose turned to me.

I shook my head. "I'm not ready to talk about it. Y'all tell me what's going on with you."

Lily nodded. "Well, nothing exciting here. I was at the theater all weekend and hung out with West."

"How's everything at work?" I took a sip of my whiskey, comforted by the sweet burn.

She shrugged. "Same. It's bittersweet because *Swan Lake* is over. That was exhausting. Amazing, but exhausting."

"Blane still behaving himself?"

"As well as he can, I guess. He's been professional, which is all I really need. I have to admit though, it's fun watching him chase after Nadia because she is one hundred percent done with him."

Rose shook her head. "I still can't believe you're friends with that c-bag."

Lily shrugged. "I don't know. I get her, I guess. We survived Blane together." She leaned forward, smiling. "She's started dating another dancer, and Blane is so bitchy about it. He does to Aaron what Nadia used to do to me, like stand across the room and try to set them on fire with his eyeballs."

I chuckled and took a drink, feeling almost normal. "How about you, Rose?"

She twisted her black hair into a knot and shook out her bangs. "Just sleep and work. I skateboarded through the park today. I swear, it's the one thing I miss about LA. I didn't have to go out of my way to skate. I could just hop on my board and take off. No one skates in New York. Too many people." She narrowed her eyes. "Okay, two things I miss. Flip flops."

Lily laughed. "Yeah, you don't wear those in New York unless you want foot herpes. I mean, in the subway? Ew."

Rose sighed and shook her head. "I used to have a permanent flip flop tan line."

"Do you ever miss it?" I asked.

She bobbled her head, her dark eyes on her drink as she picked it up. "Sometimes. I miss my friends more than I do actually living there. Like, I don't miss the traffic. New York is easy like that. Get where you need on the train without having to sit on the 405 for two hours on a Saturday to make it twenty miles."

Lily rolled her eyes. "Lies. Manhattan is convenient, but only for other stuff in Manhattan. It's like when you meet someone who lives in Brooklyn. They may as well live in Japan."

Rose conceded with a nod and a gesture with her glass.

"Is it really that far?" I asked, feeling like a noob.

"No," Lily answered, "it's not. That's what makes it so ridiculous."

"New York is funny that way." I said. "Like, I hate that the subway doesn't run east to west through the park, only north to south. What's that all about? Getting to the East Side is such a pain in the ass."

Rose pulled her legs into lotus. "I mean, the park is only three blocks wide, so it's not a huge deal."

I took a sip of my drink. "No, but to get from here to the shelter takes way longer than it should. I've been walking because the weather is so great right now, but what if it's raining? What about in the winter when it's cold, or snowing? I mean, me in snow is a whole other issue all together."

Lily raised her glass. "We should write a strongly worded email to the transit authority."

I snickered and took another drink, nearly draining my glass.

"How was work?" Lily asked.

"It was rough, long. Today was my first day with the kids, and it went well. You know, other than feeling like a dead fish."

They nodded, and we all took a drink.

I set my empty glass down and watched the ice melt inside. "I went to Cooper's after work today."

"What happened?" Lily asked gently.

"I told him that I needed time."

Rose waited through a breath. "What happened over the weekend?"

I pushed my glass to her, and she filled it up. "It was amazing. Perfect. He was perfect. And in the end, I told him I wanted to be with him. To say fuck the rules and be together, to tell West. And then, Jimmy happened."

"Fucking Jimmy." Rose passed my drink over and sipped her own.

But I just held the glass in my hands and shook my head. "So I went to Cooper's after work. I had to talk to talk to him, try to explain, you know? After all that, after making a promise, to have to go back on it …"

"How did it he take it?" Lily asked.

"Better than I thought he would, honestly. I expected him to try to convince me to change my mind, but he just let me go. I don't know if I had the willpower to say no if he begged." I spun my glass around. "He told me that he'd be waiting." I took a heavy sip to burn away the lump in my throat.

Rose and Lily exchanged looks.

"What?" I asked.

Rose shook her head. "It's just that this is so unlike Cooper."

Lily shifted in her seat. "I mean, you have to understand — Cooper gets what he wants. No, it's not even that. He can convince you to give him what he wants, and he'll even have you thanking him for convincing you by the end of it. You said he just let you go. That he wants to be with you, and he let you go. It goes against Cooper physics."

I felt sick. "Maybe he just doesn't care about me enough to put up a fight."

"He said he would wait for you," Rose said. "That doesn't sound like he wasn't putting up a fight. It sounds like he's giving you what you need so you'll come back to him. Putting your needs above his own."

I sighed. "That doesn't make me feel less pressure to make a decision." I picked up my drink and knocked it back.

"I know. But you should know that we believe he's sincere, if that's a question," Lily added.

I wiped the sweat off my glass. "I just…I don't know. I don't know how I feel about Cooper or Jimmy or even myself. The closest I can get is knowing that I'd like to drink a third of this bottle, eat a pint of ice cream, and cry myself to sleep."

Lily watched me. "What did you do with the box?"

"It's in the closet. If you want to set it on fire or anything, be my guest."

Rose poured another drink for herself. "Have you heard from Jimmy?"

"He texted me again. I haven't responded to him in months, though." I drained my drink and passed it to Rose, who took it and made quick work of filling it back up. "Now it's been so long since we've talked, I don't know what to say."

"How about, 'Go lick a hot iron real quick.'"

Rose snorted. "'Stick a paperclip in an outlet and then call me.'"

"What would you even say to him?" Lily sat back in her seat, gathering her hair up and twisting it absently.

"I really don't know. The hardest part of all of this is … well, everything. Even just seeing his handwriting. It's the same handwriting on notes passed to me in high school. The only handwriting that's ever written 'I love you.'" I shook my head. "He's the only man I've ever loved. But the entire thing was a lie, and I'm the fool who believed it. The fool who was suckered for years into thinking I'd found my dream guy."

Rose rested her elbows on the table. "You don't think he loved you?"

I dragged in a breath and let it go. "No, I suppose he loved me in his way. Loves me, if his note is true. But I don't know that he's capable of giving me what I want, giving me what he promised me when he put that ring on my finger. I believe he loves me, but I don't believe he respects me. If he did, he wouldn't have ever cheated. I just don't know why he won't let me go. Why would he do this to me? He's already hurt me enough, and it's not like I've been stringing him along. I haven't even spoken to him. I thought moving two thousand miles away would solidify my stance on our relationship."

Lily nodded. "I'm sure he's sad and hurt, feeling guilty."

My brow dropped at the thought, my hurt burning fresh. "I don't pity him. I hope he regrets what he did to me every day for the rest of his life. The more I consider his motivation for sending that fucking box — which was selfish, because of course it was — the angrier I get. I was trying to move on, get over it."

"But you weren't, really." Rose pointed out.

"No, I wasn't. But I was trying to. Pretending to. If I ignored it long enough, it would have just been behind me one day, wouldn't it have?" I knew how delusional it sounded the second it left my mouth, but funny enough, it'd always been something I'd considered an actual solution.

Rose sighed and picked at the placemat. "It doesn't work that way in my experience. Your hurt just hangs around in some dark corner of your mind until something triggers it. And then, it explodes."

I blew out a long breath, realizing how dumb I'd been. "Like last night."

"Yes, like last night." Lily paused. "Are you going to answer Jimmy? Call him?"

Dread snaked through me. "I don't know."

She picked up her drink. "I think what you need is closure."

The word sounded like a promise, laced with hope. "But how?"

Lily shook her head. "I don't know, but I think it's the only way you'll get through it, or at least the fastest way. Time can only do so much, you know? I mean, you can hide out, but look at how that's going. He sent a letter and a box full of things that you already knew existed in the world, and you hyperventilated until you passed out. When was the last time you talked to him? Like, *really* talked to him?"

"Just before I left. He came over again, and Daddy sent him packing."

Rose raised an eyebrow. "That doesn't sound like you really talked to him. What happened after the wedding?"

"He came over the next day, but I got so upset when we tried to talk that I nearly had a panic attack. Daddy told him not to come back."

"And then what happened?" Lily asked. "When did you see him after that?"

"I didn't. I stayed home a lot, avoided the places I knew he went."

"So," Rose leaned on the table, "you mean to say that you never really sat down and talked to Jimmy about everything?"

"I guess not," I answered quietly. "I didn't have to handle anything, really. Mom sent all the gifts back, Daddy handled all the money. I got through the reception and then it was almost like it never happened. Except he'd come by, text me, call me. I just ignored him. I ignored everyone, and then I ran away."

Lily's eyes were sad. No one spoke, so I kept going.

"I didn't know what to say to him. I just wanted him to go away, disappear. It's why I moved here, you know that."

"And he hasn't let you go. He's not going to either, I'd bet. Not until you deal with him." Lily said.

"So … I should call him?"

She sighed. "I don't know."

Rose took a deep breath. "You've got to find a way to face it because if you don't, it'll just keep following you around like a ghost. Just when you think it's gone, that you're better, *wham*. Something happens and kicks you straight back to rock bottom."

"Same thing happened when my grandmother died," Lily said. "I didn't cry for weeks. Spent all that time distracting myself, rehearsed extra hours, watched a ton of movies. And then, one day, I found her old scarf in my drawer, and I cried for two days straight. It's unpredictable, grief."

"But it's not so sad as someone dying."

"That doesn't mean you're not grieving. You're mourning the relationship. It's the future you constructed that died, and in the end, you still lost someone you love."

I took a breath and picked up my drink, blinking back tears. "So how do I get closure? What do I have to do? Because there has to be something. I can't just sit around waiting for another meltdown."

Rose shook her head. "If you don't find a way to shut him down once and for all then it's definitely going to happen again."

"What do I even tell him? I obviously don't want to be with him. I don't want to try again. I don't want to hear what he has to say. What if he begs? What if somehow he convinces me … tells me … what if I…"

"Go back to him?" Lily asked. "I don't think you'd do that. Do you?"

"I honestly don't even know right now. I don't trust myself, not with him and not with Cooper, and for entirely separate reasons." I took a drink, almost killing it. Rose reached for it, and I waved her off.

Lily brought a knee up. "And what reasons are those?"

"I'm afraid Jimmy will convince me to come back, and I'm afraid to care about Cooper."

"It might be too late for that," Rose said.

"Might be. But I'm scared I'll make it worse. I don't want to hurt him."

"Might be too late for that, too," Lily added.

"Which is exactly why I walked away from him today. I can't be responsible for someone else's feelings right now, not when I can't even deal with my own."

Rose sighed. "This sucks."

"Tell me about it." I tipped my drink back until it was gone and set the glass on the table. "So, I've got to talk to Jimmy."

Lily shrugged. "Doesn't seem like he's going anywhere. Ghosting him isn't really an option. And anyway, ghosting is for pussies."

"Ghosting?" I asked.

She pushed her hair over her shoulder. "Yeah, you know, when someone just disappears out of your life? Like they vanish, stop texting, unfollow you on social media. It's basically a way for people to puss out of dealing with their relationships by running away instead of facing the other person and explaining themselves. You're better than that. You can face him. Let him beg. You're not going to forget what he did to you. You won't forget the hurt. But you can close the door so you can move on."

I nodded, staring into the amber liquid in my glass. "I'm going to have to prep myself for this. Hard."

"Well," Lily said with a smile, "luckily you have all the time you need. And you have two friends armed with an offensive sense of humor and lots and lots of alcohol."

I chuckled. "Well, if that's waiting for me at the end of all this, then maybe I'll be okay."

"Oh, you'll definitely be okay," she said, and part of me actually believed it was true.

Give and Take

MAGGIE

It had been a long day.

I walked out of Susan's office that afternoon, dragging myself through the shelter like a dead woman. I'd come in on my day off, not wanting to be alone with my thoughts. I wanted to work, focus, put my heart into lesson plans and prepping crafts for the kids. So, in an attempt to be productive, I'd been cutting pipe cleaners and yarn, tracing shapes onto construction paper and organizing the new supplies Catherine sent over.

God knew what I'd have been doing if I'd been home alone. Probably crying at The Notebook and eating Tootsie Rolls, which actually sounded fantastic. Plan for the night: acquired.

I walked into the empty office, my brow dropping as I approached the table where I'd been working. I didn't see my bag where I'd left it, not after circling the table or digging through my big plastic bin of supplies in the hopes that I'd somehow lost my mind and put it in there. No bag — not on the ground, not on any of the chairs. My heart beat faster as I opened the cabinets, checked under every desk, in every corner.

It was gone.

I knew I hadn't left it anywhere else, but I flew through the building all the same, checking the common rooms before blowing through the halls, into the kitchen. Brian stood behind the gigantic flat top with about thirty chicken breasts sizzling in front of him.

His brow dropped when he saw me. "Hey, Maggie. You okay?"

"No," I heard the tremor in my voice. "I can't find my bag, not anywhere. Have you seen it? It's dark brown leather, a messenger bag?"

He called over another volunteer to take his place at the flat top before heading over to me. "We'll find it. I'm sure it's here somewhere."

I nodded and followed him out of the room. Susan had left for the day, so we searched everywhere together, and my panic grew with every minute. Everything I needed — all the things I used every single day — it was all in that bag. My phone. Keys. Books. Wallet. At least I'd left my laptop at home. I stood in the middle of the office as we checked it for the fourth time, watching Brian pull out a desk to look behind it.

"It's not here," I said softly. "Someone took it."

He looked over his shoulder at me as he scooted the desk back. "Maybe it'll turn up."

"Sure, maybe."

He walked over to me, stepped close. "Is there anyone we can call?"

There was only one number beside my parents' that I knew by heart — my brother's. And that I-told-you-so would be bitter and harsh. I wasn't equipped to deal with that, not today, not in that moment. So, I shook my head and gave him a weak smile. "I don't know anyone's number. They were all in my phone, and my phone was in my bag."

He nodded with decision. "Let me get you home. I'll catch us a cab and ride with you to make sure you can get into your apartment. Is anyone there to let you in?"

I glanced at the clock — it was almost five. Lily was still at work, and West was at school. Rose and Patrick may or may not be home. There was no way to know, and if I went all the way over there with nothing, and no one was there, I didn't know what I'd do.

But there was one person who I knew was probably home.

"I have a friend who lives a few blocks away, and he has a key. I'll start there."

His brow was low. "I don't know. Are you sure you'll be okay? I don't like the idea of you walking around Manhattan without a phone or money. Can I at least give you some cash?"

I waved a hand. "I'll be fine. If no one's home, I'll come back here and take you up on your offer."

He pulled out his wallet. "No, I insist. If you're not going to let me get you home, at least take this." He handed me a twenty. "It would make me feel a lot better to know you could at least get a cab."

I sighed. He was right. I took the twenty and folded it, slipping it into my pocket. "Thank you, Brian. Really."

"I'm sorry that this happened. I'll talk to Susan, see if we can't figure out what's going on."

"All right. I should get going while it's still light out."

"Listen, when you get home, find a phone and text yourself from the number you want me to call, just in case we find it."

"Okay. Thanks again."

"Sure thing," he said. "Come back if you need anything. I'll be here for a few more hours."

I walked out of the room and out of the building, feeling lost, naked. Alone. I never set foot out of my apartment without the things in that bag, and now I was walking through the city with nothing but a twenty dollar bill in my pocket and the clothes on my back. Walking toward Cooper's house.

Looking back, I should have taken a cab. I should have hailed a

CHASER

cab and gone home and prayed someone was there to let me in. But I didn't. Instead, I walked those blocks, thinking of all the reasons to go to him and all the reasons to walk away.

Reasons. Rules. Justifications I wore like armor to protect myself, to hide behind. I had been resolved, dug in my heels believing I was doing the right thing with every decision I made. But I didn't know what was right or wrong anymore. I didn't know what I wanted or what I needed.

I was still two blocks away when the sky opened up, first with fat, heavy drops, slow and steady, then faster, harder until it was raining in sheets. I could barely see. There was no awning, nowhere to wait out the deluge, so I hurried on, my hair hanging in my face, shoes slapping the pavement and clothes plastered to my body as I ran toward his building.

And the rain washed away my resolve. It washed away everything I thought I knew in rivulets and heavy drops, and the icy truth soaked through me, into my bones, so sharp that I split open. And what was left exposed was a scared little girl.

The doorman's eyes bugged when he saw me approaching. "Are you all right, Miss Williams?"

I wrapped my arms around myself and nodded as I stepped under the canopy. "Just a little wet, thank you."

He pulled open the door, and I ducked through shivering, my sneakers squeaking on the marble floor, across the big gold compass. He pressed the call button and stepped into the elevator, waving his fob over the pad.

"Just let me know if you need anything, miss."

"Thank you."

He tipped his hat and stepped out as the elevator doors closed. The only sounds were the chattering of my teeth and the hum of the motor as I rode up to his floor, stripped down and bare, my eyes on the seam of the doors and my heart frozen in my chest.

COOPER

he doorbell rang, and I got up, confused as I walked to the door, heartbroken when I opened it.

Maggie stood in my entryway, dripping wet, her curly hair hanging long and limp, her eyes wide and shiny. Her chin quivered, though I wasn't sure if it was from her chattering teeth or the tears brimming in her eyes. Maybe both.

I reached for her, chest aching as I touched her freezing arm. "What's wrong? What happened?"

She looked up at me, her brows knit together, voice soft, uncertain. "I … I'm sorry to barge in on you, it's just that my bag was stolen at work today, and I didn't know where else to go. I couldn't call West, and I didn't have any money or my phone or anything, and I just didn't know what else to do." The word trailed off, and she took a shaky breath.

"It's all right, you don't have to apologize. Come in." I guided her in and closed the door, glad to have something tangible I could do to help her, glad she was all right, if not cold and scared. "Let me get you a towel."

She followed me to the linen closet in the hallway, and I pulled out a fluffy gray towel. I handed it over, and she took it with trembling hands.

"What can I do?" I asked gently.

"I … don't know."

"Do you want me to take you home? Or you can shower here, and I can dry your clothes?"

She shook her head. "I don't know."

"I can't help you if I don't know what you need."

Maggie looked up at me with eyes so big, so bright, so full of pain and fear and sadness. I realized then that this wasn't just about her bag or the rain. It was about Maggie.

She leaned toward me, calling me without speaking a word.

I stepped into her, slipped a hand into her soaking hair and searched her face.

"Tell me what you need, Maggie," I whispered.

But she didn't answer, just reached for me, closed the distance between us as she drew in a breath and pressed her lips to mine.

That kiss told me she needed me. And there was nothing left to do but give myself to her.

So I wrapped her in my arms as if they could save her, kissed her as if I could replace her pain with my love.

My hands roamed down her back, and I picked her up, carried her to my bedroom and laid her down, our lips never parting. Her hands scrambled for the hem of my shirt and peeled it off, and I did the same, unhooking her bra and tossing it away. I looked down at her stretched out on my bed, laid my hand on the flat of her stomach and dragged it down to the button of her jeans.

I unzipped them. I peeled them off. My hungry eyes roamed her shivering body, down to her panties, soaked from the rain, transparent.

"Please, don't stop," she begged.

I couldn't deny her. I kicked off my pants and underwear, stripped off her panties and crawled up her naked body, my hot skin against her cold, dragging my lips up her stomach, her breasts, her neck. My knee slipped between her thighs, and the moment I lay against her, the shivering stopped. She wrapped herself around me as I flexed my hips, pressing her into the bed, my lips against hers demanding and accepting, giving and taking.

She trailed her hands around to my ass, dragged her nails across my skin, around my hips.

"Please," she breathed, her eyes sparking with emotion.

I met her urgent mouth as she pulled me into her, rolling her hips. I knew what she wanted — I wanted the same — and I shifted, resting my crown at the very edge of her. When I flexed, I couldn't breathe, just looked into her eyes, slipping in slowly until there was no space between us.

Her eyes closed with a sigh as I pulled out and slammed back in. She reached for me, pulled me down to meet her lips. And I kissed her, and she kissed me, with frantic breath and a broken heart. I felt everything — her heart, her body — and I took her and gave myself to her, claimed her and surrendered to her with every motion.

Her breath quickened, her body flexed, and then she came with a gasp, pink lips stretched, brows drawn, eyes pinned shut. I was right behind her, my hand gripping her thigh as I thrust into her again.

I buried my face in her neck as she wrapped her arms around mine, wishing I could stay just like that forever.

Her breath hitched, and I pulled away to find her crying. My hands were in her hair, my eyes searching her face, my heart aching in my chest.

"Don't cry. Please."

"I'm sorry."

I thumbed her cheek. "You don't have to apologize to me, Maggie. There's nothing to be sorry for."

"I shouldn't be here." She looked away.

"Why?" I moved her face to look at me again.

"Because this isn't fair to you."

"I don't care. You needed me."

She shook her head. "I needed your help. *This* wasn't supposed to happen."

A tingle worked down my neck. "Do you regret it?"

She didn't answer.

"Do you regret me? Answer me, Maggie."

"I don't know what you want me to say." Her voice broke.

I rolled off of her, heart on fire as I picked up my pants and pulled them on, whirling around to face her. "You said you needed time, and I told you take it. I told you I'd be here for you, and I will. But I didn't ask for this. *You* came here. You took what you wanted, and right now you're looking at me like you're ashamed of me, of us." My muscles trembled, tense and taught. "You're killing me, Maggie, and I can't pretend that everything's fine. Not right now. Not after that. I love you, can't you see that? I love you and I need you. But I refuse to just be another mistake you've made."

Her cheeks were red, lips flat as she blew out of bed and snatched her jeans off the ground. "You don't love me."

"Don't tell me how I feel."

Her face was hard when she turned around. "Everyone knows you don't fall in love, Cooper … that was the whole point. It was the only reason why I agreed to this in the first place — you don't *feel*. That was why this was supposed to work. No feelings. No strings. What happened to that?"

"Don't throw that at me, Maggie. Don't hide behind some bullshit rules that you invented to make yourself feel better for wanting me."

"Screw you, Cooper." She pulled on her pants and snatched up her clothes.

I stepped toward her, chin down. "I know you're afraid of me, of this. You're lying to yourself, and you're lying to me. You want me just as much as I want you."

"Don't tell me how I feel." She threw my words back at me and stormed out of the room, pulling on her shirt and shoes as I followed her through my apartment.

No way was I letting her walk away that easy. "Do you think this is some sort of game to me?"

She kept walking. "Track record, Cooper."

"And you honestly believe that I put you and them in the same category? That I feel for *you* what I feel for *them*?"

She reached the front door and turned on me, face hard, eyes steely. "How the hell should I know? I'm just another girl in a long line of girls. You can tell me I'm different until the end of time, and I don't know if I'll ever believe you. You don't love me. You don't love anyone but yourself." She shook her head at me. "This was a mistake. The whole thing was a mistake, and I should have known better."

There it was. The truth. I couldn't move, couldn't speak as bitter cold blew through me. I watched her for a moment, trying to breathe. There was nothing left to say.

I swallowed hard. "You should go. Bobby's downstairs — he'll take you home."

She watched me, emotion passing across her face. "Cooper—"

"Just go, Maggie. You said it yourself. I'm just a bad decision you made. A mistake. A distraction. I don't mean anything to you, so just fucking go." I opened the door.

She took a breath and stepped into the entryway. I closed the door just as she looked back over her shoulder.

My hands trembled as I walked back into my apartment, paced from one end to the other with my mind spinning so fast, I couldn't catch a single thought.

She didn't trust me. She didn't believe me.

I didn't know how it was possible after everything, after all the change in my heart and mind and *life*. I couldn't comprehend how she didn't see it. How something that was so true to me could be lost on her, the one person who I needed to understand.

She had changed me on the molecular level, and she had no idea.

In my entire life, she was the one thing that I was certain of, and I'd do anything to keep her. She was scared and confused, but I wasn't. I knew exactly what I wanted, and it was her.

I would spend the rest of my life trying to convince her that I wasn't a mistake at all. I'd convince her that she was the only girl in that line of girls. I'd convince her that I loved her far more than I could ever love myself.

I had to tell her. I picked up my phone, pulling up her contact before I realized her phone was missing.

"Fuck." I muttered and paced back through the room. *Bobby*. I pulled up his contact and called.

"Hey, Coop," he answered.

"Is she with you?"

"No, I'm still outside," he said, confused. "She never came down."

I ran a hand over my face, wondering where she'd gone. "I'll be right down."

Seconds later I was headed out the door. The doorman said he put her in a cab and sent her home, and I thanked him before trotting through the lobby and out the back door. And then we drove to her as I stared out the window, thinking of all the things I needed to say, hoping I wouldn't find West there.

I wasn't afraid of him.

I wasn't afraid of anything but losing her.

MAGGIE

The tears didn't stop in the elevator or as I climbed into a cab, not as I rode through the park with the sky on fire as the sun set. I'd stopped trying to wipe them away. More always came.

What have I done?

It was the question that rolled through my mind in a loop.

I shouldn't have gone there, not in the state I was in. I shouldn't have slept with him, but in his arms, I was safe, even if just for a moment. It was a mistake, but not like it sounded. It was a mistake because I'd hurt him.

He told me he loved me. He said it with his voice tight from his pain, his face bent in emotion. He said the words, and I threw them back at him.

I pushed him away because he was right. I hurt him because I was afraid.

Fucked up. Broken. Smashed. I couldn't be trusted with his heart. I couldn't even be trusted with mine.

The cab stopped in front of my building, and I paid him, thanking him quietly before climbing out. I walked to the building feeling like my world had stopped turning, though everyone else went about as if things were fine, normal. I climbed the stairs and knocked on my door.

Lily answered, and her face fell when she saw me. She pulled me into the apartment.

"Maggie, what happened?" She looked me over. "Where's your stuff? Why are you wet?"

"I …" I squeaked.

West stood when he saw me, flew across the room, held me by the arms and ducked down to look me in the eye. "What happened, Mags? Are you all right?"

I nodded, but my face twisted as I tried to hold in a sob, any composure I had gone. He tucked me into his chest, and I felt Lily's hand on my back.

"Where are your things?" he asked gently.

I took a breath as hot tears rolled down my cheeks. "They went missing at work."

His body tensed. "Someone stole them? Dammit, I knew that job was going to be dangerous for you."

Lily's voice was soft. "Not now, West."

He let out a breath and squeezed me tighter. "I'm sorry, Maggie. I'm sorry this happened."

I looked over at Lily, feeling her questions. I gave her the slightest nod, and she closed her eyes for a brief moment.

"How did you get home?" West asked and let me go.

"I walked."

"Why didn't you call me?" His dark brow was low, and he shook his head.

"Because I knew you'd lose your mind."

"You make me sound like a tyrant."

I gave him a look.

His face softened with his voice. "If you need me, call me. Don't walk home again with no money, no phone."

Someone knocked on the door, and shock shot through me as I spun around, staring at it like it might explode. It was him. I knew it, and when Lily looked at me, I knew she knew too. Her eyes darted to West before she walked to the door and pulled it open.

Cooper was a burning man, the pain on his face unmistakable. His eyes found mine, and my heart stopped dead.

"Cooper?" West asked, confused. "What's up, man?"

But his eyes were on me, and mine were on him. I shook my head.

"I need to talk to you," he said.

West looked down at me. "Talk about what? What's going on?"

"You shouldn't have come here." My voice trembled. Our eyes were still locked as panic rolled through me.

"Please. You have to hear me out."

The tears were back, burning my eyes. "You told me to leave, so I did."

"I was wrong." He walked into the room and toward me like

nothing could stop him.

But there was one thing that could. West stepped in front of me, cutting Cooper off. Lily flanked West, eyes wide and bouncing between the two men.

West's jaw was set. "I said, what the fuck is going on?"

Cooper finally looked away from me. "I need to talk to Maggie."

West folded his arms across his chest. "What about?"

"Let it go, West." He looked to me. "Come with me, please."

His shoulders were square, body tight. "She's not going anywhere until you tell me what the hell this is all about."

Cooper's eyes narrowed. "That's not your decision to make."

Lily touched West's arm. "Guys—"

The tension crackled between Cooper and West, and I was the only one who could defuse it. I had to defuse it. I put out a hand and stepped forward. "Stop it, both of you. I'll come with you, Cooper."

West glared at me. "Why?"

Cooper shook his head and tried to step around. "Jesus, West. Just let her go. She's a grown woman."

My eyes were full of tears, and West turned on Cooper, laying a heavy hand on his chest, his voice low and full of warning. "What did you do to her?"

Cooper's voice edged on frantic. "How do you know it was me who hurt her and not the other way around?"

"Are you …" West looked at me, confusion flickering across his face. "No. You two aren't …" He looked back at Cooper, muttering, "You fucking wouldn't. You'd never …"

Cooper shook his head, eyes open and honest, brow bent. "I love her, West," he said as if the words would absolve him, save him.

My heart broke. West's calm broke. Everything happened fast and slow somehow. The flash of West's arm as he cocked a fist and released it like a spring. The flash of blood on Cooper's face. The flash of Lily's hair as she ran to get between them. And through it all, I couldn't move, just stood rooted to the spot, watching it all happen.

West strained against Lily, who put all her weight into his chest. "Fuck you, Cooper, you son of a bitch. I can't fucking believe that you would do this. This *one fucking thing* I told you never to do. One thing. Get out. Get the fuck out, or I swear to God, I will bury you."

Lily glanced frantically over her shoulder. "Cooper, go. You shouldn't have come, not like this."

But Cooper was watching me, his eyes burning with anguish, chest heaving and nose bloodied. "You have to know how I feel about you. I've only ever told you the truth. I've been trying to prove myself to you every day — prove to you that you can trust me. That I won't hurt you. Time is the last thing I want to give you, but I will because that's what you need, because that's what you asked me for. If fighting for you means that I have to stay away, then I'll leave. But don't question my feelings for you. Don't ever question that." His voice faltered.

I wanted to run to him. I wanted to run away from him. But I couldn't bring my feet to move.

He looked back to West. "I would never do anything to betray you, and you know it, West. You know that." His eyes found mine again. "Don't let this be the end, Maggie."

"Go, Cooper. Now." West growled, fists clenched at his side.

"I'm sorry," he said to both of us.

"I don't want to fucking hear it."

Cooper's jaw flexed, and he nodded, looking to me once more for a moment that seemed to stretch on longer than it was. And then he turned and walked out the door.

West spun around, turning his fury on me. "What the fuck, Maggie? Why? Why Cooper? You had all of New York to choose from, and you picked the one guy who we all knew you couldn't trust.

Fucking *Cooper*."

I took a breath to speak, but West closed his eyes, waved a hand as he turned away.

"You know what? I don't even want to know." He stepped toward the door and muttered, "I've got to get out of here."

Lily touched his arm, but he shook her off.

"You knew about this, didn't you?"

She opened her mouth, the apology on her face clear. He stopped her before she spoke.

"You did. Goddammit, Lily. *Goddammit.*" He shook his head at us, hurt. Betrayed. And then he walked out the door, slamming it behind him.

Lily turned to me with tears in her eyes. "Fuck." She said under her breath. "Why did he come here? What happened?"

I took a shuddering breath and tried to explain. "My bag was stolen, and I had nothing. I couldn't call West, you know? So I went to Cooper's, and … I … I said some horrible things to him and then he told me to leave, so I did," I rambled, the tears falling again.

Lily sat down at the table and dropped her head into her hands. "We fucked up."

I just stared at the door, regretting everything. "No, I did."

Born to Run

looked out the window of the plane the next morning, across the tops of the clouds, down at the ground that stretched out in patches cut by roads and rivers. It was hard to grasp just how far away things were, grasp the scale of it all from so high. Everything was distorted by distance, making it feel more familiar than it was. What looked like a tree was really a copse. What looked like a house was a neighborhood.

Distance changed everything. Or at least that was what I was hoping.

I'd waited until Lily was gone, feigning sleep even as I felt her willing me to get up. And once she was gone, I packed my suitcase, wrote a letter to my friends, and took a cab to the shelter. In the wake of the explosion the night before, I texted my phone from Lily's and received a message back within minutes. One of the kids had taken my bag, hidden it in his parents' room in the shelter. Everything was intact and in place, and I hung it on my shoulder, feeling like some balance had been restored.

And so I told them I was leaving. Susan assured me that my job would be waiting for me, so long as I could work remotely on lesson plans that another volunteer would implement.

I thought about the letter I'd left on the table, the apology that wouldn't ever be enough. But it was the best I could do. I couldn't risk ruining anything else. I'd hurt everyone, exploded everything. Cooper. West. Lily. And there was only thing left to do.

Leave.

So I bought a ticket that cost three times what it should have. I boarded the plane and left the city behind. Left my friends behind. I left Cooper behind.

The clouds in the distance stretched up, casting massive shadows on the ground below. I had tried to read my book, but nothing could hold my attention. I tried to write in an attempt to purge the emotion, but nothing came. So I stared out the window with my earbuds buried in my ears as I watched the world pass by.

The only person I'd spoken to was my father, who had agreed to pick me up at the airport and not to tell West. I didn't want him to find out until Lily did — after I was long gone.

The plane descended, and I watched the roads and trees below, marveling as they came into focus that they were so much farther away than I'd realized. And we landed and pulled up to the terminal, waiting patiently as the travelers filed out in a stream occasionally broken by someone digging in an overhead compartment. The humidity hit me before I reached the door, nearly swallowed me up as I walked through the ramp and into the terminal.

My father was waiting for me in baggage — I saw him the second I stepped into the room, standing against the wall with his hands in the pockets of his slacks. He was long and lean, like a blond West with a beard to match, though Daddy's was more grey than it was blond. He saw me and pushed off the wall, eyes sad behind his thick-framed glasses.

Just the sight of him summoned the tears. I rubbed my nose, hoping I could keep them at bay.

"Hey, baby," he said as he approached, opening his arms to hug me, and any hope I had was lost.

The tears fell hot and steady as I stood the baggage claim, tucked into my father's chest as he rocked me gently.

"Shh. It's okay. It's gonna be okay."

I wanted to believe him more than anything. The worst of it had passed after a minute or two, and I pulled away, sniffling, brushing away tears. "I'm s-sorry."

He held me at arm's length, his face soft. "It's all right. Don't be sorry."

"Have you heard from West?"

"Not yet." He shook his head, not pressing me for more as we walked over to the carousel just as it dinged and began to turn. A bag slid down the metal ramp with a zip and a thump, and everyone converged to the edges of the machine with eager eyes.

I twisted my fingers together. "Thank you. For letting me come home again and all."

He smiled down at me. "You expected us to turn you away?"

I tried to smile back. "Not exactly. But I know it hasn't been easy having me popping in and out of your space over the last few months."

"Your mom and I understand. I'm just glad we can be there to hold you up when you fall. Been doing it since you started walking. Feels just as good to protect you now as it did then."

I took a deep breath and let it out.

He watched me. "You gonna tell me what this is all about?"

My eyes were on the pile of duffle bags and suitcases heading toward us. "I will."

"Because it seems it's more than just a simple visit."

"Can't a girl just miss her dad?"

"Oh, sure." He bobbed his head. "But usually that warrants more than a six hour notice."

I sighed. "I know. I'm sorry to derail your entire day."

"Quit apologizing." My bag rounded the bend, and Dad stepped up to grab it from the carousel. "Come on, kiddo. Your mom's waiting for us at home. I think she made cookies."

I laughed. "She would."

"Yes, she would."

We walked out of baggage and through the sliding doors, toward the parking lot. "How do you like the new job?"

"It feels good to be doing something productive again, you know? I feel like I've just been useless for ages, so going to the shelter and seeing the smiling faces of those kids makes me feel ... I don't know. Needed. Like I was making their lives better, somehow. It made me remember why I loved teaching."

He smiled down at me. "That right there is why I'm glad you got outta here. You needed that reminder that this isn't all there is in the world."

"I only wish I'd gotten the job sooner."

"And they were okay with you leaving for ... how long are you staying?"

"I don't know yet."

He nodded. "Well, your room's still just like you left it. Your mom can't figure out what she wants to do with it. I think she just doesn't want to admit that her kids have all left the roost permanently." He gave me an apologetic smile. "*Semi*-permanently."

We reached his vintage truck — a black and grey 1965 Ford F-100 — and he laid my suitcase down in the bed before we climbed in. The old truck rumbled when he started it and backed out of the spot.

We didn't say much on the way home. I just leaned on the door and watched out the window, everything so familiar. A few weeks hadn't changed a single thing, but everything was different. We drove into the suburbs, past the big box grocery stores and shopping strips, into the manicured neighborhood where I grew up, and came to a stop at the light into our subdivision, right across from the high school. School had just let out, and I watched the kids laughing and smiling, riding bikes, skateboarding, walking in packs. It was a walk I'd made hundreds of times with Jimmy by my side.

It was then that I wondered if coming home wasn't another mistake.

The light changed, and we pulled into our neighborhood, into our driveway. I followed him into the house I grew up in, the house that always smelled like gardenias, thanks to the multitude of candles Mom had going almost around the clock. She stepped out of the kitchen when she heard us and flew over to me.

"Come here, baby." She wrapped her arms around me and squeezed. "What in the world happened? Are you all right?" She backed away, still holding my arms, her bright eyes inspecting me.

"I'm … I'll be okay, I think."

"Well, I made cookies and sangria. You can have your pick — whichever one you think'll make you feel better."

"Maybe both?"

"That's just fine too. Come on and have a seat." She patted the bar stool at the island as she made her way to the counter.

I took a seat, watching her back as she filled the sangria glasses she'd already set out in preparation, and probably freshly hand washed, too. Because, you know, dust. She was just sort of *together* that way.

Dad sat down next to me.

"You want one too, Luke?" she asked and moved her curly black hair out of her face.

"Well, I don't want to get left out," he said with a smirk.

She smiled over her shoulder and finished pouring drinks, put them all on a tray with the cookies, and set them between all of us. She took one and leaned on the counter.

"So, tell us the story, Mags." She took a bite of her cookie, big blue eyes watching me.

I took a drink first, then set down my glass again with my eyes on an orange slice suspended in the sweet wine. "I sorta ruined everything."

"How do you figure?" Dad took a drink.

"Well …" I had no idea how to broach it. I shook my head. "I ran away from here to hide in New York. But I only just realized that I can't run away from something that's inside of me."

"Ah," Mom said knowingly. "Jimmy?"

"Partly. That's the biggest part of it, I suppose. But then … I was seeing someone."

Mom made a disapproving face.

"I know. That's not even the worst of it." I picked up my drink. "I was seeing Cooper Moore." That ice-cold wine felt good going down. I felt like I needed the whole pitcher to normalize.

Dad's brow dropped. "Pretty little rich boy, Cooper Moore? The one who won't settle down?"

I sighed. "The very one."

He shook his head. "No wonder you didn't want me to talk to West."

I slumped a little in my seat. "We tried to keep it from him, but he found out last night. I'd already ended things with Cooper. I mean, the timing was all wrong. Everything was all wrong. And then it blew up in my face. West is mad at us, even Lily because she knew. Cooper's hurt. I'm confused. I ruined everything. It just got so complicated, and I couldn't stay."

Mom watched me, adding gently. "But that's life, Maggie. It's sticky and ugly and complicated. If you keep running away, you'll never find your place."

"I know."

"What does any of that have to do with Jimmy?" she asked.

"He sent me a box of things, keepsakes, old pictures. My engagement ring. A letter. And there was no hiding from myself anymore. I just … I broke down, and I've been swinging like a pendulum ever since. I thought time would help, but after last night

… I couldn't stay. If it weren't for me, none of them would be hurt."

Dad's lips were flat. "That son of a bitch. He's done enough to hurt you, but he still keeps coming around like the goddamn tomcat he is, howlin' at the back door."

Mom gave him a look before turning to me. She handed me a cookie, which I accepted gratefully. I took a bite as she spoke. "Have you talked to Jimmy since you got the package?"

I shook my head and swallowed. "He texted me, but I hadn't decided how to handle him."

Dad gestured with his glass. "I'll handle him." He took a long sip.

"Oh, for goodness sake, Luke." Mom rolled her eyes. "Well, now you're here, so you have a whole new set of options when it comes to him. Think you might want to see him?"

"I don't *want* to see him, no. But I might need to. I just don't know if I'm ready yet."

"Honey, you might not ever be ready. Doesn't seem like you can afford to wait all that much longer."

I took another bite of my cookie, knowing she was right.

"Do you think you might stay for good?" she asked and ate the last bite of her cookie.

"I honestly don't know. I just knew I needed to get out of everyone's hair because I was all tangled up in it. Scissors were the only way out."

She dusted off her hands over the tray. "Well, your brother won't be mad at you forever. In fact, he's probably less mad at you than he is Cooper."

"Oh, he's plenty mad at Cooper — West nailed him in the face last night."

Mom snickered. "Of course he did. It's genetic. You should have seen your father when we were younger. Did you know he bloodied my prom date's nose?"

Dad frowned and pointed at her. "First off, you should have been at prom with *me*, and not Brad Wellington."

She waved him off. "I went home with you, didn't I?"

But Dad kept going. "Secondly, he was trying to Hoover your face on the dance floor, and I couldn't stand for that. You deserve better than to get mauled by that trout in the middle of a high school gym."

She gestured to him, giving me a look. "See what I mean?"

I chuckled and shook my head. "West is just so mad at all of us. Lily kept it from him because I asked her to. I shouldn't have put her in that position. I shouldn't have ever started seeing Cooper at all."

Mom shook her head. "Lily made her own choice, and I promise, West won't be mad at her for long either. You know he sees reason once he's finished seeing red. As for Cooper … well, I don't know what to tell you there."

I felt like a deflated balloon. "There's nothing to decide, not right now. I need to talk to West. I need to regroup. Lily said I need closure with Jimmy. So I've got to figure out how to chase that down."

"If he finds out you're here, you know he'll be over here in a heartbeat. Do you still want Dad to keep him away, or should we let him come?"

Dad looked thrilled. "Oh, please tell me you don't want him around."

I squirmed in my seat. "Can we decide if the time comes?"

"Of course," Mom answered.

I let out a breath. "All right."

"Well," she straightened up and smiled. "Daddy put ribs in the smoker, and I made peach cobbler, so we'll get you fed. If nothing else, your stomach will be happy."

"I will gladly eat my feelings for a few days."

"Good." She chuckled, her eyes soft. "Maggie, all of this is temporary. You'll feel better being alone, but your problems won't go away. They've got a knack for sneaking in when you're not looking to knock you on your ass. So take all the time you need, but don't hide anymore."

"All right."

She searched my face. "We just want you to be whole again, baby."

My nose burned. "Thanks, Mom."

"You're welcome. Want some help with your suitcase? I think I heard your dad volunteer."

Dad snorted and made to get up.

I waved them off and slid off my stool. "Nah, I can get it. Thanks though. I'll go get unpacked."

They watched me leave, and I felt their worry and sadness, veiled by their warmth and humor. I climbed the stairs with my suitcase, walked into the room where I'd spent my childhood, the twin bed and posters, my vintage Barbie collection along the high shelf that ran around my room. I sat down in the bay window seat and looked out into the yard.

Up in my room, I felt safe again, as if being within those walls erased my problems, exempted me from grown-up responsibility.

I only wished it were true.

COOPER

The room was almost completely dark, and I sat in the leather chair where I'd been for … I didn't know how long. I was unshaven, still in the clothes I'd slept in, scotch in my hand and an empty bottle on the ground next to me, my chair turned to face the print of Gambit and Rogue's first kiss.

Their story was bittersweet. Rogue could never be with Gambit — not without killing him. Touching him would drain his life, his memories, his power. Kissing him would kill him. But he loved her all the same, even though he'd never really understood love before. He needed her. And when he thought the world was ending, he did the one thing — the only thing — he'd ever wanted to do.

He kissed her.

But the world didn't end, though Gambit nearly died, and Rogue tortured herself. She'd learned his secrets, secrets she would rather not have known, and when they finally came back together, he asked her to enter his mind again, so she would know his truth. No more secrets. No lies. They could leave the past behind them and move on, together.

But she couldn't do it. Wouldn't risk him. So she left him.

They were pulled together and apart, time after time, again and again. I'd never forget when he asked her to trust him, even though she had no reason to. He said he'd make it right the second he was able. Told her that her heart meant more to him than his own.

I knew just how he felt.

She'd haunted my dreams. Lived in my thoughts all day. I wanted to call her. I needed to see her. But I'd resigned myself to wait. There was no way to reach her, and I had to believe she would come to me when she was ready.

I wondered where she was, what she was doing. Wondered if she'd been thinking about me all day, wishing things were different. It's all I'd done since I walked away from her.

At least I had a cabinet full of scotch to help me pass the time, to help me forget.

I sighed and stood, my body stiff as I made my way into the kitchen for a scotch bottle that wasn't empty. My hand was on the neck of the lucky bottle when the doorbell rang.

My heart stopped. *Maggie.*

I set the bottle down with trembling hands, walked to the door in a haze, my neurons firing with a billion thoughts at once. What I'd say. What she'd say. How I'd feel. I could see her in my mind, angry, happy, sad, hurt.

I opened the door, and my heart fell.

West fumed in the entry, jaw set, eyes hard.

I squared my shoulders, dropped my chin. "Did your fist have more to say?"

"She's gone, and it's your fault."

I blinked, shook my head, wondered if I'd heard him right. "What do you mean, she's gone?"

"She left. She went home." He pulled a letter out of his pocket and shoved it into my chest.

I took it and unfurled it, feeling her presence in the curve of the letters as West brushed past me and into the room.

I'm so sorry for all the trouble I've caused. If I had stayed home where I belong, no one would have gotten hurt. I've been selfish at all of your expense.

I'm going back to Jackson to sort myself out. Lily, I'm sorry that I asked you to keep my secret from West. West, I'm sorry we lied to you. And Cooper, I'm just sorry.

I just hope you'll all forgive me.

—Maggie

"Fuck." I ran a hand through my hair as I stared at the letter. "How ... have you talked to her?"

"I called my dad as soon as Lily showed me the letter. They found her bag at the shelter, and she picked it up and went straight to the airport."

I walked to the bar and dropped into a seat, my eyes still on her words.

"What did you do to her, Cooper?"

"I just wanted to be with her."

"Bullshit. She didn't leave town because you care about her."

The look I gave him must have gotten to him because he shifted, looking uncertain.

"Then why?"

I shook my head, not knowing where to even start. "Jimmy." I ran a hand over my mouth. "He sent her that fucking box and knocked her out of orbit. She asked me for time to sort through it, but she came here yesterday and needed me, then turned around and treated me like a mistake. I couldn't fucking do it anymore, West. I couldn't go on having her one minute and losing her the next. This isn't some one night stand. This isn't a fling. I love her."

He eyed me. "Do you mean that?"

I didn't answer, just met his eyes and breathed.

"How the fuck is this possible?" West rubbed his forehead. "How the fuck are you telling me right now that you're actually in love with my sister? When did this happen?"

"It's been happening for weeks. Since before that, even."

His eyes narrowed. "Since when?"

I took a deep breath and told him. "Since her wedding night."

His fists clenched by his side, ears red and lips tight. "You fucking took advantage of her on *her wedding night?*"

I put out a hand. "Calm the fuck down, West. Are you listening to anything I've said? Anything? I wouldn't take advantage of her. I wouldn't do anything to hurt her because her happiness is more important than my own. I've never felt like this … you know I don't … I can't …" I couldn't even bring myself to say the words, so I took a breath. "Maggie is a singular event in my life. I want her. Forever."

He shook his head. "I can't fucking understand this. Does she feel the same way?"

"She said she did. We were going to tell you together when we came back from the Hamptons—"

He groaned. "Of course she was with you."

I glared at him. "Is this really the worst thing that could happen? I didn't fuck her and bail — I didn't break her. I'm trying to help put her back together, for chrissake. I love her. I want to help her. What the fuck is the problem here?"

West was quiet for a moment, still angry, but he'd heard me that time. I took the opening.

"You know I'd never do anything to hurt you. I'd never do anything to jeopardize our friendship. Ever. I wouldn't risk it unless I had no other choice. And I don't have a choice, not when it comes to Maggie."

He watched me.

I watched him back. "Do you believe me?"

His fist clenched again. "Yes."

"Can you stop eyeing me like you want to hit me?"

He took a heavy breath and rubbed his face as if he would wipe the look away. "I need a drink."

"That I can do." I got up and poured us each a scotch.

West took his and sipped it. If it hadn't been a three-hundred-dollar bottle, he probably would have slammed it.

I took a sip of mine and leaned on the counter. "Is she okay?"

He sighed and took a seat at the bar, looking tired. "It's hard to say. She wasn't busted up or crying or anything, which somehow makes me worry about her even more. I don't know. We didn't talk for long, and she wouldn't talk about you at all, past apologizing for keeping it from me and asking Lily to get in the middle of it."

"So you found out about Lily, huh?"

"Yeah, I didn't handle that well either." He took a drink and sat down. "I snapped at her and blew out of there. I was just so fucking pissed and shocked and ... I don't know. I hate that she kept that from me, but I get it. Y'all had me pegged right."

"We didn't want to tell you until we were sure we wanted to

STACI HART

be together. I can't say it was innocent from the start, because deep down, that first night, I knew. I just knew it was more than that. She needed me, and I saved her the only way I knew how."

He nodded at his drink with a sigh. "I'm sorry I punched you."

"I'm sorry I fucked your sister."

He glared at me.

I smirked. "Too soon?"

West snorted and brought the glass to his lips. "It'll probably always be too soon for that." He knocked it back.

"So what now?"

He sighed. "I don't know. I think we've gotta leave her be. Let her figure it out on her own. Be there if she needs us."

I took a drink, hating the plan and knowing he was right. "I've got to at least apologize."

"What for?"

"Chasing her. Pushing her. Trying to force her hand."

He shook his head. "You can try to call her, but I don't know if she'll talk to you."

"I don't either, but I have to try."

"Maybe sober up first. Don't waste your only bullet because you'd been drinking scotch for …" he sniffed, "eighteen hours."

I chuckled. "Probably wise." My smile fell. "Do you think she'll come back?"

He shook his head and sighed. "I don't know, man. I hope so. I really do."

Chances

MAGGIE

turned the page of Stardust the next day as I sat stretched out on my window seat. Our cocker spaniel Betty lay in my lap, breathing deeply as she slept.

Is this love, Tristan? I never imagined I'd know it for myself. My heart... It feels like my chest can barely contain it. Like it's trying to escape because it doesn't belong to me any more. It belongs to you. And if you wanted it, I'd wish for nothing in exchange - no gifts. No goods. No demonstrations of devotion. Nothing but knowing you loved me too. Just your heart, in exchange for mine.

I looked out my window at the red maple that was taller than the house, watching the helicopter seeds spin to the ground.

Just one heart in exchange for another. It seemed so simple, honest and easy. But it had to be equal. And whenever, however could you know that the person you gave yours to would care for it as they would their own?

I let out a breath, and my phone rang next to me. Betty's head snapped up, her eyes still sleepy, and she looked around for only a second before dropping her head back in my lap with a huff.

My fingers went numb when I saw it was Cooper. I blinked at the screen for a moment, not knowing what to do. Knowing I was almost out of time to decide as it rang again. I took a breath and answered.

"Hey," I said softly.

He was silent for a few seconds. "Are you all right?"

The sound of his voice nearly broke me. I closed my eyes and laid my head against the wall. "Not really."

"I'm sorry, Maggie. For everything."

"Me too."

"I shouldn't have followed you."

"No, you shouldn't have."

"I just couldn't let you go. I couldn't let it end there."

"I know." I had no other words.

Silence stretched between us, and I could feel his questions. "There's so much I want to say, and I feel like I shouldn't say any of it."

I looked out the window, wiped an errant tear from my cheek. "I can't do this right now."

"It doesn't have to be complicated, Maggie. Just tell me that you believe me. Tell me that you want me."

I do. "I can't." I pursed my lips to stop my chin from trembling. "I can't say the words you want to hear, no matter how much I want to. I spoke too soon once, and it hurt us both."

Silence.

"I'm broken, and I don't want to hurt you again. The only answer I have right now is time." Tears burned my eyes.

He drew a heavy breath. "Are you coming back?"

"I don't know."

"Well, let me know when you figure it out, okay?"

The seeds spun to the ground like tiny ballerinas. "I will."

The pause was long, heavy with things left unsaid. "I meant what I said about being here."

"I know."

When he spoke again after a moment, his voice was tight. "See you around, Mags."

"Goodbye, Cooper."

I set the phone down, swiping at the tears on my cheeks, wishing things were different. But I was where I was because of the choices I'd made. It was my own fault.

Betty looked up at me.

I cupped her muzzle. "How about a walk, Betty-girl?"

Her ears perked up, nub wagging.

"Yeah, I could use the fresh air too."

I slipped on a pair of flip flops, trotted down the stairs with Betty on my heels, and grabbed her leash from the hook in the entryway, trying to push everything away, leave it up in my room. As if I could turn my problems into a place. An object. Something tangible that I could bury or smash or drop into the ocean to disappear forever.

But that wasn't how it worked. I just didn't understand how it *did* work.

I clipped on Betty's leash, and we took off, heading for adventure in the form of rogue squirrels and interesting smelling grass. Something about being outside made me feel a hundred times better — the sky, the trees, the air — even though it was already unbearably humid. My hair was so out of control, I looked like I was part sheep, and I started sweating the second I stepped through the door. But with me and Betty out walking through the neighborhood like independent women, I felt more like myself.

We rounded a corner, and I nearly ran into Courtney Dixon. She looked borderline ridiculous walking her dog in full-on workout gear, one of those fancy, expensive brands that suburban women wore to Whole Foods and Starbucks even though they probably didn't even sweat in them. I knew her workout included exactly this — walking her dog through the neighborhood, trolling for boys, using her own ass as bait. She'd been doing it since we were thirteen. Her dark hair was pulled back in a tight ponytail, and her Rottweiler, Tank, had gotten himself all tangled up with Betty.

But neither one of us cared that our dogs looked like a jumbled-up knot of fur and leash. Because one of the last times we'd seen each other, she was in the middle of getting nailed by my fiancé.

Reasons why I hate living in my home town, number two. Number one starts with *J* and ends with *bastard*.

Her cheeks flushed. "Maggie? What are you doin' here? I thought you were in New York?"

Surprisingly, I found my voice, and I didn't sound like a mouse. "Came back to see Mom and Dad."

"How are they doin'?" She flipped her ponytail and smiled, trying to look casual. She was nervous as hell. The thought gave me comfort.

I smiled, going for polite, which was hopefully the fastest way out of the conversation. "Oh, they're great."

She avoided my eyes, turning to her dog. "Come here, Tank."

She bent, trying to unwind his leash from around Betty, who stood under Tank's legs, panting. Betty flopped down on the ground on top of Tank's leash, and I'm pretty sure she smiled at me.

Courtney glanced up at me. "A little help, Mags?"

I knelt down, smiling. "C'mere, Betty." She hauled herself up and relocated at my feet. I unwound the leash and looked up to find Courtney watching me, worrying over her bottom lip.

"I'm sorry I haven't called."

I stood up a little straighter. "Don't be. I wouldn't have answered if you had."

She wound the leash around her hand, watching her fingers. "I'm sorry for what we did, and all."

That numb feeling crawled through me like it always did. "I can't tell you it's all right."

"I know. It's just that … I … I've missed you. It's been hard without you here, without you in my life."

My brow furrowed, eyes narrowed. "Are you serious?"

She looked like she'd been slapped. "Of course I'm serious. We've been best friends since we were in diapers."

"Yeah, until you fucked my fiancé. On my wedding day. You made that choice, so I'm real sorry that you miss me and all, but maybe you should have thought about that." I shook my head at her. "I can't even believe you right now, Court."

Her brow dropped, cheeks red. "Jimmy's a whore, and he always has been. He would have fucked anybody — it wasn't just me. He slept with half of Madison County, for God's sake."

My chest was on fire. "Is that supposed to make me feel better?"

She hung a hand on her hip, shaking her head. "I'm just saying, Maggie. It wasn't personal."

I could barely breathe. "Not personal? What universe do you live in? That is absolutely the most personal it could have gotten. I saw your backstabbing vagina on my wedding day, and it was full of dick. *My fiancé's dick.*" I took a few steps away. "All that just goes to show that you were never my friend. And if you hadn't been fucking him at our wedding, it would have been a year from now, five years from now. I'd rather know that you were a traitor now than later. I mean, how long's it been going on? Were you giving him blow jobs behind the bleachers in high school? On the stacks in college?"

The look on her face kicked me in mine. It was true. But I just shook my head at her. She couldn't hurt me anymore, because she wasn't real. From her hair color to her lip gloss and fancy yoga pants. From the look on her face to her dirty heart. I'd always tried to see the good in her, just like I did Jimmy. Just like I did everyone, until they hurt me and I ran away. They'd made a fool out of me, took advantage of my willingness to trust them. I believed they were better than that. But I was wrong.

I shook my head and let out a breath as I backed away. "You were never my friend, and deep down, I knew it all along. You've always known exactly how to make someone feel like a fool. I just didn't expect you'd do it to me. But you know what? It makes perfect sense. You two deserve each other."

Her lip curled. "Ugh, bitch."

I turned and walked away with my heart pounding, feeling a few inches taller and a little more together, wondering if my problems weren't more tangible than I'd realized.

COOPER

Three days. Three days since I'd heard her voice. Three days of deafening silence.

I'd woken up from a dream yesterday, heart clanging, sweat beaded on my forehead, missing her. Wanting her. All I wanted was to lie in my bed in the dark indefinitely. But I didn't. I peeled myself out of bed and took a freezing cold shower. Walked through the park to try to find some peace, hoping the sunshine would burn away the thoughts of her.

It didn't work.

I came home and sat in my living room, watching the city through my windows as the sun set and the city lights blazed, with nothing but a bottle of scotch and memories of her to keep me company. It was the same place I found myself now, the next day, watching the grey clouds roll by, the rain that intermittently fell through the day, streaking my windows, blurring the city beyond.

My phone buzzed on the table next to me again, and I scooped it up, the hope flashing through me as it did every time my screen lit up. But it was just West again.

You can't stay home forever. Let's hit the court.

I messaged him back. *It's raining.*

When has that ever stopped us?

Right now.

Come on, man.

I set my phone down again.

Time. Space. Distance. Things that she needed. Things I had to give her. Because the only way to fight for her was to not fight at all. I had to let her go and hope to God she came back to me.

But letting her go was killing me.

I thought about her back home, wondered if Jimmy had tried to see her. He'd already reached out to her and said he wanted her back. I thought of him coming to her, telling her he was sorry, pictured her in his arms. Emotion rolled through me like a storm, lightning and rain, a gust of wind. And then it would burn down again, and I'd stare south at Midtown, my eyes on the skyline, though they didn't see a single thing.

It went so much deeper than just Maggie. I'd been hiding almost my whole life, hiding pieces of myself from everyone. But I hid nothing from Maggie — it was her superpower. She saw straight through me. And when I lost her, I lost the direction she'd given me, the feeling that I belonged. She was my compass. True North. Without her, the needle spun around and around, searching for that stopping point.

But she was gone.

Someone knocked on my door, and I looked over my shoulder, confused as I stood and walked over. When I opened it, I found West and Patrick in workout clothes with duffle bags slung across their chests. West pressed a basketball into my chest.

"Come on. We're playing."

I shook my head and pushed it back at him. "How many times do I have to say no?"

He brushed past me and into the apartment with a smile. "Apparently more than you already did. Get dressed."

Patrick smirked. "You should probably just do what he says."

I scowled and turned to find West spinning the basketball on his finger. "What the fuck, man. I said I don't feel like it. What do you want from me?" I closed the door.

"I want you to quit sitting around here licking your wounds. It's not doin' you any good."

"And you think me playing basketball will make everything better?"

"No, but at least you'll have a reason to shower."

I shook my head.

"Come on." He smiled. "It'll just be for a little while and then you can come back here and get back to puppy dogging."

Anger flashed through me. "This isn't a fucking joke. It's not a crush, West. You know that."

He met my eyes, smile falling. "I know. But there's nothing you can do about it right now, is there?"

"No. Not one fucking thing." My throat closed up, and I swallowed hard.

"Then what's the harm in coming to the courts with us and not thinking about it for a few hours?"

"What if I don't want to forget about it?"

He propped the ball on his hip. "You want to wallow. I get it. Just come on for a little while, and then I swear I'll leave you alone."

My jaw flexed. "Swear?"

He held up three fingers. "Scout's honor."

"Fine." The word was flat. It would be good to work, to sweat, to forget for a minute, at least. I turned and headed to my bedroom.

West turned to Patrick. "See? Told you I could get him to go."

I rolled my eyes and walked into my closet to change into a tank and basketball shorts, grabbing my shoes on the way out. West looked pleased with himself as I sat down and pulled one on.

"Don't look so smug." I tied my laces.

"Why not? You'll feel better."

"Maybe I want to be miserable." I shoved my foot into the other shoe.

"Yeah, well, it's kind of pathetic."

I pulled the knot tight. "Thanks."

"I'm just sayin'. Mopey Cooper is pretty fucking boring."

"Sorry I can't be the clown right now, but you're a great second-string." I grabbed my bag out of the hall closet and switched out the towel.

"I aim to please."

I made my way through the kitchen, packing water and a protein bar. "Have you talked to her?" I asked quietly.

He didn't answer right away. "Yeah."

I zipped up my bag with my eyes down. "Is she all right?"

"She will be."

I finally looked at him. "You're not going to tell me anything?"

"I don't know all that much, and if I did, do you really want to know?"

"I don't know. Do I?"

West shook his head. "Why torture yourself?"

"I just want to know what's going on with her."

"She's at home, and she's trying to get her head together. That's really all I can say."

My eyes narrowed. "Did she tell you not to talk to me?"

He put up a hand. "No. I mean that's all I know."

I rubbed my face, pressed my fingers into my eye sockets. "I'm sorry. I just … it's driving me crazy. I don't know what to do."

"I think getting out of the house is step one."

I almost smiled. "Maybe you're right."

"Oh, I'm definitely right. Can we go now? Because my whole

plan revolved around us not talking about your feelings."

That one got me. I cracked a smile. "All right, fine. And get ready, Stretch, because I've got the fire in my belly to beat you on the court."

Patrick snorted. "As if that's enough to take down the giant."

I felt a little better as we left the building, though the weight of everything pressed down on me like the clouds that hung over us, the air heavy, charged with the smell of rain. I focused my thoughts on the walk to the courts, the laughter of my friends, our feet against the damp pavement.

We set down our bags at the bench, and West and I went first. I was sweating within minutes, my mind devoid of any thoughts outside of the game. The thump of the ball against the pavement. The shuffle of our feet. Our huffing breath. I shot and missed. I shot and made it. I juked and dribbled around West, my focus tight.

The rain began to fall just hard enough to make things interesting, and I tightened my concentration so I could hang on to the ball, hang on to my footing.

I shot again and made it, and West hung his hands on his hips, huffing.

"Your game, Coop."

I dribbled and shook my head, not even realizing the game was over. I could count on one hand the number of times I'd beaten West. I barely cared. Just dribbled between my legs, not wanting to lose the focus that I'd found, like I'd mainlined willpower. I shot the ball, and it passed through the hoop without touching the rim.

West and Patrick shared a look.

"No gloating?" West asked. "You even find a way to gloat when you lose."

I grabbed the ball and dribbled some more. "Tricky, you're up."

West watched me as he took the bench and Tricky took his place. I tossed him the ball, and he checked it back to me. And then, I took off.

I was up and down the court, silent as we played. I could feel their worry, the expectations pressing on me from them. From Maggie. The public. My parents. From myself. And somewhere in the back of my mind, I realized that expectation had been crushing me for my whole life.

I'd built my own cage by believing the expectations were my truth, by giving them power. And I realized that I held the power to break free. I realized I had the strength to let go.

Patrick was all over me, the game more intense with every beat of the ball. I body checked him and spun away to shoot. I made it.

Patrick panted. "Game."

My lungs burned, chest heaving as sweat and rain rolled down my face. I bent, hands on my knees, staring at the blacktop before closing my eyes.

"Coop …" It was West, and I looked up to find him and Patrick in front of me with their eyes full of sorrow.

I shook my head and looked back at the ground. I'd burned the fog down, and I could see my future. I understood for the first time what it all meant, and I knew exactly what to do.

There were two things I realized in that moment of clarity.

I had to find a way to let Maggie go, and I needed to do everything I could to be the man she deserved. And I could do it. I could be everything for her, if she came back to me.

If she didn't, if she couldn't fix herself, I would fix myself in the hopes that maybe, someday, I would get another chance.

Split

MAGGIE

It was just after dusk, and the sky was bathed in purples and indigo as the sun slipped away. The lights were off in my room, and I sat curled up in my window seat with my eyes on the big maple tree just beyond. I'd watched the tree grow from a sapling to a behemoth, climbed its branches as a girl, kissed Jimmy goodbye under them when I grew up.

I'd spent my Monday working on plans for Susan, and based on her response, I knew I'd need to make a decision soon about what I was going to do.

It was the question everyone wanted the answer to, one of the many I didn't have.

I felt split in two, and the parts of me hadn't yet mended together. No, it wasn't even that. When Old Maggie and New Maggie smashed into each other, New Maggie was obliterated. Gone. And Old Maggie was left fractured from the impact. But every day I felt a little more together. A little bit closer. I just didn't know what I was getting closer to.

Closure, I supposed, that magical land I'd find when I was whole again.

It didn't help that my days were long and quiet, filled with reading and Netflix and my thoughts. Brooke was really the only person I'd seen besides Courtney — I'd avoided going out in public at all costs after I saw her, even though I was glad I did. If every day was a step toward closure, seeing Courtney was a long jump.

Every time I picked up my phone, I thought about calling Cooper. Texting him. Anything. I wanted to know if he was out there and missing me like I was missing him.

I sighed and pulled my blanket up a little higher.

I heard the rumble of his car before I saw it — it was a sound I didn't even realize I knew. But every nerve fired at once in a shock that sent ice down my spine.

Jimmy pulled into the driveway, and when he stepped out of his car, when I saw him — the angle of his jaw, the curve of his shoulders — I couldn't breathe. When he looked up at my window and our eyes met, I felt like I'd been shot.

My heart kickstarted in a jolt, and I spun out of my room and down the stairs. Dad was already opening the door, and I stopped dead.

Jimmy stood on the porch, tall and dark with his hair a little too long and a little too messy, eyes sad. A hundred memories with him flashed through my mind in a breath.

"Is she here, Luke?"

Dad's jaw flexed, eyes narrowed, but he glanced back at me for approval. I nodded, and he moved out of the way. He looked down at me as I approached.

"You just call if you need me."

"Thanks, Daddy."

He shot a last look at Jimmy, and when I stepped onto the porch and closed the door behind me, we were alone for the first time in a long time. I didn't know what to say, standing so close to him after so much had happened. I could smell him, the familiar smell of the boy who I'd shared a thousand nights with. But he wasn't the same. He was split in two, just like me. The boy I thought I knew and the man standing in front of me.

He shifted, his eyes soft. "I … I've missed you."

I needed something to do with my hands and clasped them behind my back, squeezing them until they almost hurt. "What do you want, Jimmy?"

"I heard you were back. I had to see for myself if it was true."

"Here I am," I said simply.

"Did you get my letter?"

"I did."

He watched me. "There has to be a chance for us, Maggie."

"You ruined that chance on our wedding day."

"I've loved you ever since I knew what love was. There was a moment when I realized that I loved you, that I was meant to be with you. Did you know?" The words were gentle. He reached for my arm — my left arm — and I let go of my fingers. His big hand slipped down my forearm, to my wrist, and he held my fingers, his thumb running over the place where my ring had once been. "It was just after a game we'd won, the one against Cary, sophomore year. Do you remember?"

"Yes," I whispered.

"After they took out Ben, Coach put me in to quarterback the end of the game. I'd never been so scared in my life, never wanted to prove my worth so much. I threw that touchdown, and we won. And afterward, when I was standing at the sidelines, covered in sweat, you ran up to me, jumped into my arms. Kissed me and cried and told me you loved me. And I knew right then that I wanted you to be a part of every joy in my life."

"Jimmy—" The word seared my throat.

"I've always loved you, Maggie. I just didn't know what that meant until you left me."

I swallowed hard. "I'm sorry it took you so long to figure that out."

"So am I. You've always been a part of my life. Always. Without you here, I can't find my footing. I don't know who I am without you. I love you."

Tears burned the corners of my eyes. "But that's not how love works. If you loved me, you never would have considered sleeping with someone else, never mind sleeping with *everyone* else. Love is about respect. It's about acceptance and protection. Trust. But you disrespected me. You rejected me when you slept with every one of those girls, and that crushed me, ruined me. I will never trust you again." My hand slipped out of his.

"None of them meant anything to me. None of them compared to you."

"Then why? Why would you do this to me?"

"That's what I've been trying to figure out. I don't have any excuses to give, only apologies. Only the promise that I would never do it again."

"How could I ever trust you again? What you did can't be undone."

"There has to be a way to prove it to you. To make you believe."

Cooper flashed through my mind, and I looked over the boy I used to love, thinking about the man who I left in New York, the differences between the two sharp and stark. They were nothing alike, that was all of a sudden so clear, it was blinding. "You shouldn't have to prove anything, Jimmy. It should be undeniably clear in every action you take, in every choice you make. I should never even *consider* doubting you because the truth is plain and simple. And your truth *is* plain and simple, it's just not the one you'd have me believe. You never loved me. You loved the idea of me. You got down on one knee and asked a specter to marry you."

His brow knit together, his eyes shining. "I'm sorry, Maggie. I'll do anything."

"You already did enough. I don't have anything left to give you. You took it all — took so much that you've left me empty. I have nothing left to give anyone because of you, because of what you've done. I should have seen it. I should have known. But I believed you, and you made a fool of me in front of everyone I've ever known."

"But there has to be a way for me to make it right."

The answer was clear. "There is. Let me go. Let me go, and leave me be. You can't claim me. You say you're sorry, that you don't want to hurt me, but every time you do this, you hurt me all over again. Every single time I think I'm patched together, you come back along and blow me back up."

His jaw was set, face tight with emotion. "Change your mind," he said softly.

"I can't. I won't. I'm not yours anymore."

His eyes searched my face for a long moment, and I saw him recognize the truth in it. "I understand. Maggie, I was wrong, and I'm sorry."

It was goodbye. Relief and sadness washed over me, and when he reached for me, I stepped into his arms, curled into his chest, felt my heart let go of him.

I was instantly overwhelmed by the proximity, by my emotions, and the tears fell, my shoulders shuddering as I tried to hold back sobs. One of his hands was in my hair, clutching me to his chest, and after a moment, I pulled away, needing to get away from him. But when I looked up at him, his eyes were on my lips. I held my breath, frozen to the spot, hoping to God he wasn't about to do what I thought he was about to do.

He leaned down, and the second it was clear that he was trying to kiss me, my arms shot out, pushing him away.

"Goddammit, Jimmy." My voice cracked, tears slipping down my face. "You didn't listen to one fucking thing I said. You don't get to kiss me. You don't get to stand on my porch and remind me of what I never had to begin with. It's over. I want you to hear me right now. It's *over.*" The chains around my heart fell away with every word. "I don't love you. I don't want you. I will never be with you. And you will leave me be. Do you understand?"

"Do I have a choice?" He was hurt, and I didn't care.

"None. If you ever loved me, let me go. Move on. Let me do the same. Please."

He took a deep breath. "If you change your mind—"

"I won't."

"Well, if you do, I'll be around. I loved you, Maggie. I still do, and I probably always will. It wasn't your fault, what I did. It was … I don't know. My own issues. Something inside of me is broken, but that isn't your fault. You didn't do anything wrong. I just need you to walk away with that."

I nodded. It was all I could manage.

He watched me for a moment longer, like he was trying to memorize me, and then he walked away.

My entire body trembled as I turned and opened the door, stepped into the entryway, closed the door behind me, feeling exhausted, spent.

My parents were in the kitchen, trying to look inconspicuous — Mom moving things around on the counter, Dad pretending to read at the island. I dragged myself into the room.

Dad looked up from his tablet, his comforting smile not able to disguise his worry. "Shotgun's just in there, if you want me to grab it." He jerked his head toward the office.

I chuckled, not realizing I had it in me. "I think I got it." I took a seat next to him at the bar. "Have a bourbon with me?"

"Without a doubt." He started to get up, but Mom waved him off.

"I've got it." She reached for glasses. "Wanna talk about it?"

I took a breath. "I think it's over."

Dad smirked. "You mean it hasn't been over for months?"

I rested my arms on the cool granite. "I mean, I think I've convinced him to stay away."

"How'd you manage that?" Mom asked as she handed us each a drink.

"I unloaded all my truth on him. I think he really believed he could just patch everything up with a little bit of time and a sentimental gesture. I get the feeling he didn't think I was serious when I left. As if the several thousand miles between us was temporary."

"In fairness," Mom said, "you did come back within a few weeks."

"Only because …" I took a breath and shook my head. "Everything just got so complicated."

Dad picked up his drink and brought it to his lips. "And did coming back here make it less complicated?"

I took a sip, the taste familiar, comforting. "Nope. But I just faced my biggest fear. All this time, especially after Jimmy sent that horrible box, I wondered if he would convince me to forgive him. Worried that I'd see him and forget what he did. That thought scared me more than anything, but I didn't forget. I won't. I don't think I could even if I wanted to."

Dad raised his glass. "I'll drink to that."

And we raised our glasses to his, clinked them together. And for the first time in a very long time, I felt like everything might eventually be all right.

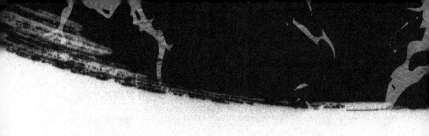

Raspberry Chip

COOPER

stepped out of the elevator on my father's floor that Tuesday morning, hands in the pockets of my slacks. The girl at the wide desk did a double take when she saw me, straightening up in her seat with a smile.

"Good morning, Mr. Moore. Your assistant called and said you'd be coming by. Your father is held up in a meeting, but he told me to send you on back to his office."

I shot her The Smile as I walked past. "Thanks."

I was back.

There were things in my life I could control, and I was ready to pour myself into them. I was ready for change.

I walked through the building, past cubicles and offices that grew exceedingly bigger, leading up to the room at the end of the hall. I opened the door and stepped into my father's office. The space was bigger than most apartments in New York, with floor-to-ceiling windows around three of the four walls, located in the center of Midtown. I stood for a long moment next to his desk, looking into the city, my eyes following the lines of the buildings, windows, the streets below.

I'd spent most of my life wondering what it was all for. When you're given everything, every opportunity, every whim, why would you work for anything? How could I decide what to do with my life when there was no need to do *anything* with it? I had no place in the world, not with the friends I'd had growing up, not even with the Habits crew, as much as I wanted to be a part of their world. I was hanging in limbo.

Until Maggie.

I'd always been adrift, floating through life, watching the shore from afar. But Maggie was an anchor, holding me steady. I couldn't float anymore — I didn't want to. I wanted to be everything for her. I wanted to prove to her, to myself, that I meant what I said. I was ready for my life to begin. I only hoped she would be a part of it.

The door behind me opened, and I turned to find my dad smiling at me.

"Hey, Coop."

I smiled. "Hey, Dad."

"What's going on? Dinner cancelled last week, haven't heard from you. We've been worried." He watched me as he stepped behind his desk and set down several leather portfolios and a small stack of papers.

"I'm … I'll be all right."

He took a seat. "So, you wanted to see me? My curiosity is piqued — not that I'm not glad to see you. It's just rare to see you *here*."

I took a seat of my own across from him and looked him in the eye. "I'm here to talk about my purpose."

His face softened, and he nodded at me with understanding. "Ah. That. Well, when it hits you, it's never subtle."

I chuckled. "Or gentle." I leaned forward. "I'd like to work for you, if it's possible."

"All things are possible. I'm glad you decided to intern here in college. The board will be pleased with that and your Columbia credentials. But

I have to ask, why here? Are you sure this is what you really want out of life? The hours are long and stressful. It's no easy job."

"I know. But this is the only place that makes sense for me. I want to be a part of this, of what you've done here. I want to follow in your footsteps, in Grandpa's. It's a legacy. It's my legacy."

He looked proud and touched, though his jaw was firm, his brow flat. "I've been waiting to hear that for a long time, Coop. But I have to ask how certain you are. I can get you a position as a financial analyst, but you'll need to do the work, put in the time just like anyone else, work your way up from the bottom. It's not going to be glamourous."

"I understand. You know, when I worked here that summer, I didn't hate it. At all. It was like the numbers, the data, it was all a pattern, a puzzle. I could see it, make sense of it."

He smiled. "I know the feeling. If you do with the opportunity what I think you'll do, some day, this office will be yours, just like it was my father's before me."

"I'm certain. And I promise — I won't let you down."

He folded his hands on his desk. "I'm more concerned that you'll let yourself down."

"I've done enough of that. Now I'm ready."

He smiled. "Well, in that case, when can you start?"

MAGGIE

Brooke and I stood at the counter of the ice cream parlor that afternoon, bent to eye the frozen goodness from behind the double-paned glass.

Her hair was piled in a caramel-colored knot on her head, held back by an elastic headband. She snickered and pointed at one. "You should get the Billionaire." She read off the plate. "*Sumptuous dark chocolate, laced with swirls of salted caramel and decadent fudge. Only for the self-indulgent.*"

I rolled my eyes and groaned. "Goddammit, that sounds so good."

"Then get it."

"Well, now I can't just on principle alone."

She shook her head and stood. "You're a mess."

"Obviously."

The teenager behind the counter smiled at us, a pretty girl with braces. "Did y'all decide?"

Brooke smiled back and leaned on the counter. "I'd like a scoop of Black Raspberry Chip in a waffle cone, please."

The girl was already reaching for a cone. "Sounds good. And for you, miss?"

I wrinkled my nose. "A scoop of Billionaire, please."

Brooke laughed. "Ha. I knew it."

"Waffle cone?"

"Why not." I sighed. "Waffle's my middle name."

Brooke snickered. She turned to me as the girl assembled our cones. "I can't believe you finally talked to Jimmy." She waved a hand. "No, what I can't believe is that it took you so long."

"I've been running away from months. I've got nowhere to go. If I'd dealt with him in the first place, none of this mess would have happened."

The girl passed over Brooke's cone, and she immediately stuck her face in it. She took a break from making out with it to say, "You weren't ready."

"I was never gonna be ready for that, Brooke." She handed me mine. "Thanks." I reached for my wallet.

"Nope, I got it." Brooke whipped a twenty out of her back pocket faster than Doc Holliday.

"Jeez. Prepared, were you?"

She smiled at me and shrugged. "I had it all planned out. We're on a date, Mags! I can't let my girl buy her own ice cream."

I laughed as we took seats at a small table next to the window.

She licked her ice cream and watched me. "Are you gonna eat that or just stare at it?"

I looked down at my Billionaire waffle cone. "I'm afraid it'll taste good."

"Isn't that the point?"

I sighed. "I should have gotten another flavor."

She gave me a flat look. "God, Maggie. Eat the damn ice cream I got for you."

I made a face at her, licking it lewdly for show, but the second it hit my tongue, I groaned. "Oh, God. That's fucking heaven in my mouth."

"Oooh, how good is your Billionaire?"

"So good. I could lick my Billionaire all day." I stuck my tongue out and licked with a seductive flare. You know, for emphasis.

She cackled, and a lady with a toddler gave her a look. "Does it taste as rich as it looks?"

"So rich and creamy. And so thick. I can barely get my mouth around my Billionaire." I closed my lips over the top of the scoop.

"Oh, my God, Maggie." She giggled.

I laughed.

She settled back in her seat, her green eyes bright. "How are you feelin'?"

I shrugged and turned the cone for a better angle. "I dunno. Better. You were right. I needed to see Jimmy and tell him I didn't want him. Say it out loud, not just for him, but for me. I feel … free."

"Think he'll leave you alone?"

"I hope so. I really think he got it. I mean, I told him straight up I didn't love him anymore. I don't know how much clearer I could be. But even if he does come back around, I feel like I'll be all right. I know I can tell him no. I know I don't want him at all. He tried to kiss me, but he may as well have been trying to feed me snakes. There wasn't a single part of me that wanted to kiss him at all."

"Good, because if you'd kissed him I would have slapped you."

"I don't doubt that. But now I know, you know? And if he comes back around, I know how to handle him. I figured out my DEFCON protocol."

"He'd better not come back around. He's done enough damage for a lifetime." She took a lick. "Figure out if you're goin' back to New York?"

"No."

"Heard from Cooper Moore?"

I gave her a look.

She raised her eyebrows and ignored me, sticking out her tongue to run her ice cream over it.

"No, I haven't heard from him."

"You gonna call him?"

My stomach sank at the thought. At least I was filling it with ice cream. "I dunno, Brooke. What would I even say?"

"How about, 'Hey, Cooper Moore, you decadent billionaire hottie, I superlove you and really want to see you and your peen soon.'"

I snickered. "It's definitely direct."

She shrugged. "I don't know, Mags. Just tell him how you feel."

"I said some horrible things to him. Cruel and horrible things. I don't know if he even wants me anymore, not after the way I treated him. I fucked it up. He's probably already got a new girl, anyway. She's probably a supermodel with mile long legs who can make up her mind and doesn't treat him like shit."

"He told you he'd be waiting. I doubt he bagged the idea in a week."

My chest ached. "I've just been such an ass. Doesn't matter that I didn't mean to, you know?"

"I'd be more worried about the rest of it. I mean, he was begging you to believe him. To trust him."

"But that's the whole thing, Brooke. I did. I do. I said all that because I was hurt. Because I was afraid that it was true, you know? My head telling me not to listen to my heart. But now I know — that's the difference between Cooper and Jimmy. Everything Cooper did was to prove to me that he *was* serious. That what I wanted or needed was more important than his feelings. Jimmy only cared about himself. Cooper only cared about me."

She watched me for a moment. "You need to tell him that."

I sighed. "I know. But I don't want to fuck up again or hurt him anymore. I need to make sure I'm ready."

"But that's the thing about love. You're not always certain. You're not always ready. I mean, that's what I've heard at least. I don't have a billionaire myself."

I chuckled and bit off a piece of my cone.

"Well," she said as she tore the paper wrapper around her cone and angled it for a bite, "I think you should call him. You can't hide forever."

"Why not?"

She rolled her eyes and swallowed. "Because that's weak as hell, and you're better than that."

"Am I? Because it seems to me that the only way I know to deal with real problems is to run away."

"You faced Jimmy."

"And Courtney too, that slag."

"Fuck that bitch. I hope she gets vagina rot."

"Gross, Brooke."

She smiled. "Okay, *treatable* vagina rot. Better?"

I laughed and sighed, licking that ice cream like it was the last I'd ever have. It was seriously so good, it did things to my girly parts. "This ice cream really is like Cooper. Sexy and rich, so good that you're sure you'll never have anything as good. Like, if I came here every day and got ice cream, I'd probably always choose this one. Because why take a risk on Raspberry Chip when you can have *Billionaire*?"

She nodded. "Mine really isn't all that great. I'm almost positive I don't look like I'm having an orgasm every time I take a bite."

I took another bite. "It really is so good."

She extended her hand. "Gimme."

I passed it over and she took a lick. Her face fell. "Motherfucker. I should have gotten some Billionaire too. God knows this as close as I'll ever get to the real thing." She took another bite.

"Hey." I reached for it.

She swatted my hand away. "Greedy. Share."

I giggled. "Get your own."

She handed it back over with a sigh. "So if you had fifty flavors to choose from, you'd choose this one every time?"

I shifted in my seat, not wanting to answer. "Are we still talking about ice cream?"

She gave me a look.

"I can't imagine picking anything but the Billionaire."

"Well, then there you go. Pick the Billionaire. Get fat on all of his dark chocolatey goodness."

I thought about calling him, and my heart bungee jumped into my shoes. "I've just got to be sure this time. I can't play games with his heart."

"You should have known from the start." She sang it and made boy band hand gestures.

I snickered. "Seriously, though. I feel like my life's a shirt that's buttoned wrong. I've got to fix it before I go back to him. I turned into a monster and pushed him away. I just shut him down and ran."

She gasped melodramatically. "Man, who knew you were such a coldhearted bitch."

"I really am."

She rolled her eyes. "Don't be dumb. You got your heart smashed to bits and lit on fire and thrown off a cliff. So you acted like a dick. You didn't do it on purpose. You didn't even realize you were doing it until, like, yesterday. You screwed up, so just fix it."

"I don't know how to fix this, Brooke."

"Well, I feel eating ice cream is step one. And then you need to grab hold of your ladynuts and call him."

"I can't reach my ovaries from here."

She gave me a flat look. "Grab your metaphorical ovaries and call him, you wuss. What are you afraid of?"

"Everything."

"Do you feel like it could be worse than what you've already been through?"

I thought about it, considered all I'd been through, everything I'd learned. "No."

"Then stop thinking about it and just jump."

"You make it sound so easy." I smiled. "Can I just carry you around in my pocket to pump me up when I doubt myself?"

"Hell yeah, you can. I'll be the best Polly Pocket in the world, especially if you pack me with booze."

I laughed.

"Everybody knows I give my best advice when I'm drunk. And anyway, you already do carry me around in your pocket. You can always call me, whenever you need."

"You should have been my maid of honor, you know."

"Uh, obviously. I've been telling you that ever since always. I will forever stand by the notion that a pact you made with Courtney when you were nine doesn't count."

"I mean, to be fair, she was basically the worst maid of honor to ever walk the Earth, so the bar was pretty low."

"Also true. But I still would have crushed it." She took a bite of ice cream, and I just watched her, my heart full of gratitude.

"I love you, Brookie. Thank you. For everything."

She reached for my hand, smiling. "You're welcome, Mags. Now deep throat that Billionaire before I do."

COOPER

don't know what else to do but wait, Astrid."

She nodded and picked up her wine. We hadn't been on one of our regular dates in a week — I'd barely spoken to her or anyone else, for that matter.

It felt good to tell her everything, like a confession. The relief that comes with sharing your burden with someone else, someone who cares.

"You haven't talked to her at all?"

"Not since I called her last week. I have to believe that she'll come back to me. She needs to work herself out, if she can. So I told her I'd wait."

"You're not going to get in touch with her at all? Just sit here on your hands? That doesn't sound like you."

I smirked. "I have a plan. There are things I need her to know, so I overnighted her something this morning. If I don't hear from her, I have a Plan B, C, D. I'll give her time, but I won't let her go."

"This is crazy, Coop. You really love her. When did this really happen?" She picked up her fork and fished around on her plate.

"I think it's been coming for weeks. But when we left everything in the city behind us, I saw the possibility. I saw what we could be, and I realized I want that. I want her, all of her — even the broken parts. Because I can put her back together."

Astrid's fork was still, her eyes wide. "Wow."

"Yeah, I know." I leaned back in my chair and took a sip of scotch. "There's more."

"More than your undying love?"

"I went to my dad's office today and asked him for a job."

She dropped her fork, and the people sitting next to us glanced over. Her mouth was hanging open.

"Oh, come on. That can't be *that* big of a surprise."

"Cooper Moore, model, playboy, one of New York's most eligible bachelors—"

"That's a national nomination, just so you know."

She shook her head, gaping at me. "A job? At your *father's* company? I mean … are you sick? Had a fever lately? Travel to any third world countries or low-end whorehouses or anything?"

"Hilarious."

"I just … I mean … I'm speechless. Really. I have literally nothing to say except that I have nothing to say."

"I can't explain it. I just want to be *better*. More. I've got a legacy, an opportunity. I'm over The Life. I've been watching everyone else grow up, West and Lily especially, and that's what I want. I can give back to my father for everything he's given to me. I can prove to myself and Maggie that I'm serious. My dad said it was about finding purpose, and I did. It's her."

She watched me for a moment. "All right. Then that's that. I'll talk to Sam. You'll start your job on Wall Street. And we'll wait and see what happens with Maggie." She took a breath. "I hope you hear from her soon."

"Me too." The familiar ache twisted in my chest, but I smiled because I had something stronger than the hurt.

I had hope.

Measures

MAGGIE

"**M**ags?" *my mom called up* the stairs, and I laid my book in my lap.

"Yeah, Mom?"

"There's a package here for you." I heard her climbing the stairs, and I got up just as she stepped into the doorway with curious eyes.

My brow quirked as I stood and made my way over to her and took the large envelope. The return address was from a PO Box in New York, the label printed rather than hand written.

I ripped it open curiously.

Inside was a proof copy of *W Magazine* in a plastic wrapper, but I couldn't see the cover for Cooper's letter. My heart beat so hard, I could barely hear as I took a seat on my bed and read his long, strong words that stretched across the page.

Maggie—
You're all I've ever wanted. Come back to me.

I looked down at the magazine cover and could barely breathe.

Cooper hung off his sailboat with Manhattan behind him in the distance, looking right at the camera like he could see through it, into me. His smile was so bright, so lovely, the line of his arms, his hand wrapped around the rope. He was carefree and alive, and it was the most beautiful thing I'd ever seen.

A Post-It stuck out of the top, and I slipped my finger in to open the magazine to the page he had marked.

It was a full spread with an interview and several photos, one entire page filled with a shot of him looking off to the side, shirtless, hanging in the ropes of the bow, rubbing the back of his neck with that crooked smile on his lips.

In the bottom corner was a quote from the interview.

Q: So what would you say to your dream girl, if you had the chance?
A: I've been around the world, and I thought I'd seen everything it had to offer until that night, until I saw you. In all my life, I'd never seen anything so beautiful, not standing in the Blue Mosque or the Taj Mahal. Not in the streets of Rome or canals of Venice. Making you smile gives me life. Making you laugh gives me hope. Making you happy is all I want, other than to keep you.

A tear slipped down my cheek. His words were about me, I knew, words he'd spoken before the Hamptons, before I knew how he felt. He'd realized it long before then. Pieces flew together as I went back, back, all the way to the first night.

As scared as I'd been, even though I'd resisted him, I knew even then. I knew it from the first time he touched me. I wanted him. I needed him. And I knew beyond a shadow of a doubt something even more.

I loved him.

I touched my lips as my tears fell freely. He'd been waiting for me since that first night, waiting for me to realize it. Waiting until I saw that he was telling the truth, that I could trust him, believe him. Waiting for me to say goodbye to my past instead of running from it, instead of letting it hurt me.

I looked up at my mom, unable to speak. I handed the magazine to her, and she read it over.

"What does this mean?"

"It's a declaration."

"And how do you feel about him?"

I took a deep breath. "The same," I answered quietly.

She smiled, her cheeks pink and eyes shining. "I figured. What are you gonna do about it?"

A smile stretched across my face as I wiped my tears. "Oh, I think I may have an idea."

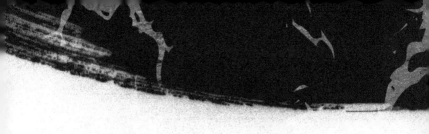

Limitless

MAGGIE

I **woke that morning feeling whole** for the first time.

My bags were packed, and my plan was set. The sun was shining, the sky a shade of cornflower blue and clouds high. It was limitless. I was limitless.

I kissed my parents goodbye at the gate. Walked through the terminal with certainty in every step, as if every single one was predestined. Like I was always meant to go back to him. As if my future had already been laid out before me — I only had to step onto the path and follow it back to him.

I'd never been so sure of anything. Not in all my life.

The plane ride back was a quiet, reverent trip that I spent looking out the window again with my headphones on. Every lyric, every song was about him, about me, about us. *First stop, Jackson. Next stop, Shangri-La,* M. Ward sang like he knew me.

When we landed in New York, I felt like I was home. I took the cab to Astrid's and sat in a chair as a makeup artist buzzed around me. I put on the most beautiful dress I'd ever worn in my life and slipped into the empty backseat of the Mercedes, sharing a conspiratorial smile with Bobby. And then we zoomed through Manhattan, back to him.

Home

Flashes strobed as I walked the red carpet at the Met Gala, hand in the pants pocket of my Armani suit, The Smile glued to my face, wondering where the hell Astrid was. She was late, which wasn't unusual for her, but she wasn't answering my texts, which was definitely unusual.

The Gala's theme was *Spellbound*, and the designers and dresses didn't disappoint. There were opulent fairy tale ball gowns, women in pantsuits inspired by period clothing, reminiscent of princes. One pop star, who was partly known for her outrageous costumes, was dressed as Rapunzel wearing a dress made out of blond hair. Her wig was connected to the dress that looked like hair wrapped around her body, peppered with flowers and braids, which was somehow not creepy. Most of the men didn't participate like the curmudgeons we were, wearing our suits like we'd wear anywhere, though I noted far more top hats in the crowd than usual.

I paused for photos as I spanned the length of the carpet and made my way inside, straight to the bar for a scotch, pulling my phone out of my pocket to check on Astrid again as I waited for my drink. A text from her waited on my lock screen.

Hey, sorry. I'll be there soon, held up with an emergency. Everything's okay. I'll explain later.

I frowned and texted her back to know I'd gotten it before slipping my phone back in my pocket. It was strange enough that she didn't want to ride together — meeting me at an event was out of the ordinary. It was the whole point of the charade, in fact. I took a sip of my drink and paced through the throng of celebrities and socialites, saying hellos, shaking hands, laying false kisses on the cheeks of the women I knew, wishing Astrid were there — my security. My partner in crime. But she wasn't, so I settled on Ash and entourage to occupy me.

But my mind wandered, my eyes roamed the crowd and the dresses on display throughout the room. It had been two days since Maggie had gotten the package. Two days of waiting patiently to hear from her. Of working for my father, grateful for something to keep me busy. I was grateful for the Gala, too. Grateful to stand next to Ash, who would keep my thoughts from her. Until the moment when I couldn't hide from her anymore. The moment when I didn't need to.

I felt her before I saw her.

I turned toward the entrance, my eyes finding her like I knew she was there, like she'd always been there. Her long earrings swung as she scanned the crowd, hanging just longer than her wild hair, and my eyes drank her in — her dress long, cut low and fitted, covered in strings of sparkling beads, draped to make her look like she was covered in a delicate spiderweb covered in dew. Her eyes burned bright and blue, lined with smokey kohl, and when they found mine, there was no one else, nothing else, not in the entire universe.

My axis shifted. Gravity took hold. My compass stopped spinning.

I don't remember moving, only that she was in my arms. My eyes roamed her face, the face that graced my dreams, my thoughts every day. I wouldn't have believed she was real if not for the weight of her against me.

"You came back," I whispered.

"I had to. I'm sorry—"

"Don't. Don't apologize. You're here."

She smiled. "I'm here."

I slipped a hand into her hair, resting my thumb on her cheek. "I didn't know if I'd ever see you again."

"I'm sorry I ran away. I was afraid. But I'm not anymore. I trust you, Cooper. I believe you. I just hope you can trust me after everything I've done. I was cruel. I hurt you to push you away, but I never doubted you."

"I know. I knew even when you didn't."

She laid a hand over mine, her eyes shining with tears.

"It was why I went after you. It's why I wouldn't stop trying. I won't ever stop, Maggie. I need you, and if there's a chance for us, I'll do whatever it takes. I'll wait. I'll beg. I'll fight for you. I'll do anything to make you mine."

"But that's what I need you to know. I've been yours from the start — I was just too broken to see the truth. But now … now I can give myself to you. I love you, Cooper, and if you want me, I'm yours."

I closed my eyes and took a breath, opening them to find her still in my arms. And then I kissed her, and she kissed me, without a single demand, a single expectation. Just a simple kiss from the girl who loved me.

I broke away, pressed my forehead to hers, smiled down at her, acknowledging distantly that people were staring and cameras flashed away. But I didn't care. There was no more reason to hide, no reason to pretend.

I was free.

Her eyes were bright and sparkling as she looked up at me smiling with her hands on my chest. "What do we do now, Mr. M?"

I squeezed her tighter. "Now? Now we drink. We eat. We dance. And then, I'm going to take you away from here."

"Where will we go?"

My fingers found a curl near her face and slipped it through my fingers. "Anywhere you want."

Her smile stretched wider. "First, take me home."

"Which home?"

"Yours," she said simply. "Home is where you are."

A breathy laugh escaped me, and when I kissed her again, I felt the truth of her words in my heart.

I was home.

MAGGIE

Cooper swept me around the crowd, introducing me to celebrity after celebrity, the upper echelon of New York society. Somehow, I didn't get ruffled, even though the whole affair was overwhelming. I just smiled and treated them like anyone else. They're just people, after all, so I shook their hands and kissed their cheeks, asked them questions about their lives without prying or acting starstruck. Even the cold ones warmed up a little.

The dresses were brilliant, and every one had a story. They all asked me about mine — Astrid's — so many awestruck by the craftsmanship, the detail. And the story was this.

In one of the many retellings of Cinderella, her fairy godmother made her dress from silken strands from spiderwebs and dew. And so Galliano designed the dress around the idea presented by Astrid — a 20s inspired gown, fitted and simple, with hundreds of strings of sparkling beads in varying sizes, all draped around the bodice and skirt to look like delicate, dewy spiderwebs that swung gently when I walked.

It was the most brilliant dress I'd ever seen in my life, never mind to *wear* it, after some emergency alterations of course. And then, there were the shoes. They were perfect — white platforms, covered in tiny crystals, just enough to make them sparkle without being showy at all. And they fit me. I swear to God, I felt like Cinderella herself when I slipped my foot into that shoe and it fit.

We walked through the exhibits featuring dresses from avant garde to historical pieces, then wandered into the dining room as dinner was announced. The moment we walked in, my eyes widened, and my chin tipped up to the ceiling. The columns lining the room were decorated to look like trees that stretched up to the ceiling, branches that wound across the open space, hanging with blankets of wisteria. Small lights were strung throughout, casting a soft glow, illuminating the canopy like tiny fairies.

"It's beautiful," I whispered.

He kissed my temple and whispered back, "It's nothing, compared to you."

I could barely breathe as he towed me across the room and to our seats, which were at one of the long tables. I took a seat, unable to comprehend where I was, what was happening. It felt like a dream.

A menu sat just in front of a fresh glass of wine, and I picked the paper up, admiring the elegant vellum and scrolling word *Spellbound*. The table was covered in hyacinth and peonies, mossy wooden displays dotted with tiny wildflowers and spotted mushrooms.

Cooper sat next to me and smiled, watching me take it all in. "What do you think?"

"It's like a real live fairy tale, Coop. They really don't do anything halfway, do they?"

He laughed. "Never."

"Cooper, I've been looking for you, man." A tall, blond man about Cooper's age approached with a brilliant smile on his face and a gorgeous girl on his arm, even if she looked incredibly bored. How anyone could have been bored there was beyond me.

We stood to greet him. "Ash," Cooper said with a smile. "This is Maggie Williams."

Recognition sparked behind his bright eyes, and he extended a hand. "West's sister?"

I smiled and took it. "I am. Pleasure to meet you."

"You too." He shook his head and shot Cooper a knowing smile. "This is the girl? West's sister is *the girl*?"

Cooper smiled back and laid a hand on my waist.

He laughed, a charming, carefree laugh. "Now I know why you weren't forthcoming with the details. He must not know, if you're still standing."

We both laughed at that, though I was curious as to how exactly that all played out. "Once I told him how I felt, it wasn't all that hard to convince him to let me live."

The girl on Ash's arm cleared her throat, and he remembered himself. "Oh, ah … sorry — this is Evangeline. Evangeline, meet Cooper Moore, one of my oldest friends."

She put on a sour smile and extended a limp hand. "Charmed."

Cooper gave it a halfhearted shake. "I'm sure."

"Looks like we're across from you. Come on, Ang."

She rolled her eyes. "*Evangeline,* please, Ash."

"Sorry, *Evangeline*. Seems like we could maybe use a little scotch, too." He smirked at Cooper before dragging not-Ang around the table to sit.

We took our seats as the dining room began to fill up. We were surrounded mostly by strangers, other than a few of Cooper's friends who sat across the table. Once we'd ordered, everyone chatted, and

Cooper and I turned to each other, feeling like we were alone for the first time all night.

He slipped a hand into my lap and threaded his fingers through mine as we leaned in. "I want to know everything that's happened since you've been gone. I feel like I've missed everything."

My brows came together just a hair, thinking back. It seemed like a million years ago. "Well, my mom fed me a lot, and I slept and read. Spent time with Brooke. Tried not to think about you or any of the mess. But then I ran into Courtney."

"Who?"

"My maid of honor."

"Oh. Her."

I sighed. "Yeah, that's pretty much how it went when I saw her too. She actually tried to tell me she missed me, as if there were a possibility that we could make amends."

"Smart girl."

I snorted. "No one would ever accuse her of that. Anyway, then it got out that I was home, and a couple of days later, Jimmy came by."

His face tightened. "What happened?"

"He tried to apologize, told me he wanted me back, blah, blah, blah. And then I unloaded on him. That son of a bitch even had the nerve to try to kiss me."

Cooper stiffened, and I smiled at him reassuringly.

"He was lucky he caught me off guard because if he hadn't, I would have either punched him or kicked him in the nuts. Maybe both."

He chuckled and seemed to relax.

I laid my hand on top of his in my lap. "But mostly, I realized that I didn't love him, not like that. I never felt for him what I feel for you. Not even in high school. It was never like *this*. I just thought I'd always be with him, as if that was just what I was supposed to do. He was a catch, and we were happy enough that I never considered it being any other way. But now? I've compared every man I've ever met to you, and not a single one measured up."

"I know what you mean. Like the bar is so high, the scale so tipped. The things I love about you are the measure for everyone else. I'll look at a woman and think, I bet her laugh isn't as pretty as Maggie's, or her hair is so dark, not like Maggie's in the sunshine. No one can compare to you. There are just too many things that I cherish."

I met his eyes and smiled, my heart so full. "Why are you so perfect?"

He laughed. "You know I'm far from perfect."

I squeezed his fingers. "Well, you're perfect for me."

Cooper reached for my cheek with his free hand. "I've never seen anything so beautiful as you are tonight."

I leaned into his hand, cheeks flushed. "Only because Astrid was my fairy godmother and had her makeup artist spray paint my face."

"No, you're always beautiful, even with your face naked, nothing to hide your freckles." He brushed the apple of my cheek with his thumb. "Where did you get this dress?"

"Astrid. It was the dress she was supposed to wear. She apparently knows one of Galliano's tailors personally, and he was waiting at her place to alter the dress for me. I didn't think it was possible, but he just snapped his fingers and said, 'Honey, give me one hour.'"

He smiled crookedly. "Fairy godmother Astrid, huh?"

"She gave me her invitation to the Gala, texted Bobby to pick me up. She got me the dress and the chariot and got me to the ball. She helped me get my prince. So, yes. As far as I'm concerned, Astrid will forever be my fairy godmother."

He laughed and pressed a sweet kiss on my lips.

A flash popped, and we both looked toward it, Cooper with narrowed eyes, mine full of shock, I was sure.

The photographer smiled. "Sorry. I'm with Getty. Didn't mean to disturb you." He nodded and made his way down the table, snapping photos.

"I thought paparazzi weren't allowed in here?" I asked.

"They aren't. He's with the press." Cooper was watching me — I felt his uncertainty when he finally spoke. "Everyone has seen you tonight. With me. People are going to wonder who you are, which means things might get crazy." He squeezed my hand. "I've lived in the public eye for years. I'm used to it. And I can protect you from a lot of it, but there will be times when it'll be overwhelming. The talk will die down after some time has passed, but in the meantime, it's going to be a lot. They're going to seek you out, ask you questions. Speculate. You might be in gossip magazines, and they're rarely kind." He searched my face. "I need to know if you're sure you want to do this."

As freaked out as I was by the thought, I smiled. "There's nothing that could keep me from you. This is part of your life, so now it's part of mine. You'll just have to hold my hand."

The relief on his face was perfectly clear. "Always."

I smiled at him. "So, what will we do now? Spend all weekend in your apartment?"

He shrugged, smiling slyly. "Or we could drive to the Hamptons in the morning, spend the weekend there instead."

I felt myself light up, unable to hide my excitement. "Oh, that sounds amazing. We'll come back Sunday, then? I go back to work Monday morning."

"Me too."

My brow quirked. "What?"

He smirked. "Work on Monday. I have to."

I blinked at him. "I heard you, but what?"

"I talked to my dad about a job and he gave me one. I started last week as a financial analyst at Moore & Co." He took a sip of his scotch like it was no big deal.

But I just gaped at him. "Cooper, that's … I mean … I don't know what to say. Whatever convinced you to do that?"

"You," he answered.

I was breathless. "But why?"

He set his drink down and faced me, his face open and earnest. "I've never felt like I've wanted more out of life than what I was living. Not until I met you." He looked down at his hand as he played with my fingers. "I want to give you everything. I want to prove that I can be serious about life. About you."

"I know you're serious, Cooper," I said softly.

"But this is a way I can show you. I found my purpose, and it's you."

I slipped my arms around his neck and pulled until my chin hooked over his shoulder, eyes closed, overcome. "I believe you can do anything."

His shoulders rose and fell as he sighed, and he shifted to kiss my shoulder.

"I mean, you convinced me to date you for a full week before I even realized it."

He laughed, the sound reverberating through my chest. I pulled back to look at him, laid a hand on his cheek.

"I'm proud of you, Cooper, and I'm honored."

He smiled and slipped a hand in my hair. "I'm glad, Maggie, and I love you."

I laid a kiss on his smiling lips. "I love you."

"Good."

I sat back in my chair, feeling giddy.

"Are you going to tell anyone you're back?"

I reached for my wine. "I'll text them later before they see us on *Perez Hilton*."

He chuckled and took a sip of his scotch. "I've barely seen anyone since you've been gone. Just West, Tricky, and Astrid. I just … I wasn't sure what to do with myself, at first. Knowing I had to wait, not knowing if I'd ever hear from you. It was maddening."

I swallowed my wine and shook my head. "I'm so sorry I put you through that. It wasn't fair."

But he only said, "There are no rules to this. You did what you felt you needed to do, and I can't fault you for that. I just missed you. I worried about you."

"I wasn't much better off, if it's any comfort."

"I wish neither of us had been unhappy. But we had to get through that to get to where we are. Worth it."

I shook my head, smiling. "Who are you?"

He smirked with an eyebrow up. "Your dream guy, all grown up."

I laughed. "Modest."

He picked up his drink again. "I don't know that I would have figured it all out without you leaving. So as much as it hurt, as much as I hated it, I'm glad for it. Because now you're all mine."

"It's true. I think I've always been yours."

His smile could have lit the whole ballroom. "Trust me, Mags — I knew."

Breathe

MAGGIE

It *was insane to be* in the room with that many people who I 'knew' but who didn't know me from Adam. But I survived the rest of the night by holding on to Cooper's arm and smiling my way through the whirlwind, through the questions and the cameras. Through the dinner that cost more than a year's worth of Manhattan rent and blew my mind. Through the afterparty's performances and raucous dance party.

But Cooper didn't leave my side, the beautiful man in the most gorgeous suit I'd ever seen. His smile filled my heart. The look in his eyes told me that everything was exactly as it should be.

We were on the dance floor as a slow song played, swaying to the music, my small hand clutched in his against his chest, my head tucked under his chin. I felt the circle close, from the first night to this one, from an ending that was a beginning to the moment we were in. But this time, we danced without fear or pain. There was no uncertainty. Nothing left unsaid.

There was only love.

He stopped moving, and I looked up at him. His blue eyes burned, and his voice was tight when he whispered, "Come with me, Maggie."

I couldn't breathe, only nodded. I would follow him anywhere.

He towed me through the crowd, down the steps of the Met with camera flashes strobing from the paparazzi just beyond the velvet rope. They called his name, asked who I was, shouted questions as we stopped at the curb where Bobby waited for us.

Cooper gave me his hand as I slipped inside, and he climbed in after me. The moment the door closed behind him, we came together, our lips finding each other in the most perfect symmetry.

I was breathless when he broke away, trailing the tip of his nose against the bridge of mine. "All night, I've wanted you. All my life, I'll want you."

I had no words, though I needed none. When I kissed him, it was like I'd finally come up for air after holding my breath for too long, so long that it hurt. But now I could breathe again.

I don't know how long it was before the car came to a stop. We barely separated — somehow our hands, our arms, some part of us was touching as we climbed out of the car and thanked Bobby, who looked happy and proud and pleased. We blew inside, across the big gold compass and into the elevator where he pressed me against the wall and kissed me again.

He could kiss me forever and ever and ever.

And then the doors opened, and we were in his apartment, and then, his room. It was almost dark, silent, and we stood in each others arms, still and reverent.

His fingers grazed my jaw and stopped at my chin. He tilted my face to his, watching me for a long moment, his eyes roaming my face before bringing his lips to mine. They were strong, moving slowly, charged with emotion. With every motion, I leaned into him, matching him, breathing him until every breath was *ours*.

When he broke away, I almost fell into him. He caught me with a smile.

I kicked off my shoes as I ran my hands under his jacket and pushed it over his shoulders. He shrugged it off and tossed it to a chair in the corner as I reached for his tie, slipping it out of the knot, out of his collar, with his hand resting on my forearm and my heart pounding in my chest. My eyes were on my fingers as I unbuttoned his shirt, tugged it out of his pants, touched his hot skin. He wrapped his arms around my waist and pulled me into him, bending to bury his face in my neck and kiss a trail up to my ear.

"Turn around," he whispered.

I did as I was told, doing my best to remember to breathe as I waited for his touch. A shock shot down my body when his fingers grazed the back of my neck and skimmed down my bare spine. A shudder rolled through me, and when he reached the zipper, he didn't hesitate, just pulled it slowly until it stopped.

"Maggie…" The word was a plea.

I looked back over my shoulder to see the emotion in every plane of his face. He stepped into me, pressed his lips to my shoulder, slipped his hands in the back of my open dress, around my naked hips, to my stomach, lower as he palmed me. I arched my back, sighing as I pressed myself into him and slipped the dress off my shoulders. It slid down my body and to the ground in a heap, but he didn't stop.

He ran his fingers up the length of me as his other hand roamed my stomach and up to my breast. His lips found my neck, his skin on fire against mine. I stepped out of my dress and moved toward the bed, and he followed until I reached the end and bent, propping myself on my forearms.

His hands trailed down my ribs, my waist, my hips, and he knelt between my legs, fingers squeezing tight as he buried his face in me, his tongue hot as he licked up the line. I gasped, rising up on my tiptoes from the shock, and he followed, unrelenting. I dropped to the bed, my cheek against the covers, barely able to keep myself standing as he ravaged me with my pulse racing, fingers twisted in the sheets.

I reached behind me, slipped my fingers into his hair and squeezed, gasping when he pressed harder, deeper into me. But it wasn't enough.

I tightened my grip in his hair, pulled his head back and called his name. He let me go, stripping off his shirt when he stood, then his pants as I lay panting. And then I felt his touch, his fingers on the backs of my thighs. He cupped them and urged me to climb onto the bed.

"I want to see your face, your eyes," he said, his voice rough as he guided me to roll over, my breath shallow as I stretched out on my back as he asked. He climbed up my body until he was hovering over me. My legs hooked around his thighs, feet tucked in the curve of his calf as he brought his hips lower and grabbed his length. He guided his tip to rest against me, and a moan passed my lips, my hips shifting to try to force him in, body aching for him.

He gripped my hip to still me, flexed slowly, and we both watched him disappear inside of me.

I sighed, and his eyes found mine as he pulled out and rocked into me, rolling his hips. Then again. And again, and again, strong and smooth, claiming and promising. He was everywhere — the weight of him against me, his hands in my hair, his lips against mine, his voice breathing my name, telling me he loved me, telling me he needed me.

And I needed him. I would always need him.

My heart beat faster, my breath shallow until I let my body go. Let my past go. Gave my heart to him as I gave him the rest of me, his name on my lips as I flexed around him fast at first, then slower until I could finally breathe again.

When I opened my eyes, they found his.

"I love you," I whispered, and his eyes fluttered closed, his body rolling in a wave, every breath deeper than the one before until he slammed into me, neck taut, a cry passing his lips as he came.

He rested his forehead against mine, hips still flexing slowly as he pulsed inside of me. I laid a hand on his chest, feeling the solid thump of his heart as he strung delicate kisses on my neck, my cheeks, my lips. And then he filled me to the hilt and propped himself up to look at me. His beautiful face was soft, and I took a long moment to memorize the shadows of his cheekbones, the swell of his lips, the cut of his jaw, the love in his eyes.

"I'm sorry I hurt you." They were words I couldn't say enough.

He touched my cheek. "I know how you can make it up to me."

"How?"

"Don't ever leave."

I smiled and kissed him, wrapped my arms around his neck and pulled him into me. And when I broke away, I pressed my lips into his ear. "I'll stay as long as you'll have me."

And he whispered back, "Forever."

COOPER

woke before her that morning, my eyes blinking open slowly, unsure whether or not I was dreaming.

I was wrapped around Maggie, my arm around her back and hand in her hair, our legs tangled together. But I didn't move, not for a long time, just listened to her slow breathing, feeling her chest rise and fall against mine as I thought about everything that had happened, everything that had brought us here.

She was mine, and I'd never let her go again.

And then my thoughts jumped forward. I daydreamed about

everything to come. Listed all of the things I wanted to show her. Pictured her standing in front of the Taj Mahal. Smiling at me from across a cafe table in Paris. Holding my hand on the streets of Istanbul.

I wanted to show her all of the things I'd seen, to experience it all with her. Through her.

I wanted to hold her hand for the rest of my life.

She stirred against me, untucked her arms and wrapped one around my ribs, slipping the other between my neck and the pillow. I squirmed, trying not to laugh when she buried her nose in my neck.

She chuckled and squeezed me. "Are you ticklish?"

"No."

She shifted her nose, and a laugh shot out of me.

I backed away so I could see her. "Maybe a little." I smoothed her hair and cupped the back of her head, kissing her forehead.

She sighed, opening her eyes sleepily when I propped my head on my hand. "I could sleep for days, I think."

"It's been a long couple of weeks."

"It's been a long year," she added, "but I feel … I don't know how to explain it. New. Like I walked outside and closed the door behind me, and now I'm looking out at the whole world."

I smiled. "I missed you."

"So much. I thought about you all day, every day."

I wrapped my arms around her. "We should get out of bed."

She groaned.

"Hamptons."

That stopped her. "Just promise me we can lie in bed all day tomorrow, and I'm good."

"I promise."

"All right, then." She pecked me on the lips and rolled away from me. I watched as the sheets fell away and she stepped into the beam of light from the window, illuminating her curly hair like a halo. I could barely breathe, and she looked back to catch me staring.

She smiled.

That smile was something I'd work for every day, forever.

Within an hour, we were showered and fed. Astrid had her suitcase sent over, and I'd packed some of her things in my duffle bag while she finished eating and straightened up the kitchen.

I smiled at her as I walked back into the kitchen. "Bobby's downstairs."

She wiped her hands on a towel. "Oh, good. Let me just grab my suitcase."

"I already packed some stuff for you. Just grabbed the rest of your toiletries."

She made a face. "What if you forgot something? Let me go check." She walked past, but I grabbed her wrist, planting a kiss on her lips when she rebounded back into me.

I looked down at her, smiling, willing her with my words. "Trust me, Maggie."

Her eyes went wide, open as they did sometimes, and she whispered, "I do, Cooper."

"Good. Now, come on. Let's not keep Bobby waiting."

She chuckled. "All right. But you'd better have packed underwear."

I winked and dragged her toward the door.

Her smile fell. "Oh, God. You didn't, did you."

"Guess we'll see."

We made our way downstairs and out the back where Bobby leaned on my black convertible Jaguar.

She stopped dead. "Where the hell did you get that?"

I raised an eyebrow, smiling. "Uh, a Jaguar dealership?"

"Obviously, but holy shit. I thought we were taking the Mercedes."

"You thought I just had one car?" I asked, amused.

"Two. The Porsche."

I hooked an arm around her neck and kissed her temple, whispering,

"That's my beach car. This is my *real* car."

She laughed as I dragged her to the car and opened the door, closing it once she was tucked in, climbing in next to her like a dream. And I had to be dreaming, I thought as she smiled over at me.

I started the car, put on my sunglasses, and pulled away. Only in my dreams would I ever imagine that such a girl could love me just as much as I loved her.

COOPER

Maggie's hand was wrapped around mine, nestled in her lap as we drove up the coast. We were in the last hour of the trip, the scenic stretch before we reached the Hamptons, and I glanced over at her, her hair flying, the Jaguar rumbling around us, top down, radio bumping. Her bare feet were on the dashboard, and she leaned back in the seat, face tilted toward the ocean, elbow propped on the door, chin in her hand.

I could have watched her for hours.

We wound around the coast, past the bay and the small neighborhoods, until we came to the driveway and pulled through the gate. The Hampton house was just as we'd left it — quiet and beautiful. The waves still crashed against the shore, the seagrass still waved in the breeze. Maggie still looked like she belonged there. But I was a different man.

We changed into swimsuits and walked the long, wooden path to the ocean. I chased her through the surf. I kissed her salty lips. I lay with her on the shore for hours in the sun, watching the clouds, watching her. Breathing and being.

We had every intention of driving into town to eat. But the

moment we walked into the house, I turned around to find her standing still in the doorway, skin a shade darker against her white bikini and golden hair. The way she looked at me made me feel like a fool and a god. I could never be enough for her, but I could be her everything. And all I could do when she looked at me that way was to kiss her. Because words weren't enough. They'd never be enough.

I took her in my arms and to my bed. I lay in her arms for hours and listened to her voice, to the sound of the ocean past the windows. We ate sandwiches in bed at eleven, and then I turned out the lights and took her in the moonlight. I gave myself to her completely. And when I fell asleep with her against my chest, I knew I'd never want another girl. I'd never love another girl. Not as long as I lived.

MAGGIE

woke up that morning before the sun rose, watching Cooper sleep in the near dark. His lips were parted, chest rising and falling slowly, dark lashes against his cheeks. My eyes traced the line of his profile, resisting the urge to touch him, not wanting to ruin the perfection. He looked like a boy, a happy, peaceful boy.

He was the most gorgeous thing I'd ever seen, and he made me feel like Cinderella, it was true. He'd been to the ball. Met all the girls. And in the end, he chose me. He chose me even when I hurt him, even when I didn't believe he was sincere. He chose me even when I said I didn't want him, when I changed my mind and pushed him away. He waited, because he loved me. And I loved him.

I climbed out of bed gently and found our bag. It was too dark and quiet to dig too much, so I grabbed the first thing I found, pulling on his tailored shirt as I walked through the kitchen. The coffee pot and supplies were easy to find, and once I'd started it, I walked out onto the back patio to watch the sun rise.

It was a little chilly, but I didn't mind, just leaned on a post on the patio with my eyes on the horizon, watching the water lap the sand and recede, listening to the steady rush of the waves, waiting for the sun.

I'd always been waiting on the sun, even when I thought I'd caught it with Jimmy. I knew now. I knew that Cooper was my sun, but I was his sun too. I didn't need to orbit him, and he didn't need to orbit me. We were a constellation, two stars connected as we moved through the heavens together, holding each other close with our own gravity.

I turned to find him behind me, tall and dark in the doorway, leaning against the frame, watching me. His hands were in the pockets of his jersey pants, his chest bare, eyes dark, his face full of love and longing. He pushed off the wall and grabbed a blanket on his way to me, opening it up. He wrapped it around his shoulders and opened his arms, and I settled into his chest, slipping my arms around his waist, pulling our bodies flush, our faces turned to the ocean.

He rocked me gently. "I imagined this moment. You. Here. The sunrise. But I never imagined I would feel this way."

My heart was so full, so heavy with emotion, and I recognized the feeling — the way he made me feel — for the first time. Compared it to every other feeling, but it was singular. Distinctive. Extraordinary. "My whole life, I thought I knew what love was. I thought I understood it, but I didn't know. Not until you."

He squeezed me tighter, took a shallow breath.

"But you knew all along, didn't you? You knew, and you tried to show me, but I fought you every step of the way."

"Lucky for us, I won."

I laughed softly, my chest aching as I pulled him even closer.

"Stay with me, Maggie."

I looked up at him.

"I don't want to be without you. Not for a minute I don't have to be. Come home with me tonight. Come home with me tomorrow night and every night."

I took a breath, lips parted to speak, but he headed me off.

"If it's ever too much, if you need time or space, it's yours. But if you want to stay, stay."

"They'll think we're crazy."

The honesty, the earnestness in his eyes overwhelmed me. "I don't care what they think. What do *you* think?"

My mind spun around, thinking it was crazy and irresponsible. Irrational. That I would doom us from the start if I agreed.

There was only one answer to give.

"Of course I will. I love you."

He smiled at me, the relief plain to see, his eyes sparkling as he kissed me. And I knew then that I'd be staying forever.

Epilogue

COOPER

We sat in habits that night with our friends, sun kissed and windblown. Maggie's arm was wrapped around mine, her smile bright as we drank and laughed after the best weekend of my life.

Lily sat on a barstool between West's legs, grinning at us. West didn't look like he wanted to hit me, so I was calling that a win. Patrick leaned back against the bar smirking, and Rose leaned from behind the bar next to him. Astrid sipped her drink, watching us sentimentally.

Lily shook her head. "I am so glad you're back, Maggie. We missed you."

"Me too. Jackson is hot, y'all. I've been here a month and I'd already deacclimated."

West laughed. "Yeah, I don't miss the mosquito hordes either."

"Not even a little."

"Mom's pie, however …"

"Never get enough," she said.

"Thank God you're back. I've had no one to watch 90s teen movies with." Rose smiled. "I'm so glad I'll have a roommate again."

Patrick had a weird look on his face, and I eyed him.

"Hey." Lily made a face.

"What?" Rose asked. "I think we can all agree you're my roommate in name only these days."

She settled back into West and blushed. "Oh, fine."

Maggie looked up at me nervously. "Well, about that …"

Oh, God. Here it goes. I squeezed her hand between my arm and ribs. West narrowed his eyes.

Maggie took a breath. "I'm going to be staying with Cooper."

A surprised laugh shot out of Lily, and West looked like he was imagining ways to decapitate me. Everyone else just gaped.

I cleared my throat. "I know it seems fast—"

"*Seems* fast?" West asked, ears red.

I gave him a look. "I live around the corner from her job. It's not like she can't come back if she wants to, right?" I asked Lily and Rose.

Lily shook her head, seemingly to clear it. "Of course. You're always welcome, Maggie. And we are so happy for you guys." She slipped off her stool, and everyone stood. Patrick clapped me on the shoulder and smiled, and the girls took turns hugging.

I stepped over to West, flashing The Smile. "Come on, Williams. You're not really mad, are you?"

His eyes narrowed, but when he looked over at Maggie, saw her smiling and laughing with the girls, something in his face changed, softened.

"If you hurt her, I'll fucking murder you."

I slipped my hands in my pockets. "I know."

"I'm not even kidding, Cooper."

"I know."

He let out a sigh. "Just make her happy."

I looked over at her, my eyes roaming her rosy cheeks, her bright eyes, the smile that changed my life, and I made him a promise.

"I will."

Epilogue

MAGGIE

pulled the boat into the wind, and when the sails luffed, I locked the wheel and turned on the engine. Cooper was already lowering the jib, the wind blowing his hair, his smile a thousand watts brighter against his deep tan. I moved past him to the mainsail and grabbed the halyard rope, pulling hand over hand until it was lowered completely.

Santorini sat just in the distance — the blue roofs and white walls lining the sheer cliff in the dusk — and I took a moment to appreciate the sight as Cooper headed back to the cockpit and pulled us into the harbor.

It was the end of May, and we'd both taken an extended Memorial Day holiday to go to Greece. We flew into Athens where we spent a few glorious days before renting a sailboat yacht much like *Midnight Caller*. First, we sailed to Mykonos, a beautiful party island, then Rhodes, full of history. Our last stop before heading back to Athens was Santorini, and I already knew it would be my favorite.

We pulled into the slip and showered, changed for dinner — him in a suit cut to perfection, me in a royal blue dress cut to keep

Cooper's eyes on my neckline. His arms were around me, his lips to my ear as we rode in a taxi up the switchback into town. His hand never left mine as we walked the streets and found the restaurant he wanted to take me to.

It was almost like a patio in that there were no window panes, just open arches that overlooked the ocean and the curve of the cliff. The white walls of the buildings glowed, illuminated by lights along the ground so they shone against the night, the domed blue roofs of each building the same shade as my dress. It was magical. The trip had been magical. My life was magical. And all because of him.

Oh, how things had changed over the course of a few weeks. I'd moved my belongings, which were mostly shoes, into Cooper's apartment. I'd gotten my own keys and had access to Bobby whenever I needed. We worked most days, and Cooper cooked dinner most nights. We watched a lot of Netflix — most recently a binge session of Star Trek: The Next Generation, since I'd never seen it and Cooper wanted to show me.

He wanted to show me everything.

It was overwhelming, at first. Obviously, the rules were gone, so the first thing he did was take me out to a string of gourmet restaurants, though I made him order for me because I was afraid to see the prices. He'd also made sport of buying me things, to make up for the time the rules *were* still in place, he'd said.

We went back to Coney Island, and I'm happy to report that this time, he kissed me in the Spook-A-Rama just as a bloody mannequin head popped out of the dark at us. And it was awesome.

But even now, as we sat in Greece after the most brilliant vacation of my life, the thing that made it right was him.

See, when I met Cooper, something in me shifted on an elemental level, as if he changed my chemistry, rearranged me. I needed him, but not in the desperate way. Being with him was a universal truth.

It was a quiet fact. Once I found him, the world made sense simply because he was in it and he loved me.

The lamb had been cleared away, and the baba ganoush was very nearly gone, and we drank our wine and talked. We laughed and we smiled. He took my hand, and I followed him through the quiet streets of Santorini.

He pulled me into an alcove on the cliff overlooking the ocean, and we could see the curve of the island, the buildings lit up in the night lining the coast and staggered in tiers below us. There were so many stars, more stars than I'd ever seen, and I tipped up my chin, my eyes on the heavens. Cooper sat on the low wall, watching me for a long moment before pulling me to him.

He looked up at me, my beautiful boy with his eyes full of stars, smiling at me sweetly before he looked down at my right hand, turning it over in his.

My free hand found his cheek, and he leaned into my palm, turning his head to kiss it as I felt him slip the ring onto my finger.

I looked down, and so did he, his fingers spinning the simple silver ring he'd placed on my ring finger. I knew the ring — I'd seen it in Rhodes at the market and admired it before putting it back. I didn't think he'd even been paying attention. But of course he was.

His voice was thick with emotion when he finally spoke, his eyes still on my hand. "I don't know how I lived my whole life without you. I don't know how I survived a single day without hearing your voice. I don't know how I woke up every morning without your face being the first thing I saw. I don't ever want to know what that feels like, to not have you."

He rose slowly, slipped a hand into my hair, searched my face. Stole my breath. Stopped my heart. "One day, I'm going to give you another ring. I'll ask you to stay with me forever, and I'll make a promise to you, to love you, to cherish you until I take my last breath. It'll be the easiest thing

I'll ever do. I love you, Maggie, and I'm yours. Be mine."

In all my life, it was all I would ever want. He was all I would ever want. "I'm yours," I whispered, the words of my heart set free.

And the kiss he laid on my lips seared my soul, branding me his forever.

Acknowledgments

To my husband Jeff — We did it. I love you. Without you, I don't make any sense.

Becca Mysoor — NOFB. Brain Twin. Partner in crime. Thank you. For everything. Tell Vinnie I said thanks by proxy, and that sharing is caring. I hear Tricky calling, so let's hold hands and get to dancing.

Brooke Cumberland — Stop yelling at me! Just kidding — never stop. Without you lending your ear, shoulder, boot in my ass, cupcakes, and chocolate, I really don't know how I could have made it through any of this. I love you. Hold my other hand and come dancing too.

To Becca AND Brooke — We're basically like a three legged stool. I couldn't do this without the both of you.

Kandi Steiner — I'll always be the Hype Man to your Polly Pocket. Thank God you haven't run screaming yet.

Angie McKeon — You, my unicorn riding princess, are an absolute godsend. You've supported me, you've given invaluable feedback, and you have become a great friend. I am so thankful for you. #Gummybears

Brittainy Cherry — I feel like if we just hang on to each other, we'll be okay. Thank you for always being there for me. Sharing this whole crazy roller coaster ride with you is kind of everything.

Christine Stanley — You have always believed in me. You've

always supported me, and without your help, there's no way I'd be where I am today. I cannot thank you enough for everything you've done for me, and I can't wait to do it again.

Rebecca Slemons — You are a saint for fixing my commas and putting up with my made up words.

Lauren Perry — You've done it again, you magical sorceress of photographical magic. You are brilliant.

Jennifer Stevens — Your sailing Cliff's Notes were invaluable. Thank you so much for fact checking me! STARBOARD, HO!

To my betas: Parrish, Melissa, Jen, Mary Catherine, Miranda, Terry, Zoe, Lex, and Brie — Thank you all so much for reading, commenting, and generally kicking my story in the face. Without your feedback, this story wouldn't be what it is.

About Staci

Staci has been a lot of things up to this point in her life: a graphic designer, an entrepreneur, a seamstress, a clothing and handbag designer, a waitress. Can't forget that. She's also been a mom to three little girls who are sure to grow up to break a number of hearts. She's been a wife, even though she's certainly not the cleanest, or the best cook. She's also super, duper fun at a party, especially if she's been drinking whiskey, and her favorite word starts with f, ends with k.

From roots in Houston, to a seven year stint in Southern California, Staci and her family ended up settling somewhere in between and equally north, in Denver. They are new enough that snow is still magical. When she's not writing, she's gaming, cleaning, or designing graphics.

FOLLOW STACI HART:

Website: Stacihartnovels.com
Facebook: Facebook.com/stacihartnovels
Twitter: Twitter.com/imaquirkybird
Pinterest: pinterest.com/imaquirkybird

CPSIA information can be obtained
at www.ICGtesting.com
Printed in the USA
LVHW091112230321
682213LV00018B/154